A 'COP FOR CRIMINALS

BURN
— THE —
DEBT

NEW YORK TIMES #1 BESTSELLER **TONY LEE** WRITING AS
JACK GATLAND

Copyright © 2024 by Jack Gatland / Tony Lee
All rights reserved.

This book or parts thereof may not be reproduced in any form or by any electronic or mechanical means, including information storage and retrieval systems without written permission from the author, unless for the use of brief quotations in a book review.

This is a work of fiction. Names, characters, places and incidents are either the product of the author's imagination or are used fictitiously, and any resemblance to actual persons, living or dead, business establishments, places of learning, events or locales is entirely coincidental.

Published by Hooded Man Media.
Cover photo by Paul Thomas Gooney

First Edition: August 2024

PRAISE FOR JACK GATLAND

'This is one of those books that will keep you up past your bedtime, as each chapter lures you into reading just one more.'

'This book was excellent! A great plot which kept you guessing until the end.'

'Couldn't put it down, fast paced with twists and turns.'

'The story was captivating, good plot, twists you never saw and really likeable characters. Can't wait for the next one!'

'I got sucked into this book from the very first page, thoroughly enjoyed it, can't wait for the next one.'

'Totally addictive. Thoroughly recommend.'

'Moves at a fast pace and carries you along with it.'

'Just couldn't put this book down, from the first page to the last one it kept you wondering what would happen next.'

There's a new Detective Inspector in town...

Before Ellie Reckless, there was DI Declan Walsh!

LIQUIDATE THE PROFITS

An EXCLUSIVE PREQUEL, completely free to anyone who joins the Jack Gatland Reader's Club!

Join at bit.ly/jackgatlandVIP

Also by Jack Gatland

DI DECLAN WALSH BOOKS
LETTER FROM THE DEAD
MURDER OF ANGELS
HUNTER HUNTED
WHISPER FOR THE REAPER
TO HUNT A MAGPIE
A RITUAL FOR THE DYING
KILLING THE MUSIC
A DINNER TO DIE FOR
BEHIND THE WIRE
HEAVY IS THE CROWN
STALKING THE RIPPER
A QUIVER OF SORROWS
MURDER BY MISTLETOE
BENEATH THE BODIES
KILL YOUR DARLINGS
KISSING A KILLER
PRETEND TO BE DEAD
HARVEST FOR THE REAPER
CROOKED WAS HIS CANE
A POCKET FULL OF POSIES

TOM MARLOWE BOOKS
SLEEPING SOLDIERS
TARGET LOCKED
COVERT ACTION
COUNTER ATTACK
STEALTH STRIKE
BROAD SWORD

ROGUE SIGNAL

ELLIE RECKLESS BOOKS
PAINT THE DEAD
STEAL THE GOLD
HUNT THE PREY
FIND THE LADY
BURN THE DEBT

DAMIAN LUCAS BOOKS
THE LIONHEART CURSE

STANDALONE BOOKS
THE BOARDROOM

For Mum, who inspired me to write.

For Tracy, who inspires me to write.

CONTENTS

1.	The Wannabe	1
2.	Diner Denied	13
3.	Evicted	22
4.	Influencers With Favours	33
5.	Sparring Matched	44
6.	House Guests	55
7.	War Council	66
8.	Police Informant	76
9.	Reparation	86
10.	Swanky Bashes	98
11.	Gym Session	109
12.	Burn A Debt	118
13.	Sinatra's Burger	131
14.	Ex-Coppers	144
15.	Visiting Hours	154
16.	Opened Vaults	163
17.	Seven Sisters	173
18.	Michael Bay's Keyring	187
19.	New Tenants	197
20.	Young Prince	207
21.	Next Steps	218
22.	Car Share	227
23.	Deals With Devils	237
24.	Weighing In	247
25.	Fight Night	259
26.	Crushing Dreams	270
	Epilogue	279
	Acknowledgements	289
	About the Author	291

1

THE WANNABE

All his life, Lavie Kaya had been told what to do.

Whether it was his parents, his teachers, even the people he laughingly called his friends, Lavie was one of the permanent hangers-on, the eternal entourage; never to be the star, always the supporting character.

And Lavie didn't like this.

Lavie was also quite melodramatic; after all, he was only fifteen years old. His uncle Ali kept telling him he had all his life to live, and that it didn't matter that he wasn't doing well right now. The problem with that was Lavie had met other people the same age as him and found they were doing much better, thank you very much. This had awoken a jealousy, something that had made Lavie decide, very early in his school career, that this was nothing more than a stepping stone to riches.

Lavie came from a second-generation immigrant family; London born and bred, but still with the name, skin tone and heritage of someone that wasn't British. Because of this, he'd suffered from bullying all of his life. Idiot little pricks with tight white shirts, collars done up at the top and no tie, telling him he needed to "go back where he came from." And when he replied that was Balham, they'd say where his *parents* came from.

He'd then reply that this was Croydon.

It was usually around then he'd get punched. Bullies didn't like being proven wrong.

Lavie had almost suggested changing his name at one point. Would he have had the same amount of bullying if his name was Alfie or Danny? He wasn't sure. All he knew were the jokes, the insults based on his name. They called him a Muslim terrorist, even though he'd been baptised Church of England, but that was also to ensure he got into a good school.

Lavie didn't care about Christianity. He didn't care about Sunni Islam, either.

In fact, Lavie had decided around the age of fourteen that school really wasn't conducive to his health. The bullying meant he often found himself injured, battered, bruised, bleeding. Never a broken bone, though; the bullies were at least considerate in that respect. He had been dangled out of a window once, a second-floor chemistry lab, while the teacher, unable to do anything, just weakly asked the bullies to stop. They did eventually, when they got bored. Then they stole one of his shoes. Not both. Just one. It was a message. They didn't want his shoes. They just didn't want *him* to have his shoes, either.

He wasn't able to hide this from his parents. His mum wanted to argue at the school, but he knew that would make it worse. *The boy whose mum came down to fight for him*, that was almost a death sentence when it came to school bullies. His dad started demanding he learned how to defend himself, explained that if you aimed for the biggest bully and punched him squarely in the face, the bully would back down, deciding respect had been given. Lavie didn't really believe this, however, one afternoon when he was being attacked once more, with nothing else to lose, he took his father's advice and swung a solid right hand into the bully, Philip's, face.

Philip was pissed off. He didn't back down or decide Lavie was someone who deserved his respect. Instead, he gave Lavie an even bigger battering than he would have before.

That was the day that Lavie realised that his father didn't have a bloody clue what he was talking about.

That was the day that Lavie stopped going to school.

NOBODY KNEW HE WASN'T GOING TO SCHOOL ALL DAY. HE DID IT cleverly. He'd dress up in his school uniform in the morning, go into school and take assembly and registration. He would then attend a class or two, making sure to be seen. But then he would take large chunks off for the day, where he would leave the school and head down to Balham High Road, down near the Army Centre.

You see, here, in a car park beside an abandoned carpet warehouse, was where Mickey hung out.

Mickey wasn't his real name. Mickey's real name was Vito, but Mickey explained to Lavie when they first met that his school life had been the same as Lavie's, with bullies calling him "Vito Corleone" from *The Godfather*. In a way, Lavie would have liked that. Vito Corleone was the *Don*. He was the head of the Mafia. Lavie liked the idea of being head of the Mafia. For a start, it meant that he could get his own back on the bullies that had made his life hell. But for some reason, Mickey hadn't liked his name and had decided when he left school at sixteen, to change it to the most generic thing he could think of.

So "Mickey" was born.

Mickey would sit on the hood of his car, tricked out and made to look like it was something from the *Fast and the Furious* movies. It had an engine that sounded like a Maserati. Lavie didn't know what a Maserati sounded like, but he'd been told it sounded like a Maserati, and therefore he took that as gospel. Mickey would spend most of his day from midday until at least nine in the evening hanging out in his car park, talking to his friends, shouting at people, leering at old ladies, and wolf-whistling at attractive teenage girls as they walked past.

Mickey was a *king*.

Lavie saw that the first time he ever met him; his clothes were expensive, his phone top of the range, and his trainers weren't shop bought. Mickey had boasted, saying that *only a mug bought trainers when they came out, it was all about the resale value,* and that it was much better when you'd find the ones that were rare.

Lavie started saving for trainers the same day. Over the weeks that Lavie sat at Mickey's learning tree, when he wasn't at school, Lavie started to understand how Mickey made his money.

Unsurprisingly, it was drugs.

But Mickey wasn't stupid. Mickey had an army of people who would do the things he needed. He'd have kids on street corners selling drugs, but the money went to some other kid, who would then let some *other* kid know to pass the drugs to yet *another* kid; always switching, always moving so as not to gain the attention of the *feds*. Mickey said he'd been taught it by someone down the line, and *now* was the time to make money. Lavie didn't understand why *now* was the time, and not a year ago, or even a year from now, but Mickey was very, very adamant that he had to make as much as possible in a short amount of time. A month later, when Lavie turned fifteen, Mickey gave him his first job, keeping an eye out for the *feds*, the local police force, who drove around looking for kids on street corners offering drugs to anybody who was walking past.

Lavie understood the role and picked it up fast; he wanted to prove his loyalty so after school he'd spend several hours with Mickey. Mickey even taught him how to defend himself; actual lessons. Mickey was a Golden Gloves boxer, an under-fourteen amateur star before he stopped, and was also a black belt in four different martial arts.

Lavie had seen no proof of these martial arts, but he didn't need to. Whatever Mickey said was gospel; Mickey was the King of Balham.

Lavie's mum wasn't happy with the fact he was spending time away from home, but Lavie had explained he was now working part-time in a sneaker shop, and this was paying for self-defence lessons every night. He'd even shown off some moves that Mickey had taught him, and that was enough to keep his dad happy, because as far as he was concerned, if Lavie could defend himself, it didn't matter where he was – and besides, at least he wasn't on the streets dealing drugs.

Lavie laughed at that; in actual fact, he wasn't, as by now he was *telling* the people dealing the drugs what to do.

Lavie wasn't stupid, he was aware the moment he started bringing money in, his parents would notice, and he wasn't going to leave it with Mickey. As much as Mickey was the

King, and Lavie looked up to him, he was also aware Mickey could at any time disappear, and if he did, then all of Lavie's money would also go.

Instead, he hid his money under a floorboard in his bedroom.

Within four months of working with Mickey, he had made almost a thousand pounds. To a fifteen-year-old boy, this was insane; he wasn't even doing much to get it. But he also knew Mickey was making a thousand pounds for every ten that Lavie was making, and by now he'd realised that above Mickey there was somebody else, and they were making even more money. He'd kept his ear to the ground as he'd learned the trade, so to speak. He'd already decided that when he was sixteen, he was going to quit school. If his parents complained, he would just give them several thousand pounds and tell them to go away.

Lavie had planned his future already. He could see the apartment he would own, the sound system he would have: speakers everywhere, connected through a solid wi-fi system. He'd have a smart home that did everything he wanted, a TV as big as a wall, his own cinema in the basement. It was dreaming, nothing more, but Lavie had already realised this was a dream that could possibly happen.

But, then one day, the dreams *stopped*.

Lavie had progressed further in the space of four months than most people did in a couple of years, and this was purely because Mickey needed people to move up and gain as much cash as could be done in a short amount of time. Eventually, people had talked, and Lavie listened to everything. One night, he heard through the grapevine *why* Mickey had always been rushing. Apparently, there had been some kind of takeover in London a few months earlier, and a gang that had run South London, the Simpsons, had been effectively castrated. There were still some lieutenants trying to keep control, but these were now feuding warlords, all watching to see who could make the most gains in the southern postcodes; while they fought, people like Mickey slipped in through the cracks, working from car parks, buying cheap, selling dear, and disappearing before the new bosses turned up.

Lavie wondered who the new boss would be; he even wondered whether it could in any way be Mickey. That would be awesome, but Mickey always changed the subject when Lavie brought this up. *There were scary people out there,* he said, *people that even he was scared of.*

But that was insane, Lavie had replied. Mickey had four black belts, was a Golden Gloves fighter, and had five illegal firearms he kept on him at various points, not to mention the various switchblades he was known for carrying. Again, all things Mickey wasn't stupid enough to show around, as the last thing he wanted was to piss off the police and get arrested before he could make his money.

There were moments when Lavie, in the middle of the night before the dawn began, would wonder whether Mickey actually *had* the weapons and the skills to use them. But that was fighting talk; you didn't say that about your King unless you were looking to take over, and Lavie didn't want to take over.

Lavie was, however, scared of who would. Then, five months after he'd first started hanging out with Mickey, he found out who was making their play.

He'd been hanging out outside a local chicken fast-food store with a couple of friends, people he'd got to know through Mickey and people he trusted. In fact, one of the larger friends, whom he just called 'Biggie', had formed a bit of a loyalty to Lavie, in the same way that Lavie had to Mickey, and had even come to school with him one day, planning to find Philip and beat the living crap out of him.

He wasn't allowed into the school, though, as the school security stopped him before he could enter, funnily enough, after finding a vicious-looking Karambit blade on him.

But Lavie had gone in. He'd still been showing his face here and there, making sure that the truant officers weren't turning up and telling his parents that he was missing too many lessons. But that was possibly a mistake, because while he wasn't there to be attacked by Philip, Philip had no one to attack. So, on the day Biggie had been banned from following him into the school, Philip had followed Lavie after he slipped back out, probably wondering how Lavie could gain new trainers; the ones Lavie would always put on after he left home, so as not to alert his parents of his sudden wealth.

With hindsight, Lavie realised Philip probably thought he could take the trainers from Lavie, and had watched him, waiting for the moment to do just that.

He never had the chance, though. Because just gone seven on a Monday evening, Lavie had a bad day.

LAVIE HAD A BURNER PHONE ON HIM AND HE WAS WAITING FOR A call from Mickey; he'd been told to be ready to meet at a moment's notice and with his crew, Biggie and another friend, Zahad. He was spending the evening killing time outside a fried chicken shop on Bedford Hill, wolf-whistling the girls as they walked past, and flipping off members of rival gangs as they drove past in their shitty little cars. Lavie was getting known now and nobody really wanted to take a piece of him, knowing who he ran with. But Philip, idiotic outsider Philip, didn't know of Lavie's rep.

It was Philip who had started it that night, walking over to Lavie with three of his own friends beside him. He'd obviously called them, told them to meet him because they were going to teach Lavie a lesson. *How dare he rise above his station?* The problem was when they arrived, Lavie wasn't scared. In fact, Lavie was actually grateful that Philip had come out of his way, it made it easier for Lavie to batter the crap out of him.

Realising this wasn't going the way he thought it would, Philip backtracked, but Lavie wasn't having it, and started following Philip as they walked away. Realising he was well out of his depth now and that this wasn't schoolyard politics anymore, Philip started running, his friends joining in, and Lavie, pulling out a wicked-looking folding knife, flipped it open and held it in his hand as he chased after him. Every time he'd been bullied was fresh in his head, and he intended to sketch a line for every single one of them onto Philip's back.

There'd be quite a few lines by the time he'd finished.

He never managed to do this, however, because as they turned into an alleyway off Balham Station, a jeep screeched in front of them, blocking their way. It was black and square, a Suzuki in the style of a Land Rover Defender. As it stopped, two older men climbed out. Lavie *said* older, but as a fifteen-year-old boy, anybody over the age of eighteen looked like they were close to death. These men were definitely not school age, however, and one of them grabbed Lavie, pushing him against the wall, as the other grabbed Biggie, slamming him to the ground, placing a knee in the small of his back as he squirmed.

Zahad, seeing what had happened to his two friends, had wisely run away.

Lavie didn't fault him for that. Lavie would have done the same as well.

With Lavie now pinned against the wall, Biggie facedown on the floor, Zahad gone and Philip and his buddies probably in a different postcode by now, Lavie watched as the passenger side of the car opened and a woman in her thirties, maybe her forties – Lavie wasn't sure about older ladies – climbed down. She was stocky, olive-skinned, with brown eyes and long black hair, straight, falling around her shoulders. She wore a denim and grey hooded jacket over jeans and Doc Martens, and her t-shirt was a graphic-designed one and showed the rapper Central Cee. Lavie didn't believe she knew a single one of his songs; she looked like a woman trying to dress younger than her age. But it also made Lavie wonder if he had accidentally aged her more than she was. Maybe she was only in her twenties or even thirties, and had had a really tough life, but he didn't get the chance to think more about it as the woman now walked over to him.

'You work for Mickey,' she said. A statement more than a question.

There was no point in lying. That they had screeched to a halt in front of him as they were running, meant to Lavie that she kind of already knew who he was. He nodded nervously. He had never dealt with men like the two now crowding him, and his arrogant belief he could cut scars into his bully's back had now turned into fear that the same was about to happen to him.

The woman leant closer, nodding to the man to drop him.

The man himself was stubbled and bald, a black bomber jacket over joggers and a t-shirt, both black. It was almost like he was in some kind of uniform, as the other man was wearing similar.

'You tell Mickey his boss turned up to say hi,' she said. 'You understand? He's been dealing with Angelo, and now Angelo is gone.'

'I don't know what you mean,' Lavie squeaked.

'You're dealing on my turf,' the woman leant in. 'My name's Becky Slade. Recognise it?'

Lavie, terrified, shook his head.

'Well, you ought to find out about it,' Becky replied. 'Because I'm taking over the south of London, and little pricks like you need to ship up and work for me, or piss off north of the Thames.'

'Yeah?' Lavie couldn't help himself, jutting his chin out. 'I work for Mickey.'

'Really? And what do your parents think about that?'

'They don't know,' Lavie shrugged, sheepishly.

Becky laughed, looking at the two men.

'Oh, look at this little baby gangster,' she said. 'Playing at being a drug dealer after school.'

'I ain't a drug dealer,' Lavie snapped. 'I'm past that.'

'You ain't nothing, unless I tell you so, Lavie Kaya,' Becky growled, leaning close. 'Whatever you've been doing, whatever you've been making, it's gone, yeah? Time to go home and play with your dollies, little boy.'

'And if I don't?' Lavie asked. It was a strange situation to be in. This woman and her friends were more terrifying and more dangerous than Philip and his bully friends had ever been in Lavie's life. Yet, where he could never stand up to Philip, he found that here, facing a woman and two vicious looking bastards who could quite probably end his life without a second thought, Lavie found his courage.

Mickey was King.

Even if Mickey *was* being taken over, usurped by this new woman, Lavie was loyal – and Lavie would go down with his King.

'You want to know what we'd do if you go against us?' Becky asked, shrugging, considering it and nodding.

'I get that,' she said. 'I'd want to know as well.'

She looked at the bald one, who had now moved away from Lavie and, as Lavie looked in horror, was putting something brass over his knuckles.

'Show the little prick what we'll do if he steps out of line,' she said. 'But don't go all the way. After all, I might need him at some point.'

She grinned.

'And after you're done, we'll have a little *chat*.'

Lavie was going to ask what the chat would be about, but then realised he'd ignored an earlier comment.

'You ain't nothing, unless I tell you so, Lavie Kaya.'

'How did you know my name?' he asked. 'You said my name. I never told you it.'

In response, Becky Slade smiled.

'I know everything about you,' she said, stepping back as one of the goons moved in.

And then the *beatings* started.

2

DINER DENIED

In the four months that had followed the Zoey Parks case, Ellie Reckless had done little.

Actually, that wasn't entirely correct.

Ellie had spent her time working for Finders and over the months had solved quite a few legitimate cases with her team of Ramsey Allen, Tinker Jones, Joanne Davey, and occasionally Casey Noyce. Occasionally, because his mum still wasn't sure about Ellie using him for her activities. Although, of late, with Ellie keeping to her side of the law and with the fact that Casey's dad's murder had now been solved – something that, even though he'd been having an affair when he died and according to Casey's mum, Pauline, was an *adulterous piece of shit* – still gave Pauline closure. Robert Lewis was still on sabbatical and, apart from the occasional message sent, usually to either Tinker or Ramsey rather than directly to Ellie, it didn't sound like he was coming back anytime soon.

Therefore, instead of taking jobs for Robert, Ellie was still working for the partners. The cases were interesting enough, and the money was good, but Ellie had felt something was missing throughout the time she'd been working cases over the last few months.

For a start, she knew it was an anti-climax to her own personal crusade.

She had begun this looking to find out who'd framed her and, well, that had eventually been discovered. Then, after that, she found she still had the favours she'd been building up, and the underworld knew and remembered this as well. She regularly had messages from people, often as subordinates knocking on her door or catching her when she was in Johnny Lucas's boxing club taking on sparring sessions or in the gym area to the side, asking when she was likely to "cash in that chit". Ellie replied the same on every occasion, that whoever it was who owed the debt should be grateful that nothing was happening, because it meant for the moment they were still safe. But she understood as nobody wanted a debt hanging over their head.

The Finder's offices were in the City, just south of Farringdon, and she had a very nice, glass-walled, ornate space to do her work, with an overly large bed in the corner for her Cocker Spaniel Millie, who spent most of the days with her. But back when she'd been working for favours, Ellie had often worked out of *Caesar's Diner*, usually a booth against the wall, maintaining a kind of separation between the work that she did ... and the work that she did for criminals.

Over the last three or four months, Ellie had still gone to Caesar's. It was a bloody good diner after all, and she would usually meet with the team for breakfast meetings there. However, on this particular Tuesday, she felt something was different. For a start, Sandra didn't serve her when she sat down. It was Ali Kaya, the diner's owner, who walked over.

'All right, Ellie?' he asked, his accent completely contrasting with his look.

Ellie nodded, looking around.

'No Sandra?'

'Sent her to the back,' Ali pointedly looked around. It was still quite empty for the day; the breakfast crowd had gone, and most of the people in the area would have gone to work by ten in the morning. There was one other person in the entire cafe, and they were as far across as you could get.

Probably too far to hear as Ali spoke.

'I wanted to have a chat,' he said.

'Are you okay?' Ellie asked.

'No, I'm not,' Ali shook his head. 'I'm really not okay.'

'Can I help in some way?'

'Well, that's the problem. You see, *you're* kind of the reason I'm not okay.'

Ellie didn't like the way this conversation was going.

'Tell me what I've done, and what I can do to fix it,' she said.

'What, use one of your favours?' Ali asked, almost a mutter as he looked away, and Ellie realised that something far worse was going on.

'Why don't you tell me what's wrong?' she continued. 'Because at the moment, mate, all you're doing is concerning me. I've been coming here for years now, and not once have you had a problem with me.'

Ali nodded, shrugging, wiping his head with a cloth.

'In all that time,' he said, 'I've never really got involved with what you do, and I appreciate that you've taken your business elsewhere for the last few months or so.'

'But we haven't,' Ellie was shaking her head now. 'We were literally here yesterday, having lunch.'

'I don't mean you and the others,' Ali replied carefully. 'I meant your *business*.'

He looked uncomfortable as he continued. This was obviously a conversation he hadn't really wanted to have.

'Look, as I said, I've never really got involved with what you do,' he carefully explained. 'But I've recognised a lot of the faces who would come here and have a chat with you as your new clients. It wasn't uncommon for you to have gangland bosses turning up for a chat, or celebrity YouTubers snapping selfies. Sandra would pick it up as well, and we knew they were asking for your help and you were providing it – whether it was for cash or favours. I don't know.'

He shook his head.

'But I also know they were wrong'uns, Ellie. I know they were the type of people that you didn't want to meet late at night in an alley, you know? I appreciate you not bringing it here but your reach, it's ...'

He paused, looking away.

'It's kind of got personal now,' he continued.

'What do you mean?'

Ali had a dishcloth in his hand, and he was wringing it slightly as he was talking. Ellie could see he was stressed and not in a good place right now.

'I've got a nephew,' he started. 'Good kid. Idiot, but good, nevertheless. He's got a good heart. But, sure, you hear that kind of thing when parents talk about their kids being dickheads.'

Ellie waited.

'Anyway, his parents, they don't really care for him that much. His dad only really cares that he defends himself, couldn't give a toss if he makes money or not. It's all about honour with him, you know?'

Ellie nodded.

'So, he started playing truant from school,' Ali continued. 'He's fifteen now, but it started about six months back. He hadn't been that happy about school; he was being bullied and his dad wasn't exactly helping. Then, for the last few months, he started hanging out with the wrong crowd down in Balham.'

'What kind of crowd?' Ellie asked.

'The kind that stand on street corners and sell drugs to idiots.' The venom in Ali's voice wasn't missed. 'He started working for some crew. I don't know all the details; he won't tell anybody. He was making money, I know this because I called him out on some trainers he was wearing. He begged me not to tell his dad, said he hid them from him and he wore them when he wasn't at home. Apparently, I'm the "cool uncle", so I get to know these things and hold his secrets for him.'

Ali paused, wrinkled his nose as he tried to work out the words, and then sighed, releasing a pent-up breath.

'So, last night Lavie, that's my nephew, is doing whatever he wants, and he gets attacked by these two men and a woman.'

'What do you mean by attacked?'

'I mean literally *attacked*. They pulled up in a car in front of him, told him they now owned the space he was on.'

'The turf?'

'Yeah, whatever, I don't know your gangland terms,' Ali spat.

Ellie held up her hands.

'Look, I'm here to help, whatever this is,' she said. 'But, I'm not the one who sent him out and I'm not the one who did whatever this is. So wind your neck back in, yeah?'

Ali glared at Ellie.

'Actually, you *are* the one who did this,' he grumbled. 'My nephew, he got a bit of a battering, told to keep off the grass, so to speak. He understood that; it's part and parcel of what happens. I don't think he was that fussed. But they knew his name, Ellie. They'd actively been hunting him. Not his boss, *him*. They smacked him about, and he didn't want to get beaten worse, so he started telling them whatever they wanted to know: who he worked for, how long he'd been doing it, what the situation was. But they didn't care. And then they started talking about the diner. This place. They asked about *you*.'

'Me?'

'Yeah, actually said you by name. "Do you know Ellie?" Lavie didn't have a clue who you were so he shook his head. She then started asking about the diner, asking how often he went in and whether there was a booth that was always filled with older people. He said there were always people in there and at fifteen, older could be anything. Then he started describing you all. Let's face it, you're all pretty recognisable. He mentioned your mate Simpson coming in when he faked his death – when the two girls took his photo. All that. She got very interested indeed when she heard his name. Started muttering "Reckless" lots. He didn't realise it was your bloody surname. He thought she was just commenting.'

He was shaking now as he mentally relived what his nephew had told him.

'And then she moved closer, told him she had a message she wanted passed. She told him to tell me, when he saw me next, that "Becky Slade said thank you, Ellie Reckless. Thank you for everything you did for her." And then she said to "tell

Ellie to keep quiet about the past, before she ended it permanently." The "she" there being her.'

'Becky Slade,' Ellie shook her head, 'I've heard the family name, but I don't think I've ever met the woman. And I have no clue what she means about the past.'

'Well, she knows you, Ellie, and the moment she made sure he knew that message word for word, she told her men to beat on him. He's a fifteen-year-old kid, Ellie, and these two men were built like brick shithouses according to Lavie. They broke his nose, they shattered a tooth, they broke his ribs, and then the woman grabbed one of those large Maglites, the ones that could be used as a weapon ...'

Ellie nodded, understanding.

'She placed him down on the floor, bleeding, battered and crying, and slammed it down on his forearm, breaking it,' Ali was angry now. 'All because she wanted to pass a message to you, Ellie.'

The diner was silent, mainly as Ellie wasn't sure what to say. A memory had come to mind of a dinner with her ex, Nathan, months earlier. He had been angry, too. The line he had spoken echoed in her head.

'You know what happened earlier this week? I was almost mugged. Some lowlife scum caught me in an alley, a couple of nights back. Thought I was going to get stabbed up for a phone and twenty quid. You know why I wasn't? Because one of them saw my face. He looks at me, and then he says "leave this one. He's Ellie Reckless's ex." That they knew you, and feared what you'd do to them, more than what I'd do? Tells me all I need to know.'

But this was different. Whereas Nathan had escaped a mugging because of his connection to Ellie Reckless, it sounded like Ali's nephew had gained one *because*. Whether he was in the wrong place at the wrong time, or on someone's turf, that didn't matter. Whoever this Becky Slade was, she had made it personal.

Ellie glanced back at Ali, who had been staring at her, waiting for her to speak. Slowly, she nodded, to show she understood.

'I don't know who this woman is,' she said. 'But know this now, Ali. You're family to me. And by her attacking Lavie, she's made herself an enemy of mine.'

She looked around the diner.

'It's because of my connection to you he got attacked, and I apologise for that. But I will find out who she is, and I will make this right.'

Ali said nothing, then seemed to shake himself out of the stupor he was in.

'You make this right, Ellie,' he said, nodding. 'I know that people who hire you, they work for favours, right? So you tell me whatever favour you need—'

'No,' Ellie interrupted, holding her hand up. 'I'm not doing this for favours. Whoever this woman is, she came at me through your family, and that's not on.'

Ali smiled. It was a weak, nervous one. But at least he wasn't glaring at her anymore.

'You have to understand,' he said, 'with these people ... I can't let these meetings happen anymore.'

'Are you barring me from the diner?' Ellie frowned.

Ali rubbed at the back of his neck, uncomfortable with the conversation.

'I just think maybe you can find somewhere different to have your meetings,' he said, before adding. 'Unless, of course, the meetings are with people solving *this* problem.'

Ellie smiled darkly. There was no humour behind the eyes as she nodded.

'Believe me, mate. We don't have any other meetings until we fix this,' she said. 'Your nephew and what's happened here, it's my priority right now, and will be until it's done.'

She rose, grabbing the lead beside her, motioning for Millie to join her. Millie had snuggled down on the ground under the table, and didn't really want to move, but reluctantly rose.

Ali looked almost shocked to see her leave.

'I didn't mean you have to go now,' he said. 'I mean, I'm sure there's breakfast and ...'

'I want this *done* now,' Ellie said. 'Don't you worry. I'll be back and I'll be keeping my breakfasts. Ramsey would kill me if I stopped coming here. He's working through the menu for a sixth time now. But I've got a woman to find. And an agenda to learn.'

3

EVICTED

Although Ali had given an effective agreement for her team to meet up in his diner in connection to the case, Ellie had decided for the first meeting a more formal location would be better and had instead called the team to the Finder's offices.

Ellie had never been a fan of these offices, even though she had been working from them most of the time for the last few years. The biggest problem was the glass-walled windows. She could see from her office into the boardroom, and into Robert Lewis's office, which for a while now had been sadly empty. Months earlier, Robert had suffered horrific injuries at the hands of Mark Lawrence and had almost died, coming out of a coma with what seemed to be recurring brain injuries. They had thought he was back to normal, but after a while he had anger and rage issues, and at one point had found himself in his office, facing onetime friend Joseph Kerrigan, a taser in his hand, almost shooting him in the face as a rage of being betrayed threw all rationality out of the window.

There had been a moment in the last case when Ellie had wondered whether there was something *more* going on between her and Robert. There had been moments over the months before; stolen glances, the usual things. She'd smiled as she remembered a moment where they had hidden behind a sofa, with Robert falling on top of her.

Nothing had happened.

And then, just as something could have, he was gone.

'Ellie Reckless, this is the right call. I need to sort myself out. I don't know how long it will take. I might be back next week. Next month. Next year.'

'You said you can still do good, and I think you can, but right now, it isn't with me.'

Ellie didn't mind that he needed to take time off. What had actually bothered her was that even though he'd promised to stay in touch, he hadn't responded to anybody, bar one or two "housecleaning" texts when needed. It was as if he had ghosted the team. The partners at Finders understood though, and had left his job open; for all intents and purposes, he was on a medical sabbatical.

But Ellie thought he would have at least tried to *call* her.

She was so deep in her thoughts that she hadn't realised Ramsey Allen had walked into her office, staring at her from the door. He was in his usual three-piece suit, pin-striped, of course, bespoke, with today's additional dressings being a blue shirt with a burgundy cravat. He was in his sixties, his hair white, his moustache trimmed, and he gave the look of an aristocratic old gentleman.

Ellie had always found this amusing. Ramsey Allen was nothing more than an East End street gutter made good; a burglar who had spent years behind bars, thanks in part to Ellie Reckless when she had been a police officer. Because she had been one of the few that had treated him right, and also one of the few that had found and caught him, Ramsey had found himself with some kind of loyalty to her. When he came out of prison, clean of the addictions that had caused him to lose his way in the first place, Ellie had given him a job at Finder's, something even Ramsey hadn't expected. And with Tinker Jones, Casey, and Joanne Davey, Ellie still had a team, even if Robert's absence was sorely missed.

'You called us in?' he asked. 'I'm guessing we have a job.'

He looked around the office.

'We're here, so I'm guessing it's paying.'

Ellie went to comment, paused at this, and then shook her head.

'Yes and no,' she replied. 'It's a favour, but not our usual type.'

Ramsey sighed, looking up at the ceiling. He'd never made a secret of the fact that he hated Ellie's favour jobs, but he understood why they had to happen. Ellie had been betrayed by a fellow police officer, and the love of her life had been murdered, with Ellie blamed for it. She'd almost gone to prison, and although she was proven not guilty, she wasn't proven innocent of all charges. It had taken years and a bag of favours gained from the criminal underworld for Ellie to fix this.

But, every time they worked for favours, Ramsey didn't get paid. Well, apart from one time when he gained a rather nice bottle of liquid gold in the process.

It still wasn't enough to stop him from complaining.

'So, who's the favour for?' Ramsey sighed. 'And why aren't we waiting for the others?'

'I called you in early because I have a question for you, and you only, first,' Ellie explained.

Ramsey grimaced theatrically, more from habit than because he was truly angry.

'Really?' he asked. 'Secret meetings? We're not back on that, are we?'

Ellie knew he was hinting at the fact that, at one point, he had been forced to spy on her, but, smiling, she shook her head.

'No,' she replied. 'The job's for a slightly different kind of client. Ali, the owner of Caesar's Diner.'

'Is he alright?' Ramsey's mock resignation turned into concern, and Ellie wondered how much of that was because of concern for Ali, or for his cafe, of which Ramsey regularly ate through the menu. Ellie never understood how he didn't put weight on with the amount of meals he consumed there.

'It's Ali's nephew,' she continued. 'He's part of some Balham crew dealing drugs.'

'So what? Ali wants us to stop him?'

'He's already been stopped, and I think he'll be reassessing his future,' Ellie shook her head. 'Ali came to me this morning, was quite insistent that our meetings at his diner have turned him and his family into targets.'

'How so?'

'His nephew was attacked last night. Two men and a woman turned up in a car. Primarily, they were there to tell him to get off their turf.'

'Balham?' Ramsey frowned. 'Nobody owns Balham at the moment; it was Simpson land until—'

'Until we got rid of the Simpsons,' Ellie nodded. 'And it's been about, what, six, seven months since then? That place has turned into the Wild West, with everybody and their dog looking to claim it for themselves. And that's not the only place, is it? We've caused disruption in the North with the

Seven Sisters, in the West with the Tsangs. Mama Lumetta offered to help us take over the West and Central London, if you remember. Johnny Lucas has stepped down from running the East while he's in Parliament.'

She leant back in the chair as the enormity of the situation struck home.

'London's all over the place, and it looks like a new player has turned up.'

'And why does this affect us and our esteemed diner owner?'

'Because when his nephew, Lavie, was attacked, the woman said my name. And then beat the living hell out of him, making sure he'd send a message. "Becky Slade says thank you."'

'Thank you for what?'

'I'm guessing thank you for opening up the South of London to her, considering the fact that she was the one who turned up demanding he back off her turf,' Ellie replied, 'I seem to recall the Slades were players at one point, probably old coppers telling me legends, but I don't recognise Becky's name, and I thought you with your contacts might have heard of her before.'

Ramsey nodded.

'The Slades were a big family, worked for the Richardsons back in the day, mainly as muscle.'

'Were?'

Ramsey nodded.

'Paddy Simpson took them out, made them his bitches, the last I heard. Had a son, thick as mince, mainly. Maybe she's the next gen? I was East London mainly, so I kept out of the south of the river politics. And I was in prison for some of that time, too.'

He considered this, looking out of the window for a long moment.

'Drew Slade,' he said. 'That was it.'

'Drew?'

'Short for Andrew. I never met him, I just remember he was a vicious bastard. And his father was even worse. Cillian.'

Now remembering the man, Ramsey was visibly unsettled.

'I seem to recall Drew was done for murder, put away. Cillian? He's dead. Maybe even killed by Drew. I can't recall, it was a while ago, before I went to prison and got clean, and definitely before you arrived at Vauxhall, which explains why you know the legends, but not the people. This woman, though, whoever she is, could be his daughter.'

He paused.

'If the Slades are making a move, Ellie, we shouldn't be getting in the middle of it. That's a fight we shouldn't be asking for.'

'I know,' Ellie nodded. 'But let's be honest here. It looks like they're coming for us first. Can you find out what you can?'

Ramsey nodded, looking back at the window where Tinker Jones had arrived, Casey beside her.

'Davey's on her way up,' Tinker said. 'I'm guessing we have a case?'

'Oh, we've definitely got a case, Tinkerbell,' Ramsey turned and smiled.

Before Tinker could say anything, Ellie rose from the chair, motioning at the glass-walled boardroom across the corridor.

'Let's take this in there,' she said, clapping her hands so that Millie, waking up, would follow them through. She couldn't help it. As she entered the boardroom, she glanced briefly into Robert's office. She knew there was nobody there, but there was just the slightest of hopes that maybe something had been moved. Maybe a jacket had been hung up to show that Robert had replied ... had returned.

There was nothing.

AFTER HEARING ELLIE'S REASONS FOR TAKING THE CASE, TINKER Jones sat back in the boardroom chair and glowered across the table at everybody.

'This bitch needs to die,' she said. 'And painfully. To hit a kid?'

'Well, he's not much younger than Casey here is,' Ramsey replied. 'And I've wanted to hit him for years.'

Casey, leaning back on his own chair, looked over at Ramsey and blew him a kiss.

'You're just sad because you're at the end of your life, and I'm just beginning mine,' he said. 'But don't worry, when you die, I will be very sad.'

He looked at his watch.

'For about ten minutes.'

The jibes between the two were pretty much the only light-hearted thing that had been said in the office since Ellie started explaining about what had happened to Lavie Kaya. But even this faded away as the others at the table – Joanna, Casey, Ramsey and Tinker – all looked towards Ellie for advice.

'I worked Vauxhall,' she said. 'And I knew the Simpsons, but I've never heard of the Slades outside of stories. Ramsey, however—'

'Is a hundred and two,' Casey interrupted, pausing at a glare from Ellie.

'Is more of a veteran of the underworld than we are,' Ellie continued. 'And while we've been talking, he's been texting his old friends for information.'

'And I have some,' Ramsey nodded now. 'Unfortunately, it's not great, and it's filled in a lot of the gaps in my memory, but not in a good way.'

Ellie waved to the table.

'Well then, the floor is yours.'

'There's not really a lecture I can give,' he replied. 'I was north of the river, and barely ventured around here. I just remember there was a guy, Drew Slade, ran a small chunk of South London twenty-odd years ago. This was when Paddy Simpson had stepped down and his son Max had taken over, so the Simpsons weren't as strong as they usually were. Because of that, there were small people who managed to start carving away at the areas. It wasn't until years later that they got smacked back down.'

'The Slades were one of these families?'

'Scottish; I think they've got traveller heritage, but I could be wrong,' Ramsey nodded. 'Cillian, the grandfather worked for the Richardsons, made a play for the turf, but the Simpsons got there first, smacked their noses with a rolled up newspaper to sit them back down, get them in line. They never did though, just walked away. Drew Slade was a bare-knuckle boxer, absolute meathead, fat and stupid when you first met him, but it didn't take long to realise that the fat was actually solid muscle. Still stupid, though.'

He opened his phone, reading a text.

'A contact reminded me that a while back, Drew had a plan to take out the Simpsons – and, as far as I know, he failed. Then, ten years back, he was put away for murder. The Slades disappeared, and apart from the odd mention here and there, they've not really been heard of again.'

'Well, now we've got a new Slade, as Becky Slade's making a play for London, ' Ellie said coldly. 'And she's making it personal. Anything on her?'

'She was around Glasgow a few years back, got in a street war with some smaller gangs,' Ramsey read from the phone. 'She's apparently a maniac, travels around bare knuckle fighting when she's not taking over small, unambitious turfs.'

'So, if she's been doing that, why the sudden shift in ambition?' Ellie asked. 'Why now aim at me?'

'That's what we need to be focusing on,' Davey said, almost to herself.

'How do you mean?'

Realising now that everybody was staring at her, Davey squirmed a little in her seat. She was still the newest member of the team, even if that had been several months now.

'Look, I come from forensics, right?' she said. 'I look at all the angles. It's the only way you can sometimes solve a case; the lateral stories rather than the obvious ones. This is a woman who's stopped playing with the minnows and is now gaining turf, yeah? She's making her way around, she's looking for places she can shore up her army. She's obviously got muscle because she had the two guys who helped her beat the diner guy's nephew. But what if there's more to that? I mean, you said she was actively looking *for* this guy.'

'You're thinking that she knew who Lavie was when she found him?' Casey asked. 'More than just his name?'

'From what the bitch told Lavie to pass on, I'd say that's a given,' Davey shrugged. 'But here's the question. You've got a woman who's trying to retake the South of London. She's effectively making sure that you know she's looking for you. You, a woman with a bag full of debts owed to her by pretty much every major player in the underworld.'

'My bag of debts isn't that extensive anymore,' Ellie replied. 'We burned a lot to take down the Simpsons, and we haven't really been taking any more over the last four months.'

'True. But there's enough there for somebody with ambition. What if she wants the debts? What if she wants you to use them on her behalf, or maybe burn them all, to stop you using them to take her out?'

'Wait, hold on,' Ellie frowned at this. 'Are you saying that Becky Slade might think I'm a rival to her?'

'Davey has a point,' Tinker looked around the room. 'We all know Mama Lumetta was eyeing you up to be a successor. You've got Nicky Simpson on speed dial if you want him. Johnny Lucas lets you spar and train in his boxing gym. And the last time we had a chat with the Tsangs, you were exorcising things for them while stopping a coup. And don't even get me started on the Seven Sisters. They owe you as well.'

'If you wanted, you could take over London,' Ramsey added. 'And this bitch knows.'

Ellie shook her head.

'I'm not liking the way this conversation's going,' she replied.

'Well, I'm sorry that's the way you feel,' Ramsey rose. 'Because there's a very strong chance this might be a situation where you have to take on a mantle you didn't want.'

'No,' Ellie shook her head once more, this time with more vigour. 'I'm not having this. I'd rather know what we're walking into, though. I want to find this woman. I want to find out *about* this woman, what she's doing, where she comes from, what her connection is to me. There's something personal here, and I don't know what it is yet.'

She stared up at Ramsey.

'Are you going somewhere?'

'I thought I'd start checking in on people,' Ramsey shrugged. 'I know a couple of faces down south still, people who used to work for the Simpsons who still talk to me, and not by text. I think it's time to find out exactly who Becky Slade is.'

'Don't get yourself killed,' Tinker said.

'Good idea,' Ellie nodded. 'Tinker, go with Ramsey. Make sure he doesn't get himself killed.'

'Oh, come on—' Tinker started, but Ellie shook her head.

'This woman beat the living shit out of a fifteen-year-old kid just to get my attention,' she muttered ominously. 'We have no idea what she'll do to any of you now she has it.'

4

INFLUENCERS WITH FAVOURS

'YOU KNOW, WHEN YOU SAID YOU HAD SOME UNDERWORLD contacts who could possibly help us here, I didn't expect to find myself standing outside this bloody place,' Tinker muttered as they stood facing the glass-windowed gym and health club owned by Nicky Simpson.

Ramsey, in response, simply shrugged.

'I don't know why *you* didn't think of this,' he said. 'Simpson's the obvious choice. His father and grandfather ran the turf when the Slades were sniffing about. If anybody knows what went on, it'll be them, and by default, Nicky.'

Tinker muttered and grumbled to herself, but Ramsey could tell she was aware that this was the only option they had right now.

Nicky Simpson had several health clubs south of the river, but only one where he had his YouTube studio, now his main business. It was a three-storey building in the middle of the recently reinvigorated Battersea Power Station, and on the expansive ground floor he had a health club and gym including a swimming pool, sauna, and steam room, and a hot-desk workspace at the front beside the café. The main offices for his media empire were on the second floor, and a penthouse had now been built into what was once the old offices on the top floor.

It was in what was known as Circus West Village; this was a self-contained estate for the elite, with new high-class shops, restaurants and entertainment venues in every direction, and with adverts for spin cycle classes being advertised on giant LED screens through the glass windows looking out.

Tinker groaned. She'd never felt more *poor*.

Inside, it looked more like an Apple store than a health club: the lobby was expansive and minimalistic, the café to the side looking modern and light, the walls an eggshell aspect against bright white, with bright orange and green chairs scattered around various square tables that looked to be made from Perspex or glass.

'The last time I was in here, we were trying to keep Nicky Simpson alive,' Tinker muttered to herself.

'But that wasn't the last time you saw him, though, was it?' Ramsey grinned. 'You ended up hanging out in his apartment with our missing magician, didn't you? Are you sure you never had a little kissy snuggle with him and Zoey Parks?'

Tinker grimaced.

'The thought of even going near that memory doesn't fill me with joy,' she replied, looking away so that Ramsey couldn't see her slightly flushed expression. She'd made a point over the last four months to avoid any situation where Nicky Simpson could be found, but it didn't stop her thinking of him.

It was annoying, to be perfectly honest. He was an arrogant, entitled prick – good looking and muscled, of course, because that was his branding – but ever since they'd saved his life, he'd actively been trying to stay legit and, in the process, had offered to help whenever he could.

Tinker remembered the last thing he'd said to her when she was at his apartment, mentioning he was about to take a shower, possibly with Zoey Parks.

'She could join me. You too, if you fancy, as I've always had a thing for the grimy look.'

Tinker had punched him in the face for that. It was instinctive, and as he lay on the floor, rubbing at his jaw in his tight white Calvin Kleins, he'd *smiled*.

It was a memory Tinker hadn't been able to get out of her mind for four months now.

Ramsey was watching her and grinned wolfishly.

'You doing okay?' he asked.

'Come on, let's get this over with,' Tinker said, already walking to the stairs.

NICKY SIMPSON'S OFFICE WAS WITH THE OTHERS ON THE second floor, if more extravagant than the others, and he rose as he saw Tinker and Ramsey enter.

'Well, bloody hell,' he said, grinning. 'Looks like all my dreams have come true at once. My two favourite people.'

Ramsey grimaced, but Nicky hadn't finished.

'How's your mum, Ramsey?'

'She's fine, thanks,' Ramsey replied cooly. He didn't like the fact that Nicky Simpson was covering his mother's costs as she stayed in an old people's home. It had begun as a business transaction; Ramsey needed to look after his elderly mother, and Simpson had wanted a spy in Ellie's department. Ramsey had, however, spoiled this arrangement by informing Ellie of what was going on. But after Simpson had been saved from the life of crime that the world now believed he was being forced into, he'd carried on paying the monthly payments – something he didn't need to do, and something that Ramsey was grateful for. Simpson, however, had already turned to Tinker, and his expression, Ramsey believed, was one of hunger.

'You've been avoiding me,' he said, waggling his finger. 'And don't tell me you haven't. I've been told you've deliberately turned down opportunities.'

'Why do I want to hang around with you?' Tinker replied calmly. 'There are much better people and places to be.'

'You're only saying that because I'm not there,' Simpson kept his smile. 'You've got no frame of reference.'

'Can we just get on with this?' Tinker said, looking back at Ramsey.

Simpson laughed.

'You know she secretly wants me, don't you?' he continued, now returning to the elderly thief. 'What she doesn't realise is that if she ever expressed the need, I'd quite happily go along. There's a curiosity, you know.'

He glanced back at Tinker quickly, winking.

'I'm all for new things,' he said.

Tinker, tiring of this, held up a finger to pause him.

'As fun as this banter is, remember the first time the Finder's team was in your office – in that case Ellie and Casey – you'd dragged them here, threatened to have them killed.'

'I never did,' Simpson argued. 'I threatened to have Saleh break some limbs, dump them in some foundations, or something.'

He shrugged.

'Saleh wouldn't have done it, I'd said it to scare her,' he

said. 'Anyway. That was a different office. A different time. A different me.'

'We'll see how long this voyage of self-discovery goes,' Tinker growled.

Nicky Simpson simply smiled in response.

'Well, now we've got the sexual tension out of the way, we've got a nice new thing for you,' Ramsey replied, stepping forward, breaking the moment. 'What do you know about Becky Slade?'

At the name, it was as if all the humour had been sucked out of the office, as Nicky Simpson now turned to face them both.

'Why do you have that name on your lips?' he asked, his voice ice-cold, emotionless.

'Let's just say it's our latest case,' Ramsey replied. 'We'd like to know where we can find her, and to be honest, Ellie would like to know so she can go and kill her, I think.'

Simpson raised an eyebrow.

'If Ellie Reckless wants to kill Becky Slade, that pretty much means they must have met. Because everybody I know who's ever spoken to the bitch wants to kill her.'

He waved for Ramsey and Tinker to sit down on two chairs facing his desk and returned to his seat, now all business.

'Energy drink?' he asked. 'E&C Macrobiotic smoothie? It's named after—'

'The Elephant and Castle, where you grew up, yes we know,' Ramsey shook his head, but Tinker nodded.

'Please,' she replied.

'You won't come and find me,' Simpson grinned as he passed one from his desk fridge. 'But you'll take my drinks.'

'If I don't like your drink, I can toss it away,' Tinker replied. 'I get the impression you're harder to get rid of.'

'Can we please stop with the flirting?' Ramsey shrugged, holding his hands up to attract their attention. 'I'd really like to get this looked into.'

Nicky Simpson turned and nodded.

'Becky Slade,' he said. 'She's about the same age as me. A little older, maybe mid-thirties, forties perhaps. Never really spent much time with her, but I know her. Her dad was Andrew Slade, known as "Drew" to anyone who had the misfortune to run into him; terrifying man. Scottish Lowland traveller heritage. Long blond hair, beard, looked like he was ripped from *Braveheart*. I didn't deal with her or him. And hypothetically—'

Ramsey held a hand up.

'Nicky, please,' he said. 'All three of us are way past the hypothetical stage. We all know what you did. We all know why you did it. We all know what the public believe and we don't care. This entire act? Just drop it. I'm not press. I am, however, a man you once threatened on a carpark roof, so I'm past the games.'

Simpson nodded, sighing as he did so.

'And I'm sorry for that, too, but again, I had Saleh next to me and I had to play the part,' he replied.

'Continue with the story,' Ramsey folded his arms.

Simpson took a mouthful of his smoothie and continued.

'So you all know that my grandfather, Paddy, worked with the Richardsons and the Krays and all that crowd, right?'

Ramsey nodded.

'And then, when he retired in early 2000, my father, Max, took over.'

Again, Ramsey nodded, as Simpson leant back in his chair, deep in thought.

'Well, my father wasn't that good at the job, you know, running the family business,' he continued. 'I mean, he was a bloody good enforcer, right-hand man, all that, but he didn't get people. He was more a Sonny than a Michael Corleone, fought first and *thought* later. Anyway, he pissed a lot of people off when he should have been winning them over, and then when he started showing Parkinsons, there was a visible weakness, right in front of them, that people wanted to exploit. It's one reason why Paddy decided to bring me on board ten years back as the heir apparent, as much as it was a mistake or not. But during the time my father was running the sweet shop, when he was starting to visibly show, Drew decided he wanted to take a shot.'

'And Drew Slade had no other reasons to do this?'

'Oh, he had reasons,' Simpson nodded. 'Cillian Slade, Becky's granddad? Well, he also hung around with the Richardson brothers and, to be honest, the Slades and the Simpsons were two of their main muscles. However, when Eddie and Charlie went down and suddenly the south of London was open for business, it was Paddy who got in first. Cillian waited a little too long to build his power base up, but Paddy, having been the accountant, knew where the money was buried ... literally. But, when Paddy was first starting off, he was vulnerable. So, Cillian Slade decided he was going to take him out before he managed to get strong enough to stop anything.'

'I'm guessing it didn't happen,' Tinker asked.

'It's a tough one,' Simpson shrugged. 'They were pretty evenly matched and then at some point in the nineties, Paddy and Cillian made some kind of truce. Lasted all the way 'til

Dad showed symptoms, and Drew thought he had a chance to do what his father never did.'

'Defeat the Simpsons.'

'Yeah. But Paddy wasn't dead, just retired, and so had a word with some people. Then, just over ten years back, Cillian Slade was murdered. Shot in the face, close range.'

Nicky Simpson held his hands up before anyone could speak.

'I didn't do it, neither did my dad. I don't even think my granddad was involved, really. There were other people Slade had managed to piss off and one day he was having some kind of a barney with his son, they then walked out into the back alley and according to witnesses Drew shot him, close range.'

Simpson leant closer, resting his elbows on the desk.

'I mean, we're talking "no way was this going to be an open casket" kind of close range.'

'So Drew went down for this?'

Simpson nodded.

'He claimed he didn't do it, but there were too many people fingering him for it. And my grandfather, possibly pissed because Cillian was dead now, or even gloating because of this ... well, he made damned sure once Drew was gone, the Slades lost any footing they had. Any plan for taking over was forgotten.'

'Until now, it seems,' Ramsey replied. 'Because Becky Slade seems to be taking on the family business.'

Simpson nodded.

'I might be out of the business,' he said, 'but I keep my ear to the ground, and I've heard similar. I barely knew the woman, and she pissed off up north directly afterwards, but she was an absolute psycho. If she's come back and decided she wants to take on things, she'll probably have Drew's blessing from Belmarsh, and she'll burn down the entire place.'

He frowned.

'Look,' he said, 'don't get me wrong, I don't like the woman, and I'd like to see her removed purely on a family basis. The Slades and the Simpsons haven't been the best of buddies, so I'm obviously going to want to see her eat dirt. But what has this got to do with you? So she's taking over the south of London. You're up in the city, that's north of the Thames. The only times you'd ever have a problem with her is if you were slumming it down here.'

'We have a client,' Tinker explained. 'His nephew was attacked in Balham.'

'Okay,' Simpson was now leaning back in the chair, his hands steepled in front of him, the tips of his fingers resting against his chin as he listened. 'So I know Balham is one area she classes as her turf. Was this client working in there?'

'Our client is a fifteen-year-old kid,' Tinker continued. 'Doesn't know any better. Some kind of street corner lieutenant for someone bigger, who in turn works for someone even bigger. You know how it goes.'

'Still not seeing why this applies to you.'

'He's the nephew of the guy who runs the diner we all meet in,' Ramsey continued. 'You remember the place? Caesar's?'

'Yeah, I enjoyed that diner,' Simpson nodded. 'There's some definite money to be made there, if they only did it right. So what, his nephew's fallen off the rails, got a beating and now you're having to leap in like white knights?'

'It's not quite as simple as that.' Tinker shook her head. 'You see, Becky Slade took a personal interest in this lad.'

'She left a message for Ellie with him,' Ramsey finished. 'Thanking Ellie for what she did.'

At this, Nicky Simpson started laughing.

'Oh, that's royal, that is,' he said when he stopped. 'Ellie Reckless took down my granddad and left a hole in South London big enough to smash a meteorite into, and now Becky Slade's taking over, so she's thanking Ellie for it. Look on the bright side, it sounds like she wants to be your ally rather than an enemy.'

'She told the boy to give the message and then beat the living shit out of him,' Ramsey replied. 'I don't think she wants to play dollies with us. We need to know where we can find her. We need to know what her plans are, what she's got on her side. And how we can negate it.'

'Negate it?' Simpson's eyes widened at this. 'Is Ellie taking a shot at South London? She's got enough debts owed to her to make a dent.'

'You know she's never wanted that,' Ramsey shook his head. 'But if this woman is going to make something personal against Ellie, we'll need to be ready. And more importantly, Becky Slade needs to be sent a message about what she did to this fifteen-year-old kid.'

Nicky Simpson pursed his lips as he considered this.

'Battering a fifteen-year-old is what we would have done to stake our claim,' he said. 'There's nothing out of the ordinary for that. You accept it as a risk of the life you take when you become a wannabe gangster on the street. But if this woman is gunning for Ellie personally, then yeah, you've got a problem. Let me make some calls. I'll find her for you. It might take a day or so.'

'Thank you.' Tinker rose from the chair, but Simpson held a hand up.

'I ain't doing this for free,' he said. 'Ellie does things for favours, and I think I should do the same. You want Becky Slade, I'll find her for you. I'll even help you, however I can, when you find her. There's no love lost between us. But in return, I want something.'

'What?' Tinker asked.

'I want a date,' Simpson grinned. 'With you. Place of my choosing. And you have to wear a dress.'

Tinker stared long and hard at Simpson.

'You do this,' she said, 'then I'll come along, and I'll wear a dress. But so do you.'

Nicky Simpson laughed.

'You playing the *Hackers* ploy at me,' he said.

Tinker didn't know what he meant by this, and so she just shrugged.

'You think I would be scared of wearing a dress in public, what with my YouTube channel, and therefore wouldn't meet you for a drink?' Simpson shook his head. 'Tinker, Tinker, Tinker. You've given me even more reasons now to find out where she is. I'll pick somewhere very romantic, and incredibly public.'

'Can we leave now, please?' Tinker glared at Ramsey. 'I think you've done enough damage for the day.'

Ramsey was chuckling as he rose from his own chair.

'Oh, believe me, Tinker,' he said. 'The damage hasn't even started.'

5

SPARRING MATCHED

Even though Ellie had been calling in old requests and even burning a couple of the smaller favours owed to her, nothing had yet come up on where Becky Slade was or could be. By the end of the day, the team was still nowhere nearer to finding a location for the woman; it seemed that currently Becky Slade was a ghost with no official address to attack.

Even Casey, coming in and working through the dark web, had found nothing more than a few messages about her, mainly from bored South London thugs who, no longer working for the Simpsons, Lumettas or Seven Sisters, were hunting new opportunities. The responses pointed out that if they were interested, the Slades would be looking for people soon. As far as Casey was concerned, it looked like she was building an army, and *that* was concerning. For a start, the number of people she seemed to hire meant she was aiming at something big, and the amount of money she was promising meant she was expecting a payout larger than anything people had been expecting.

She wasn't looking to be a warlord. She was looking to be the next Nicky Simpson. In fact, possibly even bigger.

She wanted to be *Queen*.

By now it was well past six, and Ellie decided to call it a day. With Millie following along, she returned to her Shoreditch apartment where, after feeding and walking the Cocker Spaniel, Ellie let Millie settle down in her bed, threw on some running gear, and went out into the London evening.

There was a route that Ellie liked to run; she needed to keep herself fit and healthy, but be ready for anything. Over the last year or so, she'd found herself running the same route; eastwards onto the Bethnal Green Road, south down Morpeth Street, and now through Globetown and Bullard's Place, where the red brick building known as the Globe Town Boxing Club was.

Owned by the apparently reformed East End villain, Johnny Lucas, Ellie had been a long-time visitor of the club. With Johnny gaining more than his fair share of treasure from a couple of their cases, Ellie had found herself with effectively a lifetime membership, something she tried to utilise whenever she could. Her training regime had been to run to the club, spar for half an hour, and then run, or usually walk, back home. It was two, maybe three, hours of her life that she was able to put aside from all of her concerns. It was her moment of peace and quiet. Ellie needed it more than anything now. Especially with all the issues concerning Robert Lewis over the last few months.

The boxing club was what you would expect if somebody said the words "East End Boxing Club." There was talk that back in the fifties and sixties, the Kray twins had once boxed here as teenagers, but if she was being honest, Ellie could walk into any East End boxing club that had been around at the time and be told the exact same thing. It was the same as the number of East End pubs that claimed the Krays had drunk there. Taken over years ago by the Lucas Twins, Johnny and Jackie, the club had been a hotbed for crime for several decades, only recently becoming a far more legitimate place. Gone were the battered old metal weight racks and sawdust-filled weight bags. Over the last couple of years, the boxing club had had a refit, a revamp of sorts, and now there were cardio machines and fitness opportunities galore.

Entering, Ellie could even see some kind of plastic barrel above a grating. She'd been informed that this was called a "plunge pool", filled with cold water and often ice, and the people training would climb into it for a minute or two to help with their injuries ... or whatever. Ellie wasn't the biggest fan of cold showers but understood why people did it, though felt that jumping into a bucket of ice was a little too much.

She saw Leroy, one of the younger trainers, working with a teenage boy by the punch bag. He looked up, nodded, and grinned.

'Your seven pm sparring session started ages ago,' he nodded at the clock, now showing it was almost eight. 'You're late.'

'Been a bit of a day, mate. Any chance of a quick session once you're done?' Ellie hadn't even realised the time, already walking over to the counter and picking up a pair of boxing gloves.

'Actually, we *do* have somebody who's been waiting for a spar,' Leroy replied, pausing the boxer he was working with. 'Asked if they could spar this evening. I said you were usually late, they said they'd hang around.'

Leroy grinned, looking out to the back.

'Hey, your seven o'clock is finally here!'

Ellie was clambering into the ring now, putting a mouth guard over her teeth and pulling on the headpiece as, from the back room, a woman appeared.

She was dressed similarly to Ellie, but wore no headpiece or mouth guard. She was olive skinned, with brown eyes and long black hair tied into a plait at the back, with one glove on, fixing it to her wrist with her free hand as she walked towards Ellie.

'You must be Ellie Reckless,' she said, a slight Scottish lilt to her voice. 'Good to meet you.'

Ellie smacked her gloves together to make sure the fit worked.

'Likewise. Do you have a name?' she asked, amused at the secrecy here.

The woman said nothing as she clambered into the ring, fixing the other boxing glove on and pushing the mouth guard up over her top teeth.

'Becky Slade,' she said with a smile, the act doing nothing more than to show the mouth guard which had the words *R.I.P.* written on it. 'I understand you've been looking for me.'

Ellie had a moment of fear as Becky Slade started stretching, having placed the second glove on with practised ease.

She's not here to hurt you, Ellie thought to herself. *If she wanted you out of commission, she would have turned up with a baseball bat. This is something else. This is a testing ground. She wants to see how good you are, so show her.*

'How do you usually do these?' Becky asked.

'Two-minute rounds, keeping it easy,' Ellie said. 'It's more of a cardio for me than anything else. What about you?'

'I've never started a fight I didn't finish,' Becky replied calmly, looking back at her. 'I'm a lot more used to fighting with bare knuckles than with these padded pillows on, though.'

'You should remember your head guard,' Ellie said.

'Head guards are for pussies,' Becky said. 'I won't need it. It's very unlikely that you're going to lay a punch on me, anyway.'

Ellie couldn't help it, she grinned. The arrogance was, in a way, a little reassuring.

'Let's begin then.'

The two women circled around each other to start with, Ellie throwing a couple of practice jabs to test the distance between them.

Becky didn't seem bothered.

'So, why did you come here?' Ellie asked. 'You wanted to fight me?'

'Actually, I wanted to speak to you,' Becky replied. 'You got my message, I guess?'

'Yeah,' Ellie's voice was crisp. 'I'm a bit unimpressed, to be honest.'

'I see that,' Becky nodded. 'But he was dealing drugs in my area. I had to make an example out of him.'

'Last I heard, that wasn't your turf.' Ellie dodged as Becky lazily threw a punch at her. 'Last I heard, it was open ground, and you were in Scotland.'

'I've been all over the place. Decided to come back a few months back.'

'When the Simpsons left?'

'Balham is owned by the Slades,' Becky said emotionlessly, ignoring the question. 'Tooting, Balham, all the way up to Clapham and the Oakland's Estate is Slade space. He should have known better than to peddle his shit in our area without giving us our due.'

'I'm sure he won't be doing it anymore,' Ellie replied. 'And I understand why he needed to be taught a lesson, but what the hell was the Maglite for?'

'Did you like that bit?' Becky grinned, showing the R.I.P. on her teeth once more. 'That was my little personal touch. I wanted you to understand that I'm as serious as a heart attack.'

There was a jab, a duck, and more circling.

'You wanted my attention, you got it,' Ellie replied. 'So, why don't you tell me what you actually want? Because in my experience, when somebody turns up to spar with you, it usually means they want to beat the shit out of you.'

'I'd like to talk to you about your favours,' Becky ducked as Ellie moved in, jabbing. She'd been correct. Becky was wickedly fast; Ellie was finding it hard to even get close to her face, only managing a couple of right hands into her torso, ones that had been easily blocked.

'What about them?' Ellie asked.

'I'd like them,' Becky replied, shuffling back, allowing a swing from Ellie to pass in front of her, wide. Ellie had overstepped, overbalanced, and Becky capitalised on this, ramming a hard right into Ellie's solar plexus, winding her for a second as Ellie staggered back.

That hurt. She needed to up her game.

'They're not for sale,' she said when she'd gathered her breath back. 'The favours are owed to me, not anybody else.'

'Oh, I get that,' Becky said as she paced around the ring. This wasn't a boxing move; there was no Muhammad Ali-style footwork here. Becky simply stalked her prey, her arms down, a bare-knuckle fighter who was purely there to hurt. 'I actually want you on my team.'

'Others have asked the same. They've always had the same answer,' Ellie replied.

'Yeah, but that was before everything was sorted, wasn't it?' Becky threw another punch. This time Ellie was able to miss it, but only just. 'You see, I know Mama Lumetta suggested you take on the West London area. I know the Tsangs would happily use you as an arbitrator.'

She waved around the gym.

'Christ, even East London's open for grabs now.'

'I think you'll find that just because Johnny Lucas isn't in the building doesn't mean his reach isn't here,' Ellie said.

'Reach, sure,' Becky replied. 'Let me show you reach.'

Before Ellie could say anything, Becky had swung hard upwards, catching Ellie hard on the jaw. The headpiece had taken the bulk of the impact, but it was a solid sledgehammer of a blow, and Ellie staggered back, shaking her head as Becky moved in again.

'I've got the measure of your reach now, and my reach is longer,' Becky continued.

Ellie was backing away now, realising this wasn't a simple sparring session.

'Whatever you think—' she started, but stopped as Becky had already started swinging again, quick jabs that Ellie could only absorb on the arms. It felt like she was being tenderised by a butcher.

'This is how it works,' Becky said. 'If you used all your favours, and let's be honest here, there are some big names you've got under your thumb, you could take over London. Not just south of the river. You could take over east, west, central London. You could head north, take the Seven Sisters apart. But you haven't got the balls to do it, and so I've decided that *I* should have them, because I'll know what to do with them.'

She jabbed again, but as Ellie scrambled back, she realised it was a feint.

Becky Slade was bloody playing with her.

'Now, I'd like to work as a partner with you. Ellie, you seem quite competent, and you do make the little boys shit themselves when they hear your name, so I'm more than happy to split the city with you, give you a little fiefdom of your own. But to do that, you've got to work *for* me. Give me your favours and help me.'

She jabbed twice. Ellie dodged but missed the left that came out of nowhere, catching her hard under the ribs on the right-hand side with a woof of expelled air.

Becky hadn't finished her sales pitch.

'When Mama Lumetta suggested you as a replacement, you were still trying to sort out everything going on with Nicky Simpson and his family. Now? You haven't got that over your head. The lawyer that kept you on the straight and narrow, well, he's gone for a stroll, hasn't he? All you've got is a thief, a cyber hacker and an ex-squaddie. Come on, Ellie, you ain't working for the angels anymore. Even the police, the people that were on your side, turned out to be against you. Every single bloody one of them turned out to be corrupt.'

'Not all of them,' Ellie replied, her voice croaking as she gulped in air.

'The fact you had to say, "not all of them" is bad enough,' Becky laughed, now hanging back, letting Ellie take a breath. 'Together, we could take over London.'

'And if I say no?'

'Then I'll just do it on my own and slower,' Becky said.

'And you'll become an enemy, and you don't really want to know what happens if you become my enemy.'

She sighed, smacking her gloves back together, getting ready to start again.

'So, what's it to be, Ellie? You gonna come work for me?'

'Nah, I don't play well with others,' Ellie replied. 'And there's no way you're doing this off your own back. You disappeared, and from what I can see you never went large in Scotland. Someone's backing you, funding you to do this. Care to say who?'

Becky didn't reply to this, her expression one of someone who had expected nothing else. She considered the woman in front of her, and moved into a fighting stance.

'Ballsy. I admire that. Let's finish this session and then we'll go our separate ways, then.'

Ellie went to reply, but didn't get a chance because Becky had moved in fast, bringing her arm up hard. The speed was incredible. Ellie hadn't expected it, and the glove hammered into the side of her head, sending her stumbling, sparks flying in front of her eyes.

But, before she could shake it off, Becky had moved back in again, hammering again and again, vicious shots punching into her head, her shoulders, and just as she managed to block with her arms, Becky moved in once more, hammering into her ribs, punching harder and harder, sending her staggering back.

This was not a sparring session. This was a prize fight, and Ellie was losing badly.

Ellie stumbled back, trying to stop Becky Slade, but she couldn't get an offensive move in. The attacks were continual.

'I've beaten the shit out of bigger and badder people than you, Reckless, both in Scotland with my clan, and down here,' Becky Slade snarled as she hammered down once more. 'Sometimes I even play by the rules ... but it's way more fun when I don't.'

Ellie got one blow in. It was a right-hander, and it was enough to rock Becky for a second, but that's all it was, because the moment she'd punched, she realised she'd extended her reach, and Becky, absorbing the blow, hammered hard into Ellie's face, sending her to the floor.

It felt like her legs were rubber. Her ears were ringing, and her eyes were blurred. She tried to climb back up, but Becky just crouched and hammered down hard with the glove once more into her face.

'Stay down, you bitch,' Becky snarled. 'Know your place.'

'Hey!' a male voice shouted. Leroy, realising that the sparring session wasn't going as expected, ran over. 'It's over, yeah? You're done.'

Becky rose, ready for another fight, but then realised that two of the other boxers in the gym had moved in as well, and now she was outnumbered.

'You don't want to start this, little boy,' she said. 'You don't know who I am.'

'I know exactly who you are.'

'Yeah?'

'Yeah. And you don't know where *you* are,' Leroy replied. 'The guy who runs this place—'

'The guy who runs this place is old and pointless,' Becky replied. 'And he's been battered so many times he had to go *legitimate* to hide from me.'

She laughed, rising, leaving Ellie alone on the floor.

'This ain't over, Reckless,' she said. 'I gave you a chance to stand beside me. Now you're going to lie prostrate in front of me as I march my way through London.'

She leant back down, and Ellie flinched, expecting another punch. But instead, Becky pulled off her right glove and lightly caressed the side of Ellie's headguard.

'And I *will* get your debts,' she said. 'I will burn every single one of them, use them all myself, until you have nothing. And then? Then I'll do exactly to you what I did to your little friend. Everyone will see that Becky Slade took down Ellie Reckless, and I'll finally gain the reparations.'

With this last ominous message given, Becky Slade rose and walked out of the ring.

Leroy helped Ellie to her feet, but her legs didn't want to work, and her head was still ringing.

Jesus, she thought to herself. *She was wearing padded gloves, and I had a headpiece on. How would this have felt if it were bare-knuckled?*

'Are you okay?' Leroy asked.

'No, Leroy, I can honestly say I'm really not okay,' Ellie shook her head.

She had learned Becky Slade's reach.

And she had learned that she was lacking.

6

HOUSE GUESTS

LEROY HAD TAKEN CARE OF ELLIE AFTER THE BOXING MATCH, and Becky Slade had long gone before Ellie's rubbery legs were finally able to hold her weight. She'd been moved over to a chair against the wall where she could gather her breath, down some water, and get herself ready to move.

During that time, she had noticed him making a few calls.

After ten to fifteen minutes of resting, she finally felt confident enough to get back on her feet. The confidence, however, was purely about her foot's ability to move, because Ellie no longer felt confident about anything else. She'd spent her entire career as an officer convinced that, although she wasn't the best out there, she could hold herself in a fight. She knew she would constantly have to find moments where she'd tackle or struggle with someone. In fact, several times over the last year, she had found herself in situations where she'd had to do the very same thing. But she'd never been taken apart so quickly as she was by Becky Slade. In fact, for many of the ten minutes that she'd sat at the chair, her head down almost between her legs as she gathered her breath, trying to stop the spinning and pretty much convinced she'd got some kind of concussion, Ellie had relived that moment, that one punch that threw her to the floor and Becky's face staring down at her.

'Stay down, you bitch. Know your place.'

Becky Slade was not one of the usual lieutenants that Ellie often dealt with. Becky Slade was trouble, and if she got her way, she would become the future of London's Underworld. Ellie didn't know why or how, but she knew without a doubt that this would be the worst possible thing that could ever happen. She needed to work out the game plan here. Was there someone funding her? A hand behind the pretender throne? Someone who brought her back down from her smaller life with what was likely her Traveller clan in Scotland? Becky was a fighter, but so far there wasn't much of the thinker she'd need to be.

Although she's still a step ahead of me, Ellie thought miserably to herself. *Maybe I'm the one not being the thinker this time.*

By the time Leroy had returned to her, having made his mysterious phone calls, she was already planning her next steps. Usually, Ellie would be hired to find something, solve a problem, or troubleshoot. There'd be the occasional brokering of treaties or peace deals between gangs. Finding missing magicians was one of the far extremes, but they were usually tasks that could be done easily. There was a target, and Ellie's team was brought in to achieve it. This time, though, the target seemed almost unassailable. To defeat Becky Slade, she also had to factor in Becky Slade's ambitions, and they seemed to be the biggest thing of all.

The only way that Ellie Reckless could beat Becky Slade would be to take over the role that Becky Slade wanted, and that was something that Ellie *still* wouldn't do.

Or would she?

Leroy, knowing that Ellie had run to the gym, had led her to his car, locking up behind him. Ellie had protested, but Leroy had pointed out he'd asked, and been given permission to close up for twenty minutes while he drove her back to her apartment – finally the mysterious phone call was revealed, and Ellie knew this would have had to have come from Johnny Lucas himself. Which meant at some point she'd have to deal with him too, like some overprotective ex-gangster mother hen.

Ellie had groaned and grumbled, but in all honesty, she was grateful for the opportunity. The last thing she felt like doing right now was suffering a two-mile walk back. As it was, it still took Leroy a few more minutes to lock up the boxing club, even if it was for a temporary break in the proceedings, but eventually, Ellie was placed almost carefully into the passenger seat and driven back to her apartment.

Leroy also offered to walk her to the front door of her apartment, but Ellie shook her head gingerly in case it would fall off. *She didn't need a babysitter,* she contested. *She was absolutely fine.*

Leroy was concerned. As a boxing trainer, he had seen his fair share of knockouts and concussions, and was worried this was something that was possible here. He pointed out if she started having certain symptoms appear, such as dizziness or nausea, she should definitely *not* go to sleep, and instead find somebody who could keep waking her up every two to three hours, if she couldn't stay awake, just to make sure.

Ellie didn't think she was concussed. The punch had been hard enough to stun her and send her to the floor, but she hadn't been knocked unconscious, and she *had* been wearing the protective headpiece. Again, the thought came through her mind – *what would have happened if Becky Slade had punched her that hard when she wasn't wearing such a headpiece?*

Another thing that Ellie would have to consider.

Walking up to her apartment, she paused as she noticed the door was slightly ajar. She knew she'd locked it when she'd left; the last thing she'd do would be to leave the front door open with a spaniel inside. Now, realising that in her gym gear, and with only a phone as a weapon, she was seriously under matched for whatever was in there or whoever was in there.

Ellie steeled herself, took a deep breath, and pushed open the door.

Sitting on her sofa, snuggling with Millie, was Johnny Lucas.

Currently, the MP for Bethnal Green and Bow, Johnny had, for many years, been the archetypal gangster of the East End. Ellie groaned inwardly; she should have realised Johnny would have come straight here after Leroy called.

'You shouldn't be here,' she said, closing the door behind her. She knew Johnny wouldn't be a threat; she'd known him for many years now. There was an irritation he'd broken in, but at the same time, it could have been far worse.

Johnny turned around and smiled.

'I apologise for letting myself in,' he said, a polite way of saying "picking your lock". 'But I couldn't really let a Member of Parliament be seen standing around your apartment door. Rumours could have spread, and besides, Millie was losing her mind inside knowing that I was waiting. The little girl just loves me so much.'

Ellie chuckled. There had been times over the summer

when she'd walked Millie to the boxing club, and Millie had stayed in the back office while Ellie practised her sparring. Sometimes when Johnny came to visit, purely as a social call rather than any business intention now he was a Member of Parliament, Ellie had seen him snuggling and playing with the dog. It seemed the East End gangster turned politician had a soft side after all.

'You should be in Westminster keeping our world safe,' she joked, walking to the kitchen area and grabbing herself a water. She found herself increasingly thirsty and wondered if this was again either a problem to do with concussion, or the simple fact that she'd run two miles and then got into a boxing ring.

Johnny looked up.

'Yes, please,' he said and Ellie nodded, pouring a second glass of water from a bottle. The water in her apartment was drinkable but, if she was being honest, she preferred to filter it. Walking back to the sofa, she placed a glass down in front of Johnny and sat in the chair to the side, facing him.

'Would you like to explain to me why you're here?' she asked.

Johnny shifted in his seat, turning to look at her, and Millie grumbled as she moved around on the chair.

'Leroy told me what happened,' he said. 'That you got sparked out by Becky Slade.'

His face was impassive, but his voice was cold and angry.

'Why the bloody hell were you sparring with Becky Slade?'

'Because she found out I'd been looking for her,' Ellie said.

'And why were you looking for her?'

'Because,' Ellie finished her glass of water and placed it

on the table, 'she's been looking for me. She took out a friend of mine's nephew to make a point. I decided I wanted to have a chat. Didn't realise that she was one step ahead of me, though.'

'From what I've seen, Becky Slade's one step ahead of everybody right now,' Johnny replied. 'Her entire bloody family's hot-headed, and she's been in Jockland for years. Why does she want you? I'm guessing she gave you an idea while she was punching the shit out of you.'

'It was one punch, and I wasn't ready,' Ellie muttered. 'Well, maybe a couple. No more than a few, at least. I did pretty well, thank you very much.'

'Until the moment she sparked you out,' Johnny smiled. 'Yeah, you did great there. Why was she looking for you?'

Ellie sighed.

'You know about my favours?'

'Of course I do,' Johnny replied. 'You've repeatedly reminded me I still owe you one, even after I stored God knows how many thousands of illegal bottles of gold in my boxing club, under the sodding ring.'

'Seem to recall you kept a few for yourself,' Ellie smiled. 'But yeah, it's the favours that have caused the problem. The debts I'm owed are like catnip to Becky Slade.'

'Because she wants them for herself,' Johnny asked, nodding as he understood. 'Let me guess, she's worked out the people who owe you can help her take over the South of London.'

'That's what I thought to start with,' Ellie replied. 'I know she was moving in on Nicky Simpson's area after Nicky apparently became the poster boy for the victim syndrome of gangster children. And, now, as there's no power base in South London, she's been moving back in. But I can't help thinking she's gaining help here. Financial help, a backer of some kind.'

'It won't be Drew, as her dad was a second-rate wannabe,' Johnny said, and the venom in his voice was surprising. 'He was a two-bit Scottish prick who thought he was better than he was. He tried it on with everyone, Ellie, including me and my brother.'

Ellie kept quiet at this point. It was a well-known fact that although Johnny and Jackie Lucas were twin brothers, Jackie had died sometime in the late nineties. But Johnny had some kind of mental breakdown, that meant for at least two decades he'd played the part of his dead brother, and people hadn't been sure which "twin" they would meet on a daily basis, as Johnny and Jackie had become the same person. It had only been a couple of years earlier when a detective unit, with help from Ellie, broke this.

Shortly after, the now revitalised Johnny, with all of his illegal activities blamed on his imaginary brother, now revealed to be "real" thanks to an imposter, had gone for Parliament, but that he still referred to his broken personality as "his brother" still, was a little concerning.

Johnny knew Ellie was holding back, so he leant forward, steepling his fingers.

'Just bloody speak,' he said. 'I've got no time for waiting around.'

Ellie considered this.

'She wants the entire package,' she said. 'Think about it. South of the river is up for grabs. The Simpsons have lost their power. The areas that the Simpsons didn't have are now trying to stretch into those areas and over-stretching themselves. The Simpsons' lieutenants were pretty much arrested when he was. So, anybody who's moving up to take the spot is so far down the pecking order, they don't really know what was going on. You look to the east and although the "Lucas Twins" are still a force to be feared, many people think you're toothless now.'

'Ouch,' Johnny said, but there was a smile to his words.

'Just saying it as I see it,' Ellie shrugged. 'When you ran East London, nobody pissed around. I might have hated it, being a police officer, but at the same time, I understood what was going on. Now you're on this whatever it is – this chaotic need you have to be an MP – people are paying attention to East London. There's a definite opening for someone who wants to take it. The Tsangs in West London are struggling after various deaths and Jimmy being told to piss off back to China—'

'Which I believe you did,' Johnny smiled.

'And then the Seven Sisters are still in freefall after the problems that happened with Mama Delcourt and her daughter,' Ellie continued, ignoring the comment. 'Which yeah, I know, I was involved in, too.'

'And of course you've got the centre,' Johnny Lucas nodded. 'Which has been a bouncing ground for a dozen different people.'

'Arun Nadal's now making a play, and he seems to be a nobody who has big pockets. And then you've got the Lumettas, who apparently have retired and gone legit,' Ellie continued the thread.

'Because of you,' Johnny smiled. 'And don't worry about Nadal. He's a rabid dog, sure, but he's on a leash.'

'Whose leash?'

Johnny shrugged dismissively, and Ellie sighed again.

'Whatever's happening now, I don't know,' she said. 'All I know is there's a lot of gangland heads who are no longer doing it anymore, whether it's because of me, or Monroe and his gang of happy little miscreants. I don't care; if it makes London safer, it's great.'

She leant closer, matching Johnny Lucas.

'But it's not, is it?' she said. 'People like Becky Slade are coming in. The sharks are seeing the water churning and they're smelling blood.'

Johnny said nothing, and Ellie slammed a fist on the coffee table.

'Dammit, Johnny, what am I missing?'

'You're not missing anything,' Johnny replied. 'You already know what you need to do.'

Ellie shook her head, leaning back again, almost as if to gain distance from the suggestion.

'I've had this talk with Mama Lumetta,' she replied. 'She wanted me to take over her side of the industry, become a gangland warlord. It's not my style. I'm a copper.'

'No, Ellie, you stopped being a copper several years ago,' Johnny stated. 'You became the cop for criminals, remember? The woman who would solve your problem if you gave her a favour. And before you complain, I know you had reasons to do it. But now you've *become* that person. Hell, you were cleared when Nicky Simpson dobbed his granddad in. Everything was released out into the open. You were no longer the person who killed Bryan Noyce, no longer the person who had done all these terrible things. The police would have welcomed you back with open arms. You were no longer a PR disaster; you were a PR extravaganza. They would have wheeled you and Delgado out as the Golden Girls, and yet you stayed away.'

He shook his head.

'Once a copper, always a copper, I get that. But you're not

a copper. You're an arbitrator of gangland criminals at best. You're a private mercenary force of troubleshooters with a very strange payment structure.'

There was an uncomfortable silence in the room as Ellie stared at Johnny Lucas.

'Would you back me?' Ellie asked. 'If I went for it? The arbitrator you spoke of, creating ground rules that kept civilians safe?'

She narrowed her eyes.

'Or maybe if I *did* want the whole thing? Queen of London, just like Becky?'

'I don't care what you do, as long as you don't try for East London,' Johnny smiled. 'I have my own plans for that.'

'I thought you were out?'

'You're never out, even you know that,' Johnny shrugged. 'But if I did have to pass the baton, I'd rather it was to family, no matter how distant.'

He winked at this, and settled back in the chair. However, at this, Ellie shook her head.

'I'm not gonna do it, Johnny,' she said. 'I'll burn the debts. Every single one of them, before I do that.'

'As is your right,' Johnny replied, rising from his seat. 'I'm really sorry, Ellie, but I must dash. I have a bill that needs to be voted on before ten o'clock. They're still debating it right now, but I'll need to come in and cast my deciding vote, I'm sure. I'm incredibly important now. More so than I was when me and my brother ran London.'

'I can't believe that,' Ellie laughed. 'But you've always been important to me, Johnny.'

'Flattery will get you everywhere,' Johnny paused at the door, looking back at Ellie, who had now moved over to the sofa where she was stroking Millie, snuggling him beside her.

'I'm not a gangster,' he said. 'You're not a copper. So let me give you some hypothetical advice, as if we were still both. If I was a copper, I'd want to take Becky Slade out. As a gangster, I'd look for a *permanent* way. Your decision is how you play that.'

'I won't kill anybody,' Ellie retorted.

Johnny grinned.

'But, Ellie,' he said. 'I never killed anybody either.'

With that ominous statement, far more likely to be utterly incorrect and one of the biggest lies he'd spoken that evening – and that included an upcoming debate in Parliament – Johnny Lucas left Ellie Reckless alone.

7

WAR COUNCIL

Tinker hadn't been happy about this decision, but she understood the logistics of it. With Becky Slade already showing she had information on both where Ellie trained in the evenings and where she had her breakfast meetings, it had been decided that a change of location would be optimal, especially if they were going to do things that the Finder's Agency might not be too happy about.

After all, once Becky Slade was sorted, they'd like the partners to still pay them.

Consequently, a favour once offered by Nicky Simpson was taken up. Ellie Reckless's gang now had new offices on the first floor of Nicky Simpson's exclusive Battersea health club.

It was only a couple of rooms, a phone line and an internet connection; nothing exciting. But it gave a few solid advantages over the City of London address that they'd been using.

For a start, being south of the river meant they were closer to where Becky Slade had appeared out of nowhere, and was currently working. This gave them an opportunity to speak to more people in a shorter amount of time. Second, it meant they had the advantages of using Nicky Simpson's extensive contacts list. He might no longer have been the South London gangster he once claimed to be, but he was still a man who, for several years had held that post. And whether or not his grandfather had managed to ruin things, Nicky Simpson had a contact list that Ellie could use to her advantage, especially as half of that list owed her favours as well.

She hadn't wanted to use any, but with someone like Becky Slade staring across the playing board at her, Ellie knew she had to play clever.

The first thing Ellie had done that morning had been to contact Mama Lumetta and suggest perhaps she'd like to come and sample a free trip to Simpson's Health Club. She had then contacted Kenny Tsang, offering the same situation. Kenny was less happy about this, but was aware that he also still owed Ellie a favour. And even if this *wasn't* that favour, he knew if he didn't do what she asked, she could make his life very difficult.

Thus, with the onetime South London ganglord, the West London ganglord, the onetime Central London ganglord, and on the advice of an East London ganglord, across a very expensive-looking glass and chrome board table, in a room surrounded by advertising placards for Simpson's Health Clubs and macrobiotic energy drinks, Ellie Reckless held a council of war.

'I don't understand why I'm here,' Kenny Tsang said. He was tall, slim and tired-looking, most likely as a year or so earlier he'd been shot in the chest, retired, and then came back once his cousin Jimmy moved in on his lands.

Mama Lumetta chuckled at this. Slim, with permed white hair, she looked around.

'Why do we have no one from the Seven Sisters?'

'Because Becky hasn't reached that far yet,' Ellie said. 'At the moment, she's pissing off everybody south of the Thames. But it's only going to be a matter of time before she moves up to you guys.'

'And why do you think that?' Kenny asked.

'Because last night she asked for me to give her all of my debts,' Ellie replied carefully, knowing that Kenny was one of the people that owed a favour.

'You'd better not have bloody given them to her.'

'Do you think I'd be having this meeting with you right now if I had?' Ellie snapped back. 'Becky Slade wanted me to join her. In doing so, I'd provide her with my debts, my contact list, so to speak, of people who owed me favours, and she would have used them to – in her own words – take over London. Now, I don't know for sure, but the last I saw, London covered all the areas you're involved in.'

'I'd like to raise a point here,' Mama Lumetta said, holding her hand up. 'I no longer have territory. I believe Mister Simpson there no longer has territory, and I know that our absent MP for Bethnal Green and Bow has no territory. So why are *we* here?'

'Because *he's* given us this problem,' Ellie said bluntly as she nodded at Nicky Simpson.

'Well, thanks for that,' Simpson replied coldly. He looked

at the back of the room where, keeping to the side, were Tinker, Ramsey, and Casey.

'Are you going to let her say these terrible things about me?' he said to Tinker. 'I thought you liked me.'

'Not enough to stop her saying nasty things about you,' Tinker smiled. 'I'm learning some nice words. I might gain some juicy secrets I can use against you next time you try to ask me on a date.'

'A date?' Ellie raised an eyebrow at this.

'He's going to wear a dress,' Tinker said. 'It's going to be very romantic.'

Simpson ignored her, looking back at Ellie.

'You can't pin this on me,' he said.

'I can exactly pin this on you,' Ellie replied carefully. 'In fact, I can use the date that you stepped down as head of the Simpson family as the point everything came crashing down and Becky Slade started to work on taking control.'

'Everybody always wants control,' Simpson shook his head. 'You can't say that my stepping down, or your ongoing campaign to take me out before that point, misguidedly believing that I was the murderer, was the catalyst.'

He shook his head.

'But I do agree with what you're saying. As much as I don't run the south of London anymore and for official branding reasons would never consider doing it again, Becky Slade is becoming a real pain in my arse. And I've spent years sculpting that into a thing of beauty.'

He looked across at Kenny Tsang.

'You're still in the game,' he said. 'Why don't you just send a couple of boys across the Thames, pop-pop, back of the head, done?'

'We're not having that conversation,' Ellie said.

'No? Are we going to fight her in a boxing ring, then?' Simpson glared back at her. 'Yeah, I heard. She took you out with one punch. What did you expect? She's a gypsy bare-knuckle fighter's daughter. She's a Scottish Tyson Fury, but with hair. And, well, you know, other parts.'

Ellie waited for his tantrum to finish and then, once he'd argued himself into silence, she leant forward, placing her elbows on the table.

'A few months back, Mama Lumetta said that if I wanted to go for her territory and become the new Queen of Central London she would endorse me,' she said. 'But I don't want that. Don't take this personally, but I've never really seen myself on your side of the table.'

The others simply shrugged or made accepting gestures. They understood what Ellie was saying.

'But what I have been for many years now, since I started working at Finder's, was someone very good at working *with* people like you.'

She heard a slight intake of breath and recognised it as Ramsey's. He hadn't been happy with this line of attack when she discussed it with him, but he was also aware of why she had to do it. She pressed on regardless.

'You need a police force,' she said. 'Cops for criminals to solve your problems that the police don't have to. Arbitrators of problems in the industry. My suggestion is that I and my team *become* that arbitrator. We'll be the people who *control* the people.'

'Sounds to me like you want to be a gangland leader,' Kenny muttered.

'No,' Ellie replied, looking back. 'I will expect no percentages. I will expect no tithes.'

'You do all that without the tithes and percentages, then

you're an idiot,' Mama Lumetta spoke harshly. 'Take the damned crown. Once you run London you can do what you want. Work with your friends in the police. Dismantle it. But know whatever you do, people like Slade will always wait for you to fail.'

'She's right,' Tinker added from the back. 'We don't need to take over anything, but if we don't stop her, she does, so you have to at least go for it.'

She waved around the room.

'None of these can officially help you, apart from Kenny, and even he's still part-time until his health improves.'

'But we can provide you muscle,' Mama Lumetta nodded slowly. 'Soldiers to fight the ones Becky Slade's recruiting.'

She narrowed her eyes.

'But you already knew this, didn't you?'

Ellie nodded, her face emotionless.

'I want Becky gone,' she said. 'But what happens then? Who's next? When will they stop?'

'When you burn your debts,' Kenny replied softly. 'When you are no longer a threat.'

'But she can gain new favours,' Simpson added. 'Which means she'll always be a threat. Unless ...'

He trailed off, the comment didn't need to be finished. They all knew what he was saying.

Only when Becky Slade was dead and gone would Ellie no longer be targeted.

There was a clearing of the throat, and Ellie glanced around to look back at Casey.

'You have a problem with this?' she asked, her voice tight.

Casey, who had been working on his laptop in the corner, leant back.

'Actually, yeah,' he replied. 'You're talking here about

taking her down and removing her like she's some kind of rival gang lord, but you're not a gang lord, Ellie, you're a copper. You might not think you are, but you've always been a copper. Your entire basis was to keep the law, and it still is right now.'

'That's why I'm talking about arbitrating—' Ellie replied.

'No.' Interrupting, Casey rose now, his laptop in his hand. 'That's not what you're doing. Look at who you've brought in. Name me some other people in London who can pull in three gangland leaders, even if they are retired, at a moment's notice! If you wanted to, you could have brought in Mama Delcourt, Christ, you could have had Zoom calls from people in prison. You've got power here that nobody else has, and it's going to corrupt you.'

He turned back to the other members of the team.

'Am I the only one seeing this?' he asked. 'Ellie's talking about taking out Becky Slade, and not once are we looking at how we can remove her legally!'

'If we remove Becky legally, then the message isn't given right, and someone else will take the role,' Kenny said. 'A message, a *statement,* has to be made clear.'

'That's not our concern,' Casey replied, his face reddening as he realised he was now becoming the focus of attention. 'Sure, Becky's removed, someone else turns up, that's how things always go. Before you and your brother, it was someone else, probably your father, I don't know.'

'The Turk,' Kenny replied.

'And was he related to you?'

'No, but we took him out in a drive by, about thirteen years back.'

'Exactly …' Casey paused as he realised the point he'd just had confirmed was an admission of murder, but still carried on, regardless. 'There's got to be something we can use to take this woman down, and I don't mean in a way that Ellie wants to do. Becky's grandfather was shot in the face. Maybe there's something there, maybe there's rivals in the shadows we can use, maybe there was a problem in the family?'

'They've got a history of kicking off against each other,' Tinker admitted.

'Great. Then we find something you can leverage on her.'

'I hate to admit it, but the boy has a point,' Simpson said. 'Look, you can go on about gaining an army to take out Becky, that's fine, but at the end of the day, all you have to do is *take out Becky.*'

There was a tense silence in the room. Ellie rubbed at her head, closing her eyes as she could feel a migraine approaching.

'Ellie, you're an ex-detective who solves problems with a Cocker Spaniel by her side,' Ramsey carried on, following on from Simpson's comment. 'Perhaps you don't really want to take the path you're suggesting.'

'I don't want to take any bloody path,' Ellie muttered to herself. 'But that doesn't mean it's not being made for me.'

She paused as, in the doorway, Joanne Davey appeared. She waved to gain Ellie's attention and motioned for Ellie and the rest of the team to join her outside in the corridor.

'Gentlemen, ladies, please wait here a moment,' Ellie said, rising, looking to the others, 'Ramsey, Tinks, Casey, I think our presence is required.'

WITH THE OTHERS FOLLOWING, ELLIE WALKED OUTSIDE.

'You got my message then,' she said.

'What, that we're staying here and getting healthy?' Davey passed a gaze across the corridor. 'Yeah, that's not why I'm pulling you out. There's no crime scene forensics to examine, so I've started forensically examining Becky Slade.'

'Okay,' Ellie frowned. 'What have you found that's making you look like someone's pissed on your chips?'

Davey pulled out her phone and for a moment, Ellie wondered if she was even going to show her what was on it.

'Look,' she said. 'I take no delight in this, all right?'

'What do you mean?' Ellie asked, a sense of foreboding creeping in.

Davey, in response, turned the phone, opening a photos app. She scrolled to the most recent photo in the library.

'I'm sorry, Ellie,' she said, 'but I got this from a friend. It seems like Becky Slade has allies we didn't realise.'

Ellie stared at the image. It was Becky Slade in a business suit, emerging from what looked to be an old red-brick building.

Beside her, walking slightly behind with his head held low, was Robert Lewis. Only his dirty-blond hair with a white streak along the parting gave his identity away.

'I think we now know why Robert's not been contacting you for the last couple of months,' Ramsey said as he brought his attention up from the picture. 'It appears our solicitor friend is now playing for the enemy.'

Ellie continued to look at the photo, unable to reply for a moment. It wasn't faked. Ellie trusted Davey enough to know she would have checked that before bringing it, which meant that Robert Lewis *had* been there and *had* been beside Becky Slade when the photo was taken.

'Do we know where this is from?' Ellie asked.

'No,' Davey replied, putting the phone away. 'All I can say with any guarantee is it was taken within the last month. I'm sorry, Ellie.'

'We don't know what this means,' Ellie said, looking up. 'And until we know one hundred percent that he's turned to the dark side, we are not giving up on Robert Lewis.'

She glanced back into the room where three potential allies now sat watching her, trying to work out what was going on.

'This means nothing,' she repeated. 'Don't say a word about it. Casey, have a check for us. Find out what Robert's been doing for the last four months.'

She shook her head, shaking out the bad thoughts.

'Because he sure as hell hasn't been having a sabbatical.'

8

POLICE INFORMANT

If DI Kate Delgado was being honest, the last person she expected to walk through the doors to her Vauxhall crime unit was Ellie Sodding Reckless.

They had been colleagues at one point, but when Ellie was accused of killing Bryan Noyce, Delgado had sided against her, convinced Ellie had crossed the line. Blood traces on her clothing had proven this, and she'd never believed the story that Ellie gave, that it had been a fight where blood had been drawn, coincidentally hours before Noyce was murdered.

It seemed too convenient, and Ellie had already started hanging with the wrong types by that point.

Delgado had, of course, been wrong.

Mark Whitehouse, her partner and Ellie's ex-partner, had always stood up for Ellie, claiming this was nothing more than a witch-hunt, and that Ellie was innocent. Delgado was painted as the bad guy, and then when Mark himself was proven to be the man who organised Bryan's murder and Ellie was cleared of all charges, Delgado was *still* seen as the bad guy, even though she was the one who ended up arresting her partner. She'd had to take a two-month secondment in Charing Cross and Soho to get away from the whispered accusations, and had only returned to Vauxhall once her promotion to Detective Inspector had been confirmed.

But, in the end, Delgado had stayed the course. She'd kept to her beliefs and had no concerns about people being angry with her for what she did. She'd followed the law every step of the way, and if someone had a problem with that, well, *to hell with them.*

After Mark had been arrested, and the true story of how Paddy Simpson had arranged the death of Bryan Noyce via Mark, throwing it onto Ellie to remove another thorn at the same time, had come out, Delgado had felt stupid and had even offered a hand of friendship to Ellie, only to find it ignored.

She couldn't really fault that, though, she would have done the same herself.

But here she was, facing Ellie one more time, in the reception of her police's unit – Ellie's *old* one.

Apparently, on arrival, Ellie asked for Delgado by name, and the sergeant on duty had recognised her. A veteran of the beat, he was most likely around when Ellie was a DI in the unit, but she hadn't been invited into the building; no, only *police* came into the building, and regardless of what Ellie Reckless was now, she was definitely *not* police. She'd been re-offered her role back once the authorities were happy she wasn't the criminal they'd believed her to be, and unsurprisingly, Ellie had thrown it back in their faces.

They'd wanted her to take a transfer, maybe go to a quiet, sleepy village. Ellie, meanwhile, had felt this was a way to remove her from their equation – dumped in a village and forgotten. She'd said no, walked away, and carried on with her team, working for Finders.

Delgado stared at Ellie, wondering what game was being played here.

Ellie, meanwhile, had arrived with what looked to be two takeaway cups of coffee.

She offered one forward.

'I was hoping we could have a catch-up,' she said.

'You and me, we don't have catch-ups,' Delgado replied, not reaching for the proffered cup. 'People like us, we end up trying to arrest each other, or *outwit* each other, I should say, because you can't arrest me, can you, Ellie, not being a police officer?'

'You say it like it's a bad thing,' Ellie replied. 'Look, Kate, I'm not here to fight. I actually need your advice.'

At this, Kate Delgado paused her response. She'd been about to throw some cheap jibe, but for Ellie to open herself up and ask for help, well, that was almost unknown.

'Okay,' she said, taking the cup of coffee. 'But let's do it outside, yeah?'

'I wouldn't have it any other way,' Ellie nodded at the sergeant behind the desk. 'See you later, Jamie.'

Jamie, the desk sergeant didn't reply. Like many others, he'd turned his back on Ellie the moment she'd been accused of the crime she didn't commit. And, like Delgado, he was probably a little uncomfortable being in her presence.

Still, at least he didn't have to have a bloody coffee with her.

Walking out of the Vauxhall unit, Ellie and Delgado made their way down Nine Elms Street, towards St George Wharf and the Riverside Gardens.

'So, what's this about?' Delgado asked. 'Last I heard, you were going legit. No more favours, no more crime lords. Is that still the case?'

Ellie gave a weak smile.

'Yes and no,' she replied.

'I expected nothing less,' Delgado sighed, sipping at her coffee. It was surprisingly good; even after all these years, Ellie had remembered how she took it.

Ellie paused, staring out across the Thames.

'Becky Slade,' she said.

'So, that's your favour, is it?' Delgado grimaced. 'Someone needs you to help take her out?'

'Actually,' Ellie looked back at her one time colleague. '*I'm* the one who needs to take her out.'

She sipped at her own coffee as she considered her next words.

'She's made it very clear I'm her target,' she explained. 'People close to me have been attacked. And she even came at me personally, took me out with a sucker punch I wasn't expecting. She made me an offer, Kate. I give her all my favours, my debts that I've built up, she takes over London and I get a pat on the head and maybe a percentage.'

'And so what, your advice needed from me is whether you should take this?' Delgado asked.

'Christ no,' Ellie replied. 'I've already decided I'm not taking it, told her to her face.'

'And what did she say to that?'

'Nothing,' Ellie replied with a wider smile now. 'She

punched me in my face, sent me to the floor, and then told me she was going to destroy me and everything I loved.'

She looked back across the Thames, nodding towards the north side and Pimlico.

'She's taken over the south of London, Kate, but her ambitions are going all the way over there,' she continued. 'She won't be happy until she's taken over everything. She's got a chip on her shoulder bigger than a Volvo, and she's got a lot to prove.'

She turned back to face Kate, and her eyes were deadly serious.

'Having met her, having faced her, I can tell you now ... she can do it.'

Delgado sipped carefully at her coffee as she considered the words.

'Slade appeared out of nowhere a few months back, and is now proving to be a bit of a thorn in our side,' she replied. 'Once her dad went to prison for granddad's murder, she took over the business, but no one would pay her any notice for years. They just let her play in the corner, so she went back to Scotland and pissed around up there like some gap year student, unsure what to do. There were rumours she wasn't even Drew's kid, too, so she had her fair share of scraps. Then you removed the Simpsons.'

She held up her hand to stop Ellie.

'And I'm not saying that's a bad thing. Christ, you cleared your name and removed a nasty bastard off the streets. Whether Nicky himself should have been arrested is up for grabs. But either way, you did good.'

'Bloody hell,' Ellie grinned. 'Compliments from Kate Delgado. Now I know I must be concussed.'

She couldn't help herself. Kate actually chuckled at this.

'Look,' she continued, 'Becky Slade's a bad one. She's not really bothered us in Vauxhall since she returned, but I know the lads in Peckham and Balham are having genuine problems with her. She's pushing her way up through Clapham right now, and it's rubbing a lot of people the wrong way.'

'So, how do you stop her?' Ellie asked.

Delgado shrugged.

'She's got followers, but it sounds like she gained them the same way she tried to gain you,' she replied. 'Scares them into silence and goes the extreme route; shock and awe, to create an army of followers. They're not followers as such, though. They're just there because they've been told to.'

She shook her head.

'As much as I hate to admit it, the days of gangsters like Mama Lumetta, or Jackie and Johnny Lucas, you know, charismatic leaders who gain loyalty, those days seem to be gone.'

Ellie frowned at this.

'You're not nostalgic for the old days, are you?' she asked. 'We're both too young for that.'

'The world's changing faster than we wanted,' Delgado replied coldly. 'The gangs coming up now aren't the same as they were ten, twenty years ago.'

She paused.

'Have you spoken to any of the others yet? The Tsangs, Lucas, Mama Lumetta, Mama Delcourt ...?'

'Most of them,' Ellie nodded. 'I haven't gone to the Delcourts yet. North London's a little too far north, I think, for Becky's ambitions right now.'

At this, Delgado shook her head.

'You'd be surprised,' she replied. 'Becky's made alliances. You ever heard of a player called Arun Nadal?'

'Here and there, but nothing that stood out. Should I be looking into him?'

Delgado sipped her coffee.

'He's a gutter-shit player who suddenly has a lot of sway and influence,' she said. 'Nobody understands how. It's believed he's hired high-level hitmen and has wiped out *and* stolen soldiers from people like Frank Maguire in Southend.'

'Maguire's not London, though,' Ellie shook her head. 'He's more Essex-based.'

'Just because you're Essex doesn't mean you don't want a chunk of the pie,' Delgado raised an eyebrow. 'All I'm saying is that Nadal is hungry and will make alliances with whoever can help him. And, right now, Becky Slade is somebody who can do that. If he came in from the North, then that's a pincer movement on Central London.'

There was a long moment of silence as the two women stared across the Thames. Eventually, it was Delgado who broke the silence.

'You could go against her, you know,' she said. 'Take your debts, build an army. You could run London before she could.'

'So others keep telling me,' Ellie smiled. 'Still doesn't make me want to do it.'

'Oh, I get that,' Delgado replied. 'Heavy is the crown and all that. But if it isn't Slade, it'll be someone else.'

Ellie turned to face Delgado now, her eyes narrowing in curiosity.

'Are you telling me, DI Delgado, that I should make a play to take over all of London as its gangland leader?'

'You hang out with the wrong people, anyway. It's no skin off my nose,' Delgado smiled faintly. 'And, if I'm being utterly honest, if you're running it it's a lot easier to find you and arrest you if you get out of line.'

She turned away, staring across the Thames once more as she finished her coffee.

'You're a gamekeeper turned poacher, Ellie Reckless. You know the rules, and you're on the other side. If anyone's going to take over, it should be you. I'm not happy about it, but I'm also aware that if it's not you, it'll be a Becky Slade, another Nicky Simpson, an Arun Nadal. The names are all lining up.'

She kept her eyes fixed on the Thames as she spoke her next lines.

'I'm guessing you know who she has on her side,' she said, a matter of fact rather than a question.

Ellie knew what she was leading to.

'You mean Robert?'

Delgado nodded.

'We picked up chatter a while back,' she admitted. 'It seems that Robert Lewis left your company a few months ago and joined hers about two months back. He's been working for his old company Bradwell Associates again, and through that he's signed on as her *consigliere*, they say. Maybe you deciding you didn't want to take over London showed him he couldn't work with you? I know he had … mental issues after Mark's attack.'

Ellie shook her head.

'There's more to it,' she replied coldly. 'Robert Lewis wouldn't turn on us like that. If he's working for Becky, there's an angle going on. Either he's trying to do something, or she's forcing him.'

'You might have something there,' Delgado walked over to a nearby bin, tossing her empty cup of coffee aside into it. 'Every time he's been seen, he looks like a bulldog chewing a wasp. He's not happy about what he's doing, but for some reason, she's keeping him beside her. Whether he owes her a debt, or ...'

She shrugged, looking around.

'Or maybe he's just sick of having the life he had. If I had to face you every day, Reckless, I think I would as well.'

'Always a pleasure, Kate,' Ellie said. The coffees were drunk. The catch-up was now over. 'But I'm lost here. I don't know what to do. My friends are confused. My allies, if you can call them that, think I should take over. You? Well, you're completely impartial because you don't care what I do.'

'No, I do care,' Delgado interrupted, holding a finger up. 'I care you keep to the law. If you move out of line, if you hurt anybody, I will come down on you.'

The finger came down, and Delgado seemed to soften slightly.

'However, you could be a means to an end. And for that, I'm willing to give you that chance.'

'A means to an end?' Ellie frowned.

'Say you take over London,' Delgado continued. 'Hypothetically, you would control all the crime. You would control the actions of the people underneath you. But you're still an officer of the law, deep inside. You'd find a way to make it a little more legitimate. It's hard to explain, but I almost think that with you in control, we'd be back to how it was in the sixties, with the Krays and the Richardsons.'

'And you think that is better than this?' Ellie was surprised by the statement.

Delgado, however, didn't react, simply continuing.

'Ellie, the world we're living in right now makes them look like children,' she said. 'My best friend and partner, your *ex*-best friend and partner, turned out to be a murderer, and had sat there looking at me like he was innocent while you took the rap for Paddy Simpson's commands. And don't tell me you knew all along, Ellie, because he was the one person you thought was on your side. If someone like Mark Whitehouse can be a traitorous bastard, then anybody can, and now you're going to get players like Slade, and Nadal, and a dozen others all coming out of the woodwork, all gutter scum, fighting for what they think is theirs, and London will turn into a battleground. More people will die and be hurt, and that includes innocents. And if you, selling your soul to the devil, means that it *won't*, well then, as far as I'm concerned, that's win-win.'

'How in God's name is that win-win?' Ellie asked.

Delgado smiled as she turned back towards the street and the Vauxhall Crime unit. 'Because I'm not the one making the deal,' she said. 'Stay on the side of the law, Ellie. Don't make me come after you. And take care of yourself, yeah? I don't want to lose any more friends.'

9

REPARATION

'You know it's a strange world when we end up working with Kate Delgado,' Ramsey muttered as Ellie filled them in on what she'd found out. It was now late in the afternoon, and most of the last hour had been spent in debate. Casey had come up blank with working out where Becky Slade was living and working from, whereas Ramsey claimed his more analogue style of investigations would save the day.

Ellie, Ramsey, Tinker, Casey, and Davey were sitting around a small briefing table, life-sized stand-ups of Nicky Simpson around them.

Tinker still didn't look comfortable sitting there.

'I'm not happy with this,' she said. 'We're missing something, I know it.'

'You're just annoyed you haven't had a fight yet,' Ramsey replied.

Tinker took the comments and shrugged.

'Well, you're not wrong,' she said. 'I'd really like to have a chance of punching out Becky Slade for what she did to Ellie.'

'If anybody's punching Becky Slade out, it's me,' Ellie muttered angrily. 'I think I'm the one who has the right for that.'

'With the best will in the world, Ellie, the last time you tried, she punched you onto the ground,' Ramsey smiled. 'If you're going to go for it properly, someone's going to have to give you a *Rocky* montage.'

'I think I might have to give you a clean-up on the training I used to give you,' Tinker added. 'You went in for a sparring session last time. Becky Slade went in for a fight. Next time, play dirty.'

She held her finger up to stop Ellie.

'If you don't think she's going to play dirty, then you're more naïve than I thought you were.'

Ellie smiled, remembering a line Becky had spoken in the ring.

'Sometimes I even play by the rules ... but it's way more fun when I don't.'

'Trust me,' she replied, 'I know how she plays, and I've got no concerns about playing dirty. My question is, how dirty do I play?'

'As dirty as you can possibly go,' a voice said from the door, and Ellie turned to see Nicky Simpson standing there. He'd obviously been listening for a while.

'Sorry to break up your little bonding session,' he said. 'I didn't mean to interrupt as such, but Ellie, can we have a chat?'

'Anything you need to say to Ellie can be said in front of all of us,' Tinker growled, half rising from the chair.

Simpson looked at Ellie, who nodded.

'Seriously, Nicky,' she replied. 'Anything you want to say, you can say in front of these. What's on your mind?'

'Okay,' Simpson scanned the room before replying. 'So, I've been looking at your debts.'

'You've what?'

'The debts you've got owed to you. I've been looking into it, working out who owes you what and why.'

'And how did you manage that?' Casey looked up, confused.

Simpson smiled.

'Well, for quite a few months ...'

He trailed off, as if this was a comment he didn't want to continue.

Realising this, Ramsey continued.

'For the first few months, as you know, I was spying for Nicky Simpson,' he said to Ellie. 'Part of my job was to tell him who owed you and why.'

Ellie nodded, understanding now.

'And what about afterwards?'

'I ran a criminal empire,' Simpson grinned. 'It wasn't that difficult to find out who owed you. I just listened for the people complaining.'

'Okay, so hypothetically, let's say you *do* know who owes what,' Tinker spoke now, drawing everyone's attention over. 'What's this got to do with you now you're retired?'

'I wondered what I would do if I was Becky Slade,' Simpson said, walking into the room now. 'Look, it's very simple. You said that she mentioned she wanted to take over London with the favours you have owed to you, yes?'

Ellie nodded.

'She couldn't.'

'What do you mean?'

'I looked at the people who owe you, Ellie,' Simpson shook his head. 'When you did this, you were trying to clear your name, not take over entire cities. The favours you've gained for yourself were specifically aimed at getting you what you needed to solve a case, not take over empires. Even if you gave Becky Slade every single debt you're owed, she still wouldn't be able to do this. It's simply too large. Added to the fact you always make your little speech ... how does it go?'

Ellie sighed.

'One favour, given without question or argument at a time or place of my choosing,' she replied. 'If I solve whatever problem you have, you owe me whatever I ask for, but know it'll always be within your remit and something you can afford, and most of the time these favours are burned to further other cases.'

Simpson nodded slowly.

'There. "Within your remit and something you can afford." That's the part I mean. You can't get Kenny Tsang to step down for you to take over, as it goes against the deal parameters. Sure, it might be in his remit, but it affects the affordability. That's why when we all met this morning, they were more than happy to chat about you being an arbitrator, but not a rival. And Becky Slade? She'd be coming in cold, using someone else's favours. She'd have doors slammed in her face the moment she stepped above her pay grade.'

Ellie looked around the group.

'I hadn't considered that,' she said.

'But here's the thing,' Simpson added. 'Becky *should* have considered this the moment she decided to come for you.'

At the statement, Ramsey held a finger up to gain attention.

'Why exactly would Becky Slade know that?'

'Because for the last two months, she's had Robert Lewis working with her,' Simpson replied. 'And, as you all know,

Lewis knows your list of debts better than Ellie does. He could have told her at any point the debts wouldn't leave her controlling London, without some serious help.'

Ellie considered the statement. Nicky Simpson wasn't wrong. And the new information that Robert Lewis was now working with Becky Slade had thrown a large spanner into the works.

'Hypothetical question then,' she said. 'Say Robert Lewis knows the debts that I've got owed, and he's working loyally for Becky, why is he letting her go after me?'

'Maybe he's not,' Casey said. 'Maybe he's being forced to do it, and he's not giving her the information she wants.'

'No, I think there's more to it,' Simpson said, now sitting down at the table. 'Tell me again what happened when she sparred with you.'

'You want to know the part where she punched me to the ground, or the part where she carried on punching me?'

'Actually, as much as that's incredibly enjoyable to hear, I'd actually like to know what she said.'

Ellie frowned.

'She told me that if I didn't help her, she'd take me down and then take over London a lot slower.'

'No, that's paraphrasing,' Simpson replied. 'Tell me exactly word for word, because that's not what you told us when you spoke to the families.'

Ellie leant back in the chair, considering the statement.

'This ain't over, Reckless, I gave you a chance to stand beside me. Now you're going to lie prostrate in front of me as I march my way through London. And I will get your debts. I will burn every single one of them, use them all myself, until you have nothing. And then? Then I'll do exactly to you what I did to your little

friend. Everyone will see that Becky Slade took down Ellie Reckless, and I'll finally gain the reparations.'

'She said she'd use up my debts, show everyone she beat me and gain her reparations.'

'And what did you expect that to mean?'

Ellie shrugged.

'I was expecting her to mean that she was going to get some kind of reparation against me,' she said. 'Revenge, you know, take it out on my team.'

Nicky Simpson nodded at this and then placed his elbows on the table, leaning forward, resting his hands on his chin.

'What if I was to tell you there was something else?' he asked. 'Something that I think she's looking for instead of London?'

'It has to be a pretty big thing to stop her looking at London,' Ramsey muttered.

'How about five million pounds worth of something?'

'I could stop looking at London for five million pounds,' Tinker said.

Nicky now sat back on his chair, stroking his chin.

'What do you know about the reparation fund?' he asked.

'I'm guessing not as much as I will in a couple of minutes when you tell us all about it,' Ellie replied.

Simpson nodded, looking around the room as if addressing a class.

'It happened after Johnny's brother returned,' he said.

Ellie remembered this very well. Jackie had returned, back from the dead and larger than life, making efforts to take over London, and the various gangs, including the Seven Sisters, the Simpsons and the Tsangs had found themselves in a situation where old deals and memories were being brought to the surface and the skeletons were falling out of the closet.

In the end, it turned out that it wasn't Jackie; it was, in fact, another close relative of Johnny Lucas, using the identity for their own gains.

Ellie had been involved in this, helping then-DCI Alexander Monroe and his team at the Last Chance Saloon to solve the crime. But she hadn't realised this had set up any kind of chain of events.

'Go on,' she said, waving Simpson on.

'We realised then we needed some kind of mutually armed deterrent,' Simpson replied. 'We met up, and we had a conversation.'

'When you say "we", who do you mean?'

'Mama Delcourt, although she had a couple of the other Seven Sisters with her, mainly because they didn't trust her to make her own decisions at that point; Kenny Tsang, although at the time he was also grieving the loss of his brother and he was pretty much zooming from a hospital bed; me, Mama Lumetta and Johnny Lucas.'

'Johnny went legit after this,' Tinker said.

'He did,' Simpson agreed. 'But not immediately. And he knew while he went legit, he still needed to make sure his territory was looked after. MPs are voted in every election, and there was every chance that within a couple of years a by-election, or a General Election could go against him. Somebody could bring something out that caused him to step down. I mean, his bloody estranged sister Anita turned out to be one of the Seven Sisters, remember? The next thing he'd know, he's no longer an MP, and he's back on the streets. Always good to have a back-up plan.'

'So North, South, East, West and Central,' Ellie said. 'Five gangland leaders. Carry on.'

'We decided we needed a deterrent to stop us kicking off again and causing more bloody idiot behaviour,' Simpson replied. 'We all invested a million pounds each into what was called the *reparation fund*. The plan was if one of us went for somebody else, or took out someone's area, the wronged party would gain the five million. We had our own little arbitrators who would decide. Each of us provided somebody.'

He shifted as he scanned the room.

'The idea was that none of us wanted to lose a million pounds. So if you're going to kick off against, say, Mama Lumetta, it's in my interest to stop you as much as it's in my interest to see you take her down. The destabilisation that could gain me advantage in building my empire would be lost by the money I would lose,' he smiled. 'And, of course, while we did this, the money would sit in the high-interest bank accounts and make us ten percent a year.'

'Interesting,' Ramsey said.

'What, the reparation fund?'

'No, the fact you found a bank account that gives you ten percent a year,' Ramsey smiled. 'I'd love to know which bank that was.'

'So, here you are with this magical fund,' Ellie said, ignoring Ramsey, 'which means if somebody takes over someone else's area, the wronged party gains the money.'

'And it's still valid even now,' Nicky added. 'If one of the signatories, and by that, I mean the Tsangs, Lucas or Mama Lumetta, even the Seven Sisters, if they go for my land, even now I'm legit, I'd gain that money back. There's been talk about splitting it back up now we're all retiring, but ...'

He shrugged.

'... having a deterrent is quite nice.'

'But Becky Slade's not part of this?'

'No,' Simpson shook his head. 'So, if she does take over land, we don't gain any money. Sure, we could speak to the signatories, and there's a case to be said that if she takes over our land, and the money isn't used, does she effectively own the money? But that's not the point.'

He reached into his pocket and pulled out a piece of paper.

'Each of us had somebody who would speak on our behalf, someone we trusted. When reparations were needed, these five men and women would meet up, discuss the situation, and decide what reparations needed to be made. Five was deliberate, an odd number, which meant we could never have a tie-break. They weren't allowed to abstain. And, with none of us around, it felt that it was a lot fairer.'

'Did you have much call for it?'

'As far as I can recall, they never needed to meet,' Simpson smiled. 'We loved each other too much.'

'Yeah, well, that one we can discuss down the line,' Ramsey said. 'Who were the five?'

'Mama Lumetta had suggested Marco DeLuca,' Nicky said. 'Kenny Tsang had given Wei Chen as his choice. Mama Delcourt, Darnell Thompson. Johnny Lucas had picked Ronnie Carter. And I had given them Fiona Byrne, who had worked for both my grandfather and my father before me. And I trusted her to do the job.'

Ellie frowned.

'I recognise those names,' she said, 'and I don't mean one or two, I mean I recognise all five.'

Ramsey nodded.

'Darnell needed help tracking down a shipment of illicit goods that was stolen during transit,' he started. 'De Luca? I think that was a blackmail issue. Carter had a rival gang attack one of their safe houses, leaving several gang members injured and supplies stolen, and he asked us to check it out before Johnny got involved. Wei Chen had a gambling problem, and Fiona …'

'Fiona had problems with her financials,' Casey added. 'I went through her self-assessment form with her.'

He sat back in his chair.

'Every single one of these people owes Ellie Reckless a favour,' he said.

There was a moment of stunned silence.

'Now we said before that the favours you had didn't mount up enough to take over London,' Simpson added, 'but what if she's *not* using you to take over London? She could be using you to gain the favours that pressurise these five into making a decision that she wants.'

Ellie whistled.

'She did say "I'll finally gain *the* reparations", rather than "your" or "my". It makes sense.'

Tinker nodded, now understanding the situation.

'Do they have final say over the money?'

'They all have the right to sign over the money. We have no say in it,' Simpson replied. 'All five have to sign the paperwork, but if they all worked together, they could gain themselves five million without trying. A million each, I'm sure they've thought about it, but loyalty runs deep and we didn't just pick any normal person, we actually found people we *knew* would work for us.'

Simpson looked around the room.

'However, as you can understand, loyalty to us is one

thing. Half of us are gone now, and if Becky Slade gains their debt, they're going to do what she says.'

Ellie slammed her fist onto the table.

'So, it's not about power, it's about money,' Davey said, shaking her head with disgust.

'I'm sorry to break this to you,' Casey smiled. 'But money *is* power. Think about it. She's taking over London slowly. Five million in her pocket would be a very good war chest to have. If she gains that, she can hire a ton of people. And the remaining debts that Ellie has, she can use to destabilise other areas.'

'With all of Ellie's debts *and* five million pounds, she has a chance of doing everything she wants to do,' Tinker growled.

'Or this *is* just about the money,' Ellie shook her head. 'Even more reasons we need to get this bloody woman out of our hair.'

'I think I might have a way of doing that,' Casey said.

'Yeah, you found her?' Ellie asked. 'Because currently we've been having a shit time with that.'

'I went a different route,' Casey smiled. 'You see, we might not know where Becky is, but I can tell you where Robert Lewis is.'

'What do you mean?' Ellie leant forward at the hearing of Robert's name.

Casey shrugged, tapping at his laptop, which had been on the desk in front of him.

'When Robert left, he didn't change his password,' he said. 'I can see his calendar. Can't get into his emails, but I'm sure if I really wanted to try—'

'We don't need that,' Ellie shook her head. 'But his calendar would be interesting.'

She frowned.

'Hold on. This is the same calendar he had when he was here?'

'Why wouldn't it be?' Tinker asked.

Ellie looked back at her.

'Because every thirty days, Robert would change his password. He was paranoid about people breaking in. It's been months now since he left.'

'Maybe he forgot?'

'No,' Casey shook his head. 'Robert never struck me as the kind of person who'd forget.'

Ellie looked back at Davey.

'You've seen him the most recently out of all of us.'

'I wouldn't say I've seen him,' Davey replied. 'I've kept in contact with him, but it's mainly text messages here and there, and I haven't heard from him for the last couple of months, ever since it looks like Becky Slade's been working with him. It looks like he cut all ties.'

She smiled.

'Maybe this was deliberate? Maybe he was counting on Casey being a sneaky little brat and getting in? It's his way of helping us.'

'There are better ways to help us,' Ramsey muttered.

'Not if she's watching him constantly,' Tinker argued. 'And I wouldn't put that past her.'

Ellie stared back at Casey.

'Find me the next time he's out with Becky Slade,' she said. 'I think it's time to find out what the hell's going on with Robert Lewis once and for all.'

10

SWANKY BASHES

As it was, they didn't have to wait long to find an event where Robert would be as, after checking through Robert Lewis's calendar, Casey saw the following morning had Robert and Becky at some kind of networking event in Camberwell, not far down the road from the Elephant and Castle, and smack bang in the middle of Nicky Simpson's old hunting grounds.

From what he could find with the help of a couple of search engines, it was the launch of a book connected to an old South London boxer named Eddie "The Hammer" Harris, someone who had gained minor notoriety in the British welterweight boxing scene half a century ago but had grown up in a land full of gangsters. It was very much a "my time learning how to box with the Richardsons living round the corner" kind of book. The gangster connections gave it an interest outside of sports, the publishers were having an event to promote it, and somehow Becky Slade had gained an invitation, most likely because of her connections through the bare-knuckle fighting industry.

Also interestingly, however, was the fact that Nicky Simpson had also been invited, something that caused him great interest and amusement when he learnt he was the only person who could go out of the current "team", of which he now included himself. Ellie had pointed out he wasn't the *only* person going as she would be his plus one, whether he liked it or not.

Thus, the following morning, and after yet another sleepless night for Ellie, one filled with dreams of being hunted by boxers with RIP mouth guards, Nicky Simpson and Ellie Reckless went to a book launch.

THE EVENT WAS BEING HELD IN THE SHACKLETON PUB, SLIGHTLY southeast of The Oval Cricket Ground. An old, Victorian-looking pub with an upstairs function room – a function room which, Ellie learned to her surprise, was actually a boxing ring with space around it for an audience, and a bar at the back.

As they entered, Simpson took in a deep breath, sighing with delight.

'Can you smell that?' he asked, grinning as he looked back at her. 'Sweat. Exertion. Ambition.'

'All I can smell is money,' Ellie replied, looking back at the suited people standing around. 'And who the bloody hell puts a boxing ring upstairs, anyway?'

'This is a South London tradition,' Simpson replied proudly. 'Many places in South and East London had boxing rings back in the day.'

He nodded at the ring in the middle.

'That ring there, that was rescued from the *Thomas a*

Beckett on the Old Kent Road when it was sold and turned into a Thai restaurant and flats. Henryy Cooper himself trained in that ring when he prepared for his fight with Muhammad Ali.'

'Let me guess, the Krays and the Richardsons and all the others did the same?'

'It was a massively famous pub on the Old Kent Road,' Simpson's smile had drifted off now. 'So yeah, they probably did.'

Ellie decided that baiting Simpson wasn't the best idea right now as they started looking around.

It was a late morning brunch affair more than either a breakfast or lunch event, possibly because the start had been delayed by an hour for some reason; probably the fact that Eddie "The Hammer" Harris already looked pissed up and ready for another bottle. There were some local press, a few journalists, and a bag full of fitness influencers, all waxing lyrical about the book into their iPhones, or expensive-looking cameras held by friends. But Ellie didn't care about that. She recognised a few familiar faces – South London *wrong'uns*, so to speak. Even Simpson himself gained a few nods from familiar faces. Ellie found this amusing to start with – there were quite a few people in the room who owed her favours, as well as a few people she had used those favours on. The book might have been the reason for a lot of people there, but it certainly wasn't the focus of attention.

Ellie had never felt so of interest, and at the same time, so unwanted. It reminded her of her time in the police, dealing with the same people from the other side of the law. Nicky Simpson, meanwhile, was eating up the attention, laughing to himself and waving to the occasional reformed gangster.

But then, shortly after they arrived, and when the interest

in the two arrivals was waning, things took a turn for the worse.

Becky Slade and Robert Lewis entered.

At the start, Ellie hadn't wanted to believe this; that Robert Lewis would betray her for someone like Becky Slade. Even the photo she'd seen could have been manipulated or created digitally. But seeing Becky Slade walk into the room, dressed in a business suit, looking like authoritarian money, with Robert Lewis a few steps behind her, head down, subservient to the woman in front of him, made Ellie's skin crawl. It was almost as if she was part of some alternate world where things weren't quite right, and she hated it with every fibre of her being.

Becky Slade was playing the part of a politician today, it seemed, shaking hands with various people as she moved through the room, but Ellie noted that many of them didn't seem happy to be shaking her hand back. It seemed, as far as Ellie could see, that the people in the room were tolerating Becky Slade rather than appreciating her.

Good.

'You know why she's here, don't you?' Simpson muttered, just loud enough for Ellie to hear.

Ellie shrugged.

'I'm guessing it's because of her dad or something.'

'It's her heritage; she's a bare-knuckle fighter,' Simpson nodded. 'Cillian Slade sparred with Eddie Harris back in the day. I'm sure the book won't state any of the wonderful things the Slades have claimed they did over time, however. They do love a tall story, that crowd. But with Drew in prison and with Granddad dead, Becky's really the only member of the family who can come by now.'

Ellie glanced at Simpson.

'Is your grandfather in the book?' she asked.

'Probably, he knew Harris too,' Simpson nodded. 'Even had him break a couple of arms when the boxing came to an end. I bet that's not in it, though.'

'You going to read the book?'

'I know enough shit about my family, I don't need to dredge up more.'

Ellie nodded and started towards Becky Slade, currently shadow boxing for an influencer, laughing as they aimed a camera phone at her, but Simpson grabbed her arm.

'Don't,' he said. 'Not here, not now. You get smacked down in a boxing ring owned by Johnny Lucas? It doesn't go far. You get taken out on her home turf? This'll be everywhere.'

He nodded to the side, where the influencers and reporters were watching.

'People know who she is and people know what's going on,' he continued. 'I've had my fair share of people taking photos of me since I've arrived, and I can tell you now they're watching to see what goes on, waiting for the inevitable car crash.'

'You think?'

'Oh, hell yes,' Simpson nodded. 'Anyone in the know is waiting to see a fireworks display. Anyone who doesn't will just be watching to see what happens, anyway.'

Ellie shook his hand off.

'I'm not going to speak to her,' she said. 'I'm going to have a word with *him*.'

'And what makes you think he's going to have a word back?' Simpson turned Ellie to face him. 'Look at him. He's staring at the ground. He's fiddling with his watch. He doesn't want to be here any more than we do. Whatever Becky's got on him, it's something that's made him betray you, and also turn up to something he doesn't want to turn up to.'

Ellie turned and looked back at Robert. It was the first time she'd seen him in four months. His hair was still dirty-blond and unkempt in a stylish, trendy way, with the white streak down the parting a visible reminder of the attack he'd endured from Mark Whitehouse. The suit he wore was muted, the tie grey and monochrome. It was as if the man she'd known had had all the colour, the vibrancy leeched out of him and had been left to rot in a world of monochrome mediocrity.

This was not the man she knew. And she needed to know why.

Pulling once more away from Nicky Simpson, she started purposefully towards Robert and Becky.

It was Becky who saw her first, a smile blossoming across her face. Becky knew why Ellie was turning up, and Becky was savouring the moment.

'Ellie Reckless,' she shouted, loud enough for the people around to hear, and realise what was about to happen – if they had any idea who Ellie Reckless was. 'You've got some nerve coming to my party.'

'Last I heard, this wasn't your party,' Ellie said, looking around. 'Unless your name is Eddie "The Hammer" Harris, and you used to box with the Richardsons.'

'I'm a donor to the novel. I helped fund it,' Becky replied casually. 'I didn't see your name on the list at all.'

'No, but mine was,' Simpson said, stepping up beside Becky. 'Hello, Becky.'

'Christ, Nicky Simpson, I thought they'd cancelled you.'

'Not yet,' Simpson smiled warmly, turning to face Robert. 'Mister Lewis, good to see you again.'

Robert didn't look up, just nodded silently.

'Oh, that's quite rude,' Simpson turned back to face Becky. 'You've not been feeding him right, he's off his food.'

'He's not a thoroughbred horse or anything like that,' Becky snapped back.

'But that's what you know best, isn't it, really, with your heritage,' Simpson's voice had darkened, and Ellie realised he was mocking the traveller's side of her history. This wasn't the direction she wanted to go right now, but Ellie realised a little too late that Simpson and Slade still had history.

'Mister Simpson,' Robert spoke now, looking up at him, still avoiding Ellie. 'I wanted to speak to you. I'd like to cancel my gym membership. Miss Slade has found me a far superior location where I can exercise alone.'

'You had corporate membership through Finders,' Simpson replied coldly. 'As you don't seem to be employed there anymore, your membership is void anyway.'

He turned back to Becky.

'And as for you—'

'I'm not here to see *you*,' Ellie said quickly to Becky, interrupting. 'And funnily enough, neither's he.'

Simpson held up his hands, backing away.

'I'm here to talk to Robert Lewis,' Ellie continued. 'We used to work together. I have some questions about an old case.'

'You can do it during his business hours,' Becky replied, as Robert looked away. 'He's busy working for me right now; has been for a couple of months. I do hope you did his exit interview correctly. I would so hate for you to have not known that the man you were so close to has been working beside me for so long.'

She turned and caressed her hand along Robert's cheek, and Ellie saw a slight flinch as she did so.

'We're as close as lovers, you know,' Becky continued with a smile. 'Me and Robert sitting in a tree ... well, you know the rest.'

Robert didn't seem to agree with this and glared up at Becky. It was a momentary look, but then as she glanced back at him, his eyes flickered back down, the fire and fight now dissipated.

'Whatever she's done to you, I can help,' Ellie said to Robert.

Robert didn't reply.

'I'm serious, Robert, whatever's happened.'

'I'm sorry, Miss Reckless, but you seem to be confused,' Robert said, looking back up at her, fixing her with his gaze. 'I left your service because of emotional trauma; trauma gained while working for you. Trauma gained at the hand of a man that you claimed was once your friend. Trauma that left me in a coma. I returned to my old company; I think it's the best thing for me.'

Ellie winced as the words were spoken. Every single one of the barbs aimed at her were true, but to hear Robert say them with such viciousness, such vitriol ... it hurt.

'You see?' Becky slapped Ellie on the arm. 'Robbie here wants to be with Becky Babes, not with Ellie Belly and the whatever God knows crappy energy you give out. He's my toy to play with, not yours, so I suggest you take your blow-up doll here ...' this was aimed at Simpson, '... and piss off back to wherever the hell you came from. I have no need for you anymore. You've made your point and I don't need you.'

'Are you sure about that?' Ellie asked.

'Oh, I don't need you to give me your favours,' Becky leant closer now. 'I'll get them myself, one by one, and I'll use them all.'

'That's a good idea,' Ellie said. 'Unless I burn them first.'

There was a moment of confusion flitting across Becky's face as she realised what Ellie was suggesting.

'Burn them?'

Ellie, not wanting to give any advantage, continued on.

'Yeah, sure, why not? You said when we last met I didn't really need them anymore, and they're just an albatross around my neck,' Ellie smiled. 'If it's not you, it'll be some other wannabe gangster with Mummy issues coming along, demanding them.'

'You think I have Mummy issues?'

'No, I think it's all Daddy issues with you,' Ellie shrugged. 'Anyway, I was thinking of maybe asking some people to fulfil their debts with some pointless small actions – you know, make me a coffee, or sing happy birthday to me.'

'Is it your birthday?'

'Does it matter?' Ellie said. 'I thought I'd start with a few people like Wei Chen, Darnell Thompson, maybe even, oh, I don't know, Fiona Byrne – have a little chat and burn those debts before anybody else gets them.'

At the names, Becky Slade's eyes narrowed, and Ellie knew that Becky knew now ... that Ellie *knew*.

'Looks like I'll have to deal with you a little quicker then, won't I,' Becky muttered, straightening. 'I'd hold those debts if I were you, Reckless, because I think those are the only ones keeping you alive right now.'

'I'm quaking in my boots,' Ellie replied. 'Bigger and badder people have tried and they've failed, so you take your new toy and you go play with the ex-boxers. I know where I stand and I know who my friends are.'

She looked at Robert.

'And it looks like I know who aren't anymore as well.'

Before Robert could reply to this, Becky nodded at the ring in the middle of the event.

'I'd ask if you wanted to have a rematch right now, but I wouldn't want to embarrass you in front of all these people,' she said. 'Not after last time.'

She turned to one of the serving staff walking past.

'Got any cider?' she asked.

'Sorry, only beers and wines.'

'Well, I don't want beer or wine,' Becky snapped back. 'So I suggest you go find me a pint of cider and black. Bring it from the pump, not the bottle.'

The server glanced across at one organiser of the event, who nodded, obviously aware of who Becky was, and Ellie shook her head.

'You can't help yourself, can you?' she replied. 'No compromise for Becky Slade.'

'Why should there be?' Becky replied. 'When you're queen, you get what queens deserve.'

She looked back at the ring and then turned back to Ellie.

'My dreams were made in boxing rings,' she said. 'But the lessons I learned before I started to dream? They were taught on the streets, in rings made of rope, or people standing in a circle, with me in the middle, battering the shit out of whoever was in my way, while dogs barked in the background.'

'Fun childhood. Explains a lot,' Ellie replied dismissively as she turned to Nicky Simpson.

'I'm going to go back to the office,' she said. 'Feel free to schmooze and hang out with the people here. I know it's your thing more than mine.'

And with Simpson simply watching after her, Ellie

stormed out of the party, the boxing ring, and as far away as she could from Robert Lewis and Becky Slade.

She lasted all the way to the car, sitting behind the driver's seat before the shakes began. The adrenaline she'd held back, the constant memories of Becky Slade punching her, of Robert looking up at her—

'Mister Simpson, I wanted to speak to you. I'd like to cancel my gym membership. Miss Slade has found me a far superior location where I can exercise alone.'

Ellie leant back in the seat, calming herself down as she considered Robert's words. And, after a moment, she pulled out her phone, dialling a number.

'Casey, it's me,' she said. 'Do me a favour. Go into Robert's diary again and see when his next gym session is booked.'

This order given, Ellie started the car and drove off, away from the event, Eddie "The Hammer" Harris, Nicky Simpson, Robert Lewis and Becky Slade.

This wasn't over.

11

GYM SESSION

In the grand scheme of things, Tinker liked to get in fast, cause as little fuss as possible, and then leave. Her reputation as a fighter was only because of desperation or circumstance; her preferred method was to avoid fighting whatsoever.

However, there were some times when fighting wasn't only required but actively encouraged, usually when she faced people she really wanted to hit.

After Ellie had returned with information gained at the book event, and the order for Casey to check out Robert's gym membership, Casey had checked the diary. Ellie had been right. An hour after the event's ending time, Robert Lewis had scheduled a solo session in a gym just south of Clapham. It was a lunchtime session – more a case of just after lunch, if Tinker was being pedantic – but she supposed that when you worked for someone like Becky Slade, who kept odd hours at the best of times, you got your gym time in when you could.

As it was, she arrived at the *Titan Strength and Condi-*

tioning Gym a good fifteen minutes before Robert's schedule had started.

The gym itself was off the Brixton Road, south of Clapham and housed in a renovated warehouse with a medium-sized car park out front. The website claimed it was an old gym brought into the twenty-first century, featuring state-of-the-art equipment, spacious training areas, and a dedicated boxing ring. It was advertised as a hub for fitness enthusiasts and aspiring boxers alike, offering a range of classes from high-intensity interval training, or HIIT, to traditional boxing and strength training.

Tinker could see why Becky Slade liked it and she smiled at the thought of telling Nicky Simpson about it, especially if it was better than his.

She watched as a car of what she could only call thick-set goons appeared, pulling up in the car park, two goons emerging from the car and entering the gym and within a matter of minutes, the other gym-goers were leaving en masse. All Tinker could assume was they'd encouraged the gym-goers to perhaps find a *better* time to work out, or suffer the consequences. Either way, by the time Robert Lewis's car turned up ten minutes later, the only people anywhere near the gym were two thick-set goons standing outside.

Robert was already wearing a pair of running shorts and a shirt, a towel over his shoulder, and a water bottle in his hand as he exited the car's passenger side. He'd been driven there, Tinker noted, wondering whether this meant that Becky Slade didn't trust him to drive himself.

Perhaps *this* was the situation; an empty gym wasn't for his own personal enjoyment, it was to stop him from talking to someone. Driving on his own would give him the opportunity to make phone calls or perhaps make a stop. Being driven somewhere meant that, once more, Becky Slade was controlling the narrative.

Robert looked around and couldn't have missed Tinker's army jeep, a vehicle he'd driven in many times with her over the years, but he scanned past her and carried on into the gym, where through the glass windows she saw him place his bags down in a locker, take the towel and start working on a cross-trainer.

The two goons stood at the front of the gym, almost like bouncers, barring anybody from entering. Tinker hadn't liked the way they'd evicted the other gym-goers, and if she was being perfectly honest, she'd had a pretty shitty couple of days following what had happened to Ellie, and definitely after what Lavie Kaya had gone through, deserved or not. So, cracking her neck and flexing her fingers, getting as many knots and tight muscles out as she could, and after watching for the car driver to leave – two-on-one was a far better series of odds than three-on-one, after all – she climbed out of her jeep, grabbed an aluminium water bottle from beside the seat and walked over to the front of the gym, acting as if she was going into the gym for a session.

If the two men at the front of the gym had been informed about anyone turning up, they obviously hadn't been given a description, because Tinker was pretty obvious, recognisable in her green army coat, baseball cap, and distinctive hair. But as it was, the goons simply glared at her.

'Gym's closed,' the first of the two goons snapped, as the second held his arm out to block her.

'No, it's not,' Tinker said, as if the man was completely incorrect, no doubt in her voice whatsoever. 'I've got a class in fifteen minutes.'

'Yeah, class is cancelled,' the goon repeated, and the arm blocking her way stayed there.

Tinker stopped, looking confused.

'What's going on?' she asked, her voice softening, giving them the impression that she was no threat.

'Look, why don't you just—'

The second guard didn't finish his words, his sentence turning into a strangulated scream, as Tinker grabbed the wrist that was blocking her way and twisted it hard, hearing the wrenching *crack* as the motion moved up his arm and dislocated his shoulder.

As the second goon staggered backwards, the first goon, realising that something bad and unexpected was suddenly happening, moved in quickly, pulling out an extendable baton from his hip pocket. However, the element of surprise was on Tinker's side, and before he could do anything, she moved in. She'd been holding the aluminium bottle in her hand, something unobtrusive, and now she slammed it upwards, striking the mouthpiece into the first goon's throat, sending him scrabbling backwards as his windpipe, more bruised than crushed, caused him immediate panic.

The second goon, still grabbing at his shoulder, went down even quicker as Tinker kicked him hard between the legs, slamming her knee into his face as she grabbed the back of his head and pulled it down simultaneously, breaking his nose with a *crunch* as he collapsed to the floor.

Tinker turned back to the first goon, who was now calming, realising that he hadn't had his throat crushed. But Tinker moved in quickly from behind, grabbing him in a chokehold, bringing him down to the ground now as she patiently choked him out.

With both men on the floor, she opened the door to the

gym's main reception, dragging both in, dumping them to the floor, and then walking over to the side to pick up a couple of resistance bands to hogtie them. This now done, she turned and walked into the main gym area, where Robert Lewis was still working on the cross-trainer.

'You're a tough bloody guy to speak to,' she muttered. 'Do you want to tell me exactly what's going on?'

Robert Lewis turned to face Tinker, and she was quite surprised to see that his face had scrunched up in furious anger.

'It's good to see you, Tinker!' he shouted, angrily pointing at her, gesticulating wildly as he walked towards her. 'I'm really glad you got the message! I'm guessing Casey hacked my calendar!'

'What the hell is all this about?' Tinker replied, backing away slightly in confusion.

Robert walked over to her, still gesticulating, and with both hands pushed her visibly backwards.

'Don't stop now!' he shouted. 'Shout back at me. Have a go at me! Look angry!'

'Why in God's name would I do that?' Tinker said, her voice rising into anger, effectively doing what Robert had asked.

'There's a camera in this gym, but there's no sound!' Robert shouted. 'She can see me, but she can't hear me, so all she can do is work out what's going on from what she sees!'

'Why, what's happening?' Tinker pushed him away but Robert, in response, waved at the door, as if telling her to piss off, before turning and walking away.

Tinker, now understanding what was going on, followed him, waving her own arms for dramatic intent.

'Why did you drop us for the last four months?'

'I didn't drop you for the last four months,' Robert said, ignoring her, keeping his back to her. 'I had a break for two months, and then she turned up on my doorstep, with a whole load of men beside her.'

'And that was enough to make you turn?'

Robert turned, and for the first time, the anger on his face was genuine.

'I didn't turn on anyone!' he shouted. 'She showed me pictures. She knew how close I was with Ellie, knew I could help her and she had information on all of you, stuff that I couldn't have found out if I'd tried. Ramsey's mum in the bloody home, all the people you give a shit about, she had people watching them! She told me I could either come to work with her, or watch everybody I knew get hurt bad – you, Casey, Ramsey, even Davey. If I didn't go with her, rejoin Bradwell and do what she needed, you all fell. And she told me Ellie would be killed. *Ellie*, Tinker! What the bloody hell was I supposed to do? She blackmailed me with your lives!'

He moved close again.

'She's insane, and I can't do anything about it until she's stopped. But I've not been able to contact you, or see anybody. She controls everything I do, as if she's keeping me in a box, waiting for the right moment to let me out. I'm a trinket, and I think she wants me because Ellie once had me.'

At this point, he swung a punch.

Tinker hadn't been expecting it, but he'd choreographed it so slowly and telegraphed the move that she was able to swoop back, allowing him to stumble forward, all part of the act.

'The guards are going to wake up in a minute,' he said. 'You need to tell Ellie something for me. But first, you need to hit me.'

'What?'

'I need you to hit me. Hard-way knuckle punch to my eyebrow. It's what wrestlers do when they want to draw blood without using blades.'

'Since when did you become a wrestling expert?'

'I've always loved wrestling. That's not the point. Hit me hard. Split my forehead. I need a physical wound.'

He waved around the gym.

'Ellie's mental sidekick turns up and starts kicking off, decides she's going to take me on for leaving Ellie alone. I fight back. I get knocked to the floor. It's very simple. It gives you a reason to come here, gives me a reason not to be targeted by Becky, which means *you* get a chance of not being targeted by Becky.'

'We can deal with Becky!' Tinker shouted, now swinging hard, catching Robert in the eye. He staggered back, gripping his head.

'Jesus, I'm sorry,' Tinker said. 'What was I thinking? You've got a head wound.'

'Don't worry about the head wound,' Robert said, falling to one knee and grabbing at his skull. Tinker could see the blood in his hands. 'You've done enough. Tell Ellie I'm doing my best, but she needs to stop Becky from getting the money. She already knows about the reparations; she gave some names in the event earlier on. She needs to get those people out, and she needs to remove Becky before she does even worse.'

He looked up.

'It's not just the money,' he said. 'She wants her dad out of prison as well, but I'm not sure why. I don't even think he's her real dad.'

'We're doing everything we can,' Tinker replied, mentally

filing away the comment Robert had just made, and noticing that the two men were now struggling, waking up. She couldn't do much more without them recognising it.

She grabbed Robert, dragging him up by his top.

'What else can you give me?'

'Look into the death of her granddad,' he said. 'It was blamed on Drew, but it wasn't him. And keep digging in my calendar, and also keep an eye on Arun Nadal. He's got issues with the Slades too. That's all I know.'

He pulled away, staggering backwards.

'And tell Ellie I'm sorry.'

With this said, he screamed.

'Guards! Guards!'

Tinker saw two cars pull up outside. The driver had also returned, staring at her through the window. He had a coffee in his hand and had obviously gone to pick it up; on returning, he'd seen what had happened and had called for help.

'We'll get you out of this,' Tinker said, and then, as a bonus, she kicked him in the ribs, a light tap that looked worse as she pulled it, allowing Robert to take the blow and roll across the floor.

'There you go,' she said. 'You could be a professional wrestler if you tried. Well, apart from, like, a major head injury, and all that.'

She ran for the main entrance, bursting through it and sprinting for the Jeep. As the goons ran into the gym, Tinker leapt in, gunning the engine, and speeding off down the street.

She hoped that what she'd done was enough to shake off any ideas Becky Slade might have that Robert Lewis was still working for them. And, as she stared down at her blood-stained knuckle gripping hard on the steering wheel, she hoped to Christ she hadn't given Robert Lewis yet another concussion or minor brain injury.

One thing she was happy about was that Robert Lewis was on their side still and had given them vital information about their loved ones.

The problem was, though ... how did they *move* them without causing Becky Slade to suspect?

12

BURN A DEBT

'So,' Ellie said, leaning back in her chair. 'What do we have?'

She stared at her team as they faced her across the Simpson's Health Club boardroom table.

Ramsey shrugged.

'It looks like Robert's on our side at least,' he said. 'Although he can't publicly be *seen* on our side.'

'It sounded to me like Becky had something major on us, and was using our deaths to blackmail him into working for her,' Tinker added. 'She's had it over him for a couple of months now, poor sod.'

'He could have left us a message,' Casey replied suddenly, sullenly.

Ellie turned to face him.

'He did,' she said. 'He left you his calendar. It's not my fault you've not looked at it for the last two months.'

Casey held his hands up in a surrendering gesture.

'You usually tell me not to look at peoples' calendars,' he said. 'You've got to decide one day, Ellie. Either

I'm allowed to do what I want, or I've got to follow the rules.'

Ellie waved off the comment. She knew she was being angry and turned to face the group again.

'Look,' she said, 'this is on me, and I'm sorry that you've all been involved in this, and I'm sorry that your loved ones have been involved. But if Becky Slade is making a move, she's been planning this for ages.'

'Ever since Nicky Simpson stepped down, most likely,' Ramsey replied.

'What I can't work out is why now?' Tinker suggested. 'I mean, everything seems to be moving quickly. But she's had months. It's been, what, five, maybe six months now since Nicky stopped being the criminal under-lord of South London and Paddy was arrested. It's been four since Zoey Park, when we kicked Jimmy Tsang out of London.'

She looked around the room for support.

'I mean, these have to have been the reasons she went for this now, but she could have done it a month ago, she could have done it a month *from* now,' she continued. 'But taking out Lavie, and passing the message, finding Ellie the following day ... what's the need here?'

'The need is she wants to take over London,' Ramsey suggested.

'No, Tinker's right,' Davey had been scribbling on a notepad, but now looked up, addressing the group. 'Forensics. Always look at the angles. The one thing I learned while working for Doctor Marcos and the Last Chance Saloon—'

'Oh, please,' Ramsey muttered to himself. 'Please tell me again about working for the amazing DCI Monroe and the Last Chance sodding Saloon.'

'Hey,' Ellie held her hand up. 'I worked for Monroe. Don't

for one second think that anything Davey's about to tell you isn't relevant.'

Ramsey muttered to himself, settling back in his chair. Ellie knew the reason he was uncomfortable and irritated was because Robert had suggested that Ramsey's own mother was in Becky Slade's crosshairs, and this was something they needed to address.

'We'll get your mum somewhere safe,' she said, continuing. 'We'll make sure she's out of Becky Slade's eyesight, yeah?'

Ramsey didn't reply, just nodded, his eyes tight.

Ellie looked back at Davey.

'Carry on.'

Davey shifted for a moment, before continuing.

'Look. We thought she wanted to take over London, but now we know she's looking for specific debts,' she said. 'She wants five million. We understand that. Half the cases that we ever had in Temple Inn involved money. From what I've seen with you guys, it's pretty much the same here. If it's not Nicky Simpson demanding money owed from Danny Flynn, it's the Lumettas boiling up gold into weird little liquids; it's land grabs, life insurance policies, you name it. As the young boy says …'

She nodded at Casey with a smile.

'… Power is money. But again, she could have done this now, a week ago, a month from now. If anything, I would have been trying to get it done quicker rather than later, because anything could happen to that money.'

'Nicky Simpson might decide he wants to take it back,' Tinker suggested.

'Exactly. Or Johnny Lucas might decide he wants to use it for his next election campaign,' Davey replied. 'Kenny Tsang might decide he wants it back because nobody else is using it. Mama Lumetta's retired. Now granted, this could mean that this is the perfect time to grab it. But it's all about the dates.'

'So, we need to find something else then,' Ramsey replied. 'What other dates are lining up?'

'I think I've got something,' Casey still stared at his laptop. 'Cillian Blake.'

'What about him?'

'Cillian Slade was shot ten years ago,' Casey said, reading the notes. 'It was believed that there was some kind of fight in the alley of a pub. And, in the end, it was Drew, his son, who was arrested and charged with the crime.'

Casey looked up.

'From what the evidence is saying here, Drew did it in front of witnesses. A proper Kray twins versus George Cornell job. But whereas with the Krays, people were too scared to say anything, everybody was quite happy to throw Drew to the wolves.'

'So Drew killed his father. Do we know why?' Ellie asked.

Casey shook his head.

'Nothing came up during the trial,' he replied. 'But I'm not a lawyer. I don't know how these things work … but that's not the relevant thing here.'

'Go on,' Ellie frowned.

'He's up for appeal. Claims there's fresh evidence. Defence says that it was self-defence.'

'What kind of evidence?' Ramsey asked.

'No idea,' Casey replied. 'I'm just going on what the notes say. But, it says here that tomorrow, Drew Slade will be back at the Inner London Crown Court in Southwark, and his case will be appealed as a mistrial.'

Ellie started tapping her chin.

'So, you're the granddaughter of a well-known villain who's killed by his son – your father. He's appealing his charge and at the same time, you're doing your best to gain five million pounds.'

She looked around the table.

'Thoughts?'

'When Drew gets out, he gets a payout,' Ramsey suggested.

'How likely is Drew to get out, though?' Tinker added. 'There's every chance he could lose.'

'What if it's not about the appeal?' Davey now spoke. 'What if it's about giving her dad a new life? Five million's enough to gain a crew to break him free. A couple of million in his pocket, he pisses off to Spain, never seen again, lives his life in luxury.'

Ellie slowly nodded.

'That is scarily, incredibly believable,' she said. 'Becky Slade takes the five million, saves her dad, sets him off somewhere, uses the rest to help take over London.'

'That's if she's even looking at London,' Ramsey replied. 'If this is the case, it could be a pure smokescreen. Everything she's doing right now is to get her dad out of prison.'

'But why?' Davey held a finger up. 'And not because she loves her dad or anything like that. Her dad killed her grandfather. Why would she want him free?'

'Also, if we're listening to Robert, Drew might not even be her father,' Ellie added.

'She knows something that we don't know,' Tinker suggested, shrugging. 'Maybe there's more to the murder – or the self-defence, as his lawyers are claiming.'

'You said it was public,' Ellie said. 'Who else was there? What witnesses?'

'I'll look into it,' Casey said, already tapping on the keyboard.

'Let's find out what actually happened that night,' Ellie nodded. 'Delgado even told us to check it out. And now there's every possibility that tomorrow's appeal is conveniently timed. Things like mistrials usually mean something that was solid then is now questioned. It could be a witness, the arrest ...'

'Actually, I might also have something about this,' Tinker said. 'After Robert told me Drew's parentage was questioned, I asked about. Nothing too deep, I didn't want it getting back, but apparently, Drew got together with Becky's mum, Charity, when they were young. She was only fifteen when she became pregnant, but this wasn't uncommon in the traveller social scene at the time.'

'Okay, so how does this affect parentage?' Ramsey frowned.

Tinker pulled out her phone and scrolled to a photo.

'I was sent this,' she said. 'It's Drew and Charity about twenty-five years ago.'

She showed it to the group; both Drew and Charity were wearing hideously coloured tracksuits, standing by a racetrack.

'Horrifying,' Casey said. 'People could wear things like that?'

'It's not the clothing you should look at,' Tinker insisted. 'It's the pair of them. He's blond, she's ginger.'

'And that's a crime now?' Davey, who was red-headed, frowned.

'No, but Becky isn't either of those,' Ellie nodded, understanding where Tinker was going. 'She's dark-haired, olive skin. Sure, it could be genetics, but I can see the Slades jumping to conclusions here.'

She smiled.

'Maybe we can use that to our advantage somehow,' she continued as she rose from the chair. 'Right, we have a plan for a change. Casey, find us somebody we can talk to. Ramsey, Tinker, hit the streets. See if you can find anybody in the south of London who'll talk to you.'

'What do you want me to do, boss?' Davey asked. 'Still a lack of bodies, or evidence to look at.'

Ellie smiled, turning back to her.

'You're coming with me,' she said. 'Let's go burn some favours.'

As they walked through the underground car park under the building and climbed into Ellie's car, Davey waited for a moment, before she turned and faced Ellie, her expression curious before putting the seatbelt on.

'Go on then,' she asked. 'What's your plan?'

Ellie said nothing, attaching her own seatbelt and starting the engine.

'I'm serious, Ellie. What is it?' Davey repeated. 'You didn't need me for this. You could have brought Tinker or Ramsey or even Casey. You put me here because you wanted somebody who wasn't part of the original team. What exactly is your plan?'

Ellie slumped a little as she placed her hands on the steering wheel.

'Becky Slade's watching everybody that I love,' she said.

'And their families. If we try to move them, she'll know we've been told and not only will she probably go in fast and hard, but she'll also take out Robert. Which means we have to find a way to *not* have this happen.'

'Again, with the *why me* question,' Davey smiled.

'Because you're analytical,' Ellie explained as they started down the street. 'Sure, you've been with us a few months now, you've seen how we work and you've built relationships. But before you, it was Casey who was the new kid, and even he'd been with us for several months by the time you turned up. Ramsey and Tinker, I've known them for years. The two of them, well, let's just say they're family.'

She leant back, allowing the car to drive through the London traffic.

'Also, when Becky spoke about my team, she didn't mention you,' she continued. 'She would have gathered the intel from Robert, but I think he deliberately neglected to name you.'

'Risky. If she found out…'

'He could claim it was around the same time he had a head wound,' Ellie shrugged. 'But I think he gave us wiggle room through you. They watch us, but thanks to Robert, he made sure you, the analytical one who's good at working through problems can make moves.'

She turned down a side road.

'When did Tinker tell you what Robert had said?' she continued.

'Pretty much as soon as she arrived.'

Ellie nodded at this.

'And how long did it take before you'd worked out the list?'

'List?'

'This isn't a time to play coy,' Ellie chuckled. 'Analytical mind and all that. The moment Tinker told you our families were in trouble, you'd have been finding out exactly who these people are and *where* they are. You'll know that Ramsey's mum's in a home. You'll know where Casey's mother lives. You'll know—'

'Where your ex, Nathan is living?' Davey interrupted. 'I didn't bother. I guessed you probably wouldn't care too much if he was beaten up.'

Ellie couldn't help herself and actually laughed at this.

'Nathan might be a prick, And he might have left me the moment he thought I was a murderer,' she said. 'But if he's on Becky Slade's list, we need to monitor him as well. So, do you have one?'

Davey smiled and reached into her pocket, pulling out a sheet of A5 paper.

'Casey's mum, his aunt, Ramsey's mother, Tinker's sister, and her cousin. My parents, but that might be irrelevant if what you're saying is true.'

'I'd still keep them there, in case I'm wrong.'

As they slowed at a set of lights, Davey showed Ellie the list.

'They were the ones I thought Becky would make a first move against; people who were important to us. I've also added Robert Lewis's parents as well just in case she decides to take them out as well. The only one I didn't have was you.'

'That's because *you're* my weak spot,' Ellie said. 'All of you.'

She looked at the note and nodded to herself.

'It's pretty much what I saw as well.'

She looked out of the window, indicating right and turning towards the Thames.

'I've got a lot of debts owed to me,' she said. 'I'll need five or six of the smaller ones I own cashed in. Get people to quietly keep an eye on the ones we love. This way we don't move them until we need them to, and Becky doesn't realise. It'd work better that way.'

She paused, looking at Davey.

'In the glove box, you'll find an external drive. Take it.'

Davey did so.

'What am I looking for?' she asked.

'There's a folder on it,' Ellie replied. 'It's a special one, for me only. It's a list of my debts and who owes them to me.'

'I've seen your list,' Davey frowned. 'Casey has—'

'Casey had a version of the list,' Ellie replied. 'The ones that I've gained with Finders. But that's not my entire list of debts. I have some I gained on my own. Some that were owed to me from when I was a police officer. Every single debt that I have owed is on a file on that drive.'

'Tell me you have it somewhere else,' Davey paled. 'I don't want to find that if I just toss this out the window, you're suddenly screwed.'

'It's elsewhere,' Ellie smiled. 'But that doesn't matter. I need you with your analytical brain and knowledge of London to go through it. Pick some debts you think I can lose, but at the same time could do what we need. Provide muscle who are clever enough to keep silent and out of the way. I'd suggest looking at people outside of London. Maybe, if we have to go into the city, north of the Thames.'

'Why me?'

The lights ahead were red, and Ellie didn't speak until she pulled up to a stop.

'Because Robert Lewis is having to work for Becky,' she said. 'Chances are he's having to give her what she wants. Which means he's informing on her about me, but hasn't informed about you. Added to that, she's a sharp player. She'll have a list very similar to this. Maybe not as complete, but as good as the one you've seen here. She's intelligent enough to look at the list and work out who I'd burn. So, go the other direction. Take the debts and domino them. Find ways to burn a debt for something completely irrelevant, while providing the service I need.'

'Shell companies but through debts.' Davey nodded. 'I get what you're saying. And how long do I have?'

'About ten minutes,' Ellie said. 'Because we'll be hitting our first favour around then.'

They arrived at a pub near St Paul's, and Ellie pulled up, double parking on the street.

'Who's in the pub?' Davey asked.

'Desmond Palmer,' Ellie replied.

Davey glanced at the list, now connected by USB to her phone, thought for a second, and then nodded.

'Des Palmer. Counterfeit goods seller. Owes you because you recovered a stolen motorbike,' she said.

'He owes me for several things; one of those is that,' Ellie nodded. 'He also works with the Cooper gang—'

'Of which I can see here, Tony Cooper owes you a favour. Something about a girlfriend being harassed?'

Ellie nodded.

'And Tony Cooper is a friend of Bobby Hill, who nobody

else knows. I helped him with a house sale, believe it or not. And Bobby Hill has three men under his control he can loan to me without losing anything for a few days.'

Ellie smiled.

'Do you see where I'm going now?'

Davey grinned back.

'You push Des to honour the favour, to tell Tony to then tell *Bobby* that you need something going on,' she said. 'Three favours burned. It's a high cost.'

'It saves people,' Ellie replied, 'There's no higher cost. You did the same thing two or three times, and the debts can cover all of you.'

'You're happy to burn this many?'

'Joanne, I've burned them for a cab home for someone once. Another was to get me dog food when Millie was left on my doorstep. I'm happy to burn these for something important.'

Ellie checked her phone as it buzzed; another message had come through.

'Rain check on that,' she said, pulling out a notepad and writing something down. 'Take the drive and my list. Do what you need to do. Don't tell me who you burn, or what you use. Go off-grid until it's done. Make sure everyone's safe.'

'They're not just going to let me ...'

'Yes, they will,' Ellie said, passing her the note. 'This tells anyone you speak to, that you're here on behalf of me, and that they should listen to everything you say. That's all they'll need. Get someone ready to extract each of our loved ones the moment we pull the cord. I'd prefer not to know who and how, but if you have to contact me, you know where to find me.'

'And what about you?' Davey asked, nodding at the phone. 'What's the special message?'

'Casey found us a witness,' Ellie smiled darkly. 'To the murder of Cillian Slade. I intend to have a chat with them, maybe take Ramsey with me. He does love meeting old criminals, after all.'

13

SINATRA'S BURGER

ARTHUR DAVENPORT LOOKED LIKE SOMEONE HAD GOOGLED THE term "incredibly old skinny man" and turned it into a life choice.

He was stick-thin, giving the impression of someone who had somehow managed to avoid food for most of his life, and his almost translucent skin was painfully stretched over his bones, making him look more like a cadaver than a human. His teeth were yellow, seen briefly between puffs of his vape, and his hair, what was left of it, was an almost dirty yellow, the colour that you would often see on pub walls when smoking was still allowed. In fact, there wasn't a single piece of Arthur that Ellie could have said was endearing in any way whatsoever.

He had a throaty chuckle, and his voice sounded exactly as you'd expect from someone who smoked twenty a day for decades, before moving to vapes. As Ellie and Ramsey entered the pub, walking over to him and sitting down, he smiled.

'I've been told you want some answers,' he said, tapping

at the tumbler in front of him with the gold signet ring he wore on his right hand. The ring itself looked like it was worth more than everything else he owned.

Ellie looked down at the tumbler.

'Would you like another?' she asked.

'Yeah,' Arthur nodded. 'A double, but no ice. Makes it taste like shite.'

He looked over at the bar, dinging his signet ring against the glass, until the barman looked up.

'They're buying me a double,' he said. 'But no ice. Makes it taste like shite.'

'Yeah, I know, Arthur, I know,' the barman muttered, turning around and putting two generous squirts of whisky into it. Ramsey had walked over, placing a ten-pound note down and picking up the glass, bringing it back and placing it down in front of Arthur.

'Should you be vaping in here?' he asked.

'Medicinal. They allow it. So what do you want to know?' Arthur asked. 'Don't worry about the people in here. None of them give a shite about me. And I'm too long in the tooth for anybody to care about if I inform on anyone. You police?'

'Used to be,' Ellie said. 'Not anymore.'

'What about you, fancy man?'

Ellie stifled a chuckle as Ramsey Allen, gentleman thief, stared in abject horror at Arthur Davenport.

'How in God's name would you think I was a bloody copper?' he said. 'I'm Ramsey Sodding Allen!'

'I don't know who you are, do I?' Arthur said, taking the tumbler off Ramsey and downing it in one quick swig.

Placing it down, he tapped his ring upon the side.

'Same again?'

Muttering to himself, Ramsey snatched at the glass,

walking over to the bar and slamming it down. Ellie took the moment to stare again at the broken, dirty man in front of her. This was a man who didn't care anymore. He didn't care how he looked, how he sounded, or how he acted. He probably cared even less what people thought about him. And yet, there was an element of pride. The ring, the one he'd rapped several times on the glasses, was still clean and shiny. It had been taken care of. The silver ring on the finger next to it was tarnished and darkened. But the gold could have been brand new.

'Where's the ring from?' she asked.

Arthur looked at the signet ring on his finger and grinned, showing his yellow, rotting teeth.

'Frank Sinatra gave me that,' he said.

'You've met Sinatra?'

At the question, Arthur Davenport raised himself up straight, as if he was trying to regain a lost dignity.

'You don't think that Sinatra would hang around with the likes of me? I wasn't always like this, missy.' He shook his head. 'I used to hang around with all the bigs: Krays, Richardsons, Sinatra and the others when they would come over.'

He looked around the bar as a mischievous glint came to his eye.

'Do you know how to make a Sinatra burger?' he asked. 'He told me himself.'

'There's a special menu, is there?' Ellie asked.

Arthur smiled wider.

'Yeah, do you want to know it?'

'Sure, why not?'

Arthur Davenport leant closer, and Ellie almost regretted asking, because the man definitely hadn't brushed his teeth in a while.

'So this came from Dean Martin's recipe,' he explained. 'Sinatra called him Deano. Had a big thing about ground beef and bourbon, and drinking while eating, boring bloody recipe. Never cared much for Deano. But Dean Martin and Frank Sinatra, they ran around a lot, yeah? Dean wasn't a fan of the more criminal classes like Sinatra was, but they still hung around. So, when you want a Sinatra burger, step one, call for Deano. Step two, tell him to make you a goddamn burger. Step three …'

He paused as Ramsey walked over with yet another filled tumbler. He took it from him, downed it in one go, slamming the glass back onto the table.

'Step three, drink his goddamn whisky.'

This was apparently the funniest joke that Arthur Davenport had ever told, and as he rocked back-and-forth laughing, Ellie decided she'd had enough.

'Mister Davenport,' she said coldly, 'do you know who I am?'

'Not really. I know you're not a copper, and the flash pants there who says he isn't a copper is Ramsey somebody.'

'Let me introduce myself then,' Ellie whispered. 'My name, Mister Davenport, is Ellie Reckless.'

She had spoken it softly, no louder than the immediacy of the area, yet it was almost like the oxygen had been sucked out of the bar.

Arthur Davenport had *heard* of Ellie Reckless.

He paused, his eyes widening, staring at her.

'You here about a favour from someone?' he asked quietly. 'Is that why you're here?'

'No, Mister Davenport,' Ellie smiled, a dark, humourless one, as she moved forward, placing her arms on the table, risking the smell of his breath once more to make the point. 'I'm here to offer you one.'

'What's that supposed to mean?'

'It means, Arthur, we need some information from you,' Ramsey said. 'And, if you can help us, Ellie Reckless will be in your debt.'

'Oh, I like that,' Arthur said, the smile now returning. 'Go on then, Miss Reckless, what do you need from me?'

'Tell me about the night Cillian Slade died.'

Arthur narrowed his eyes.

'I wouldn't know,' he said. 'I wasn't—'

'You were there. We know you were there.' Ellie's voice was quieter now, but cut through the space. 'Now, I don't really have time to screw around, Mister Davenport. You now know who I am, and you know what I can do if I get pissed off. I don't *want* to get pissed off. Not at someone who's got Sinatra's signet ring and knows how to make a Sinatra burger. It's not quite the same as shaking hands with Sinatra, but you know what I mean. All I want to know is *who killed Cillian Slade.*'

'The police did a case,' Arthur said, almost accusatory. 'They said who did it. His son, Andrew. I mean Drew.'

'Yeah, but why?' Ellie asked. 'Why would Cillian's loyal son kill him?'

'Maybe they had a falling out.'

'You have one last chance,' Ellie said. 'I want to hear everything. And while you consider whether or not you're going to tell me, why don't you have another double?'

Arthur Davenport licked his lips, but it seemed more from nervousness than anticipation of another drink, as he leant back in his chair and stared at both Ramsey and Ellie.

'How much do you know about South London? Ten years back?' he asked.

Ellie and Ramsey shook their heads.

'I was East London, mainly,' Ramsey replied. 'I knew the players, but didn't hang around with them that much.'

'I'd just started at Vauxhall,' Ellie added. 'So I saw the players as they were. At that time, Max Simpson was changing over to Nicky, although officially nobody knew about this.'

Arthur Davenport laughed.

'Max Simpson? "Old shaky" we'd call him, because of his Parkinson's,' he said, shaking his head. 'Shit way to go, if you ask me.'

'You talk about him like he's dead,' Ramsey said. 'He's not, he's living in Spain.'

'Yeah, exactly,' Arthur Davenport replied. 'Running off to Spain. Such a cliché, you know. Stay here, see it out, right to the end.'

Ellie kind of understood what Arthur was talking about, but let the man carry on, regardless.

'Anyway,' he said, 'Max was bad, not doing great. Cillian at that point, he was old, past his prime, a bit like Paddy was, you know. Paddy Simpson and Cillian, they hated each other. Beef that went all the way back to when they both worked for the Richardsons. Cillian had always been pissed that Paddy had beaten him to the punch when it came to taking over the south of London, especially as Cillian was a lieutenant and Paddy was the sodding accountant.'

Ellie nodded. She already knew Paddy stepped in purely because he had a reputation as a quiet man, a safe pair of hands. It was likely someone like Cillian Slade and his likely wave of violence would have been rejected.

Arthur was continuing on.

'I mean, he'd managed to grab his own little areas, so it wasn't like Simpson owned all of London. But even if Cillian had had more streets, more control, more postcodes even, Paddy was the first to publicly claim he was the Richardsons' replacement, the King of South London.'

The barman walked over, placing another double in front of Arthur. He went to drink it, but then paused and placed it back down on the table, as if deciding he'd wait until he'd finished.

'Anyway, so we're looking at ten, eleven years back,' he said. 'At this point, Paddy's retired, twelve years at this point, I think, maybe longer. Max has been in control, and he's sometimes as good as his dad was, but other times he's an absolute nightmare. Very much "strike first, ask questions later". Pisses away all of dad's goodwill, especially after he starts to get the shakes. There were rumours Paddy was annoyed at him because of this, and then of course you've got nineteen-year-old Nicky, fresh as a daisy, ready to play gangster.'

He chuckled, deciding then to take a sip from his drink.

'Little prick turned out to be a fair bit worse than his dad ever was, didn't he? But you'd know about that, Reckless. You're the one who started all this.'

'Well, that's unfair.'

'You think?' Arthur looked around the pub. 'This place used to be Simpson-owned, yeah? You'd pay a monthly "subscription", shall we say. No problems kicking off because of that. Since you took out the Simpsons, it's fair game for any group of wannabes to turn up and try to cause shit. The bouncers don't want to get involved and, well ...'

He shrugged, sighing.

'Let's just say it's not as good as it used to be.'

Ellie frowned. One thing that she'd realised in recent months was the level of organisation and authority that some of these gangs had held in their areas. By removing gangs, she had effectively caused a cultural shift – and one not for the better.

'Okay, hypothetical,' she said. 'Once this is done, say Becky Slade disappears, what would you want to see happen?'

'I'd want someone in charge who isn't a psycho,' Arthur said. 'Someone who remembers the old days, yeah? Don't care who it is, as long as we're looked after. Not threatened by kiddies with butterfly knives.'

'I'll do my best,' Ellie said. 'I'll speak to some people.'

'Oh, you're the Godfather now?'

Ramsey leant in closer.

'You might be surprised to learn that there's a pretty good chance she could be if Becky Slade is removed.'

Arthur smiled, a wide, beaming grin that showed off all of his knackered teeth.

'Count me in, then,' he said. 'I've heard about you, Reckless, there are worse people out there.'

'I didn't say I was going to be the Godfather,' Ellie muttered. 'And we're going off track here. You were telling me about Cillian Slade.'

Arthur nodded reluctantly.

'Yeah, so, ten years back, Paddy Simpson forces Max to step down. He gives the land to his grandson, who, unknown to everybody else, he's been subtly grooming for the last year or two. Max is unhappy about this, as you can guess, but the reason he was removed was because he was dropping the ball. More importantly, he'd been dropping the ball so bad that the Slades thought they had the chance of taking him out.'

He took another sip of whisky, frowned, and then looked at the bar.

'This is the good stuff?' he asked.

The landlord flipped him a finger, and Arthur chuckled, looking back.

'Cillian Slade was past his prime, but his son, Drew? He was still pretty solid. He wanted to try to take over before Max was removed himself. Max was a weak leader. There was every opportunity the Slades could do something, and they were making steady progress, gaining land from the Simpsons in the year before Max was deposed. We weren't up to full-on war yet, but there was a nibbling of the edges, shall we say.'

Ellie nodded as Arthur held up the tumbler, staring into it.

'Drew Slade was becoming a problem to the Simpsons, yeah, but Cillian didn't want any of it, kept telling Drew to back down, stay in his lane, claimed that although he'd always been able to go toe-to-toe with the Simpsons, Drew was nothing but a bare-knuckle fighter. He was muscle more than brains. There were other issues, too—'

'To do with Becky's parentage, perhaps?' Ramsey enquired.

'Yeah, that didn't help, either. There was talk his wife, stupid Gypsy name, can't remember what it was, cuckolded Drew with the Turk's son.'

Ellie held a hand up to stop Arthur.

'The Turk had a son?'

Arthur shrugged.

'Never met him, kept the hell away from the Turk, too. Tsangs did us all a service, wiping that prick out. But there was talk. Baris, his name was. Dealt with the Slades to help destabilise the Simpsons, but ended up ...'

He shrugged.

'Destabilising Slade's wife until she fell underneath him,' he winked. 'Anyway, all that aside, back when daddy was telling Drew to shut the hell up and behave himself, Drew was unhappy about this. I always got the impression there was more to it than just dad not believing in his son, though.'

'How do you mean?'

'I'm not sure, but if you ask me, I think Paddy had had a chat with Cillian and convinced him somehow to take a step back, maybe promising something else, I don't know.'

'Are you sure about this?' Ramsey asked.

'All I know is that Drew turned up all piss and vinegar one night in 2013, claiming that the Simpsons couldn't stop him, and he was damn well sure his dad couldn't stop him.'

He stared off out of the window.

'It was in the Lord Palmerston in Deptford,' he said. 'Used to be on Childers Street, but it's long gone now, probably turned into apartments or something. That's the problem with gentrification, all the cool stuff disappears, and spit and sawdust pubs become a thing of the past.'

'We're not here to talk about cultural shifting,' Ramsey leant closer, tapping the glass. 'You were saying ...'

Arthur Davenport nodded.

'I was finishing up a pint in the pub that night,' he said. 'Cillian had turned up with a couple of his friends and was mouthing off, buying rounds for everybody, playing the big hoo-ha. Someone had said that Cillian wasn't the King anymore, and it was now Drew, and Cillian had taken offence. There'd been a fight, well, more of a beating. Cillian might have been an old man by then, but you still didn't go one-on-one with the big guy.'

Arthur sighed, lost in the memory.

'Anyway, I didn't want to get involved and so I said my goodbyes, walked out the door and, as I was there, I saw Drew pull up in his car. Someone had obviously called him, said what had gone down. He was furious, shouting and screaming, his daughter, Becky – or whatever the hell she was to him – she was beside him trying to pull him back. She was only twenty, if that. She was training for the Olympics, I think. First Slade to actually box with gloves on, although I hear she's still pretty good without them.'

Ellie winced at this; she knew first-hand how good Becky Slade was without gloves on.

'Anyway, I know Drew goes into the pub, they're shouting and screaming, I pause across the street and then I hear a noise at the back of the pub. Cillian's dragged Drew out into the car park behind it, and he's beating down on him. There's a twenty-year difference and Drew's a good foot in height on his pa, but it didn't matter. Cillian was fired up, had enough and then ... well, there was a gunshot. Next thing I know from the alley at the side, Becky and Drew are running, they get in the car, they drive off. My curiosity got the better of me, so I run down the alley and I find Cillian Slade laying on the floor, a hole in his head where the bullet had hit, all his friends claiming Drew did it.'

There was a moment of silence, almost as if Arthur Davenport was giving it to Cillian's honour.

'The problem was that nobody saw it happen,' he said. 'I

heard later that Cillian's friends, they hadn't gone out with him, they'd been told to stay back, as it was father and son only. Even Becky was told to stay in the room, although apparently she never listened to orders. They claimed it was Drew because who else could it be? Drew was arrested. And after a couple of days, he admitted to the murder, said it was self-defence. Cillian had pulled the gun, and in the struggle, Drew had shot him. Didn't matter though, Drew had enough things against him to throw him in jail for a long time. You know, longer than a *DFS sale* length of time.'

Arthur drew himself back up, taking a deep breath.

'So yeah, that's what I saw. Probably not what you were hoping for.'

'Actually, in a way, it's better,' Ellie replied. 'Let me get this straight; as far as everybody was concerned, Drew, Cillian and Becky were out in the alley. Nobody else there? So it could have been Becky that killed her grandfather.'

Arthur didn't seem surprised by the suggestion, and Ellie realised he'd probably considered this himself over the years.

'Yeah,' he nodded. 'It could have been her. She was there, she had the opportunity. And there was no love there, considering who her other granddad was, if the stories were true.'

'Did you ever give a statement?'

'Of course I did.'

'Do you remember who you gave the statement to?'

'Oh yeah, absolutely.' At this, Arthur Davenport grinned. 'You see *that* name's popped up a lot over the years. The person who took the statement, and in fact was lead in this case, was a young Detective Constable, fresh on the beat, working with DI Hays, who we all knew was corrupt as well.'

He watched Ellie as he spoke the name.

'Detective Constable Mark Whitehouse.'

Ellie stared at Arthur.

'Mark Whitehouse was on the case?'

'Oh yeah,' Arthur replied. 'And I've heard what happened to him recently, who he worked for back then. Makes you wonder, doesn't it? Who exactly was working for who ...'

'And who wanted Cillian Slade dead the most?'

14

EX-COPPERS

If she was being brutally honest, Ellie hadn't expected to be speaking to Kate Delgado again so quickly. The moment they left the pub, with Arthur Davenport drinking his final double whisky on their expenses, she was already sending a message, demanding a meeting. As it was, it looked like Delgado had been expecting this because it was only a matter of seconds before a text appeared on her screen.

Marshall's Diner. Stockwell. One hour.

Checking a map on her phone, Ellie realised that even making the diner at that time was going to be close in the early afternoon traffic. But, leaving Ramsey to his own devices, she decided to meet up with her onetime colleague once again.

The diner that Delgado had chosen was very much a trucker's diner, as far removed from the Caesars Diner-retro 1950s City of London base as you could get. Ellie didn't mind this. If anything, she was surprised that Delgado would pick such a location. She'd always seen her more as a wine bar, or gastropub kind of woman.

Ellie took a booth at the far end. Although "booth" was a polite way of explaining a wide plastic bench placed on either side of a similarly utilitarian table. She chose tea and a ham sandwich from the laminated menu, conveniently providing photos of each item, in case you weren't too sure what each menu item text meant, and sat back to wait.

While she did, she ruminated on what she'd learnt already. Becky Slade was playing several games at once, it seemed. First, she was trying to gain the favours to force five arbitrators to sign across five million pounds' worth of reparation money. Second, she was looking to use this to somehow assist her father in his upcoming appeal in Southwark. Whether this meant by breaking him out beforehand, or by helping his appeal, Ellie didn't know yet.

Third, Drew might not be her father, and someone needed to see what had really happened between Charity Slade and Baris ... well, whatever Baris's surname was. She was sure calling him "Baris Turk" would be classed as borderline racism.

Fourth, Becky Slade had ambition, and whatever money was left over was likely going into some kind of war chest to take over at least the entire southern half of London. Currently, with Robert Lewis by her side, reluctant as he might be, Becky Slade was in the lead.

Ellie wasn't sure how on earth she was going to get this done.

And then there was Drew Slade, who may have killed her grandfather, and was likely claiming a mistrial, as the detective who arrested him was Mark Whitehouse.

She'd heard nothing from Joanne Davey, which was

understandable; she'd told her to go off-grid. Checking her watch, she hoped that by now at least some of the Finder's crew had their families being looked after. She knew Casey was examining the calendar, so if Robert *was* on the side of angels, he'd leave more clues.

Ellie leant back on the plastic bench, and for the first time that day she felt optimistic. She knew by the time she returned to the makeshift offices at Simpson's Health Spa, her team would likely have a better idea of what Becky's plans were.

Until then, she needed to keep moving forward, and that involved Mark Whitehouse.

No longer a police officer, Ellie couldn't just phone the prison up and demand a meeting. She had to go through the public routes, and had already checked through the online messaging portal while waiting in the diner, requesting a time as soon as possible.

She was hoping Delgado could help push this through, though.

Looking up, she saw Delgado enter the diner, exactly one hour after the text had been sent. Ellie couldn't help herself – she actually found herself wondering whether Delgado had been waiting outside just to make sure this point was held.

Delgado said nothing. She walked up to Ellie, nodded, and then sat down facing her.

There was a long, quiet, uncomfortable moment between the two women before Ellie spoke.

'How long have you known?' she asked.

Delgado shook her head.

'I don't know what you mean.'

Ellie slammed a fist on the diner's table, which not only

surprised Delgado but also gained the attention of several diners around them.

'I have just about had enough of this,' Ellie snarled. 'You said to me, when we met last time, that I should look into the death of Cillian Slade. Well, I *did* look into the death of Cillian Slade. And the first thing I found was that the arresting officer was Mark Whitehouse, who had just been made Detective Constable.'

She leant closer.

'Now, this was around the time I joined, but I wasn't on this case. We hadn't been partnered up at this point. If anything, I was still gophering for Monroe. But you seem to know way more about this than I do, even though you started after this happened. So why don't you explain to me how you know this?'

Delgado gave an almost-sneer as she sat there, smiling back.

'What, so we're once again saying that I'm corrupt?'

'No,' Ellie shook her head. 'What we're saying is that you know more than you're telling me, and I'm sick to death of having to jump through hoops to get it. Please, Kate, I'm asking. As a favour, as a friend. As we used to be, at least.'

Delgado sighed, rubbing her eyes with her hand.

'Look,' she replied. 'When Mark was found to be corrupt, it landed on the entire unit, you know? *No smoke without fire. Surely someone must have known.* There you were, brave Ellie Reckless, on her own against the entire department. And we're blindly sitting there as Mark Whitehouse apparently takes us all for a ride. We had to be involved. We had to be part of this.'

Ellie nodded.

'I'll be honest, I thought you were,' she said. 'It's not too difficult to think that others would believe the same once Mark was found out.'

'Yeah, well, we weren't, were we?' Delgado snapped. 'I've never been corrupt. I might have been wrong in my thoughts and my beliefs, and I'll hold my hands up to that, but I never took a bribe. I never looked the other way.'

'Apart from when I was claiming my innocence.'

'Damn it, Ellie. Are we going to go back over that now?'

Ellie held her hand up.

'Sorry, please, carry on.'

'So the first thing that happens is I'm moved. And yeah, I know I told you I'd decided I needed a break from Vauxhall, but the fact of the matter was Vauxhall didn't want me. I was dirty. I was corrupted goods. I had to move over to Charing Cross and Soho for two months to get away from that stink. And even *they* didn't bloody want me, because the next thing that happens is Kenny Tsang and Jimmy Tsang fighting again, and once more I'm looked at as the person who's causing this shit. Once more Ellie Reckless is there. And so what do I do? I return to Vauxhall. Suck up the insults. The side eyes. Go back to the Detective Chief Superintendent and ask if I can have my old job back.'

She leant back, puffing out her cheeks before continuing.

'And,' she laughed, 'not only did they give me the job, they let me keep the sodding promotion. That was nice of them. But the first thing I had to do was go through every single one of Mark Whitehouse's cases. All the ones he did with you, all the ones he did with me, all the ones he did before either of us were his partner. One by one, checking them through, making sure that we hadn't missed out on something, or that we hadn't put somebody innocent in prison because of Mark Whitehouse's corrupt-as-shit word.'

'And what did you find?' Ellie asked.

'Honestly? Quite a few,' Delgado admitted. 'They're all in the system at the moment. Internal Affairs is now looking into it. There's going to be quite a few quashed convictions and I think there's going to be a few civil actions – the police are going to be making a few payouts because of Mark Whitehouse. Luckily for me, none of the cases *we* did together were on this list. Probably because he was trying to hide the fact he was a corrupt prick at that point.'

Ellie frowned, but before she could speak, Delgado smiled.

'And so you don't need to worry, there was only one case that the two of you did together that's being looked into.'

'Which one?'

'I don't have it to hand,' Delgado replied. 'But I'll find it. You should know about it because I'm sure you'll be pulled in as a witness. But when I went back further, all the way to the start, I saw the murder of Cillian Slade pop up on the list. I saw that not only was Mark Whitehouse the Detective Constable that was first on site, he'd actively waived away any uniforms. That was the first clue. Once I found out that Cillian had been dealing with Paddy, I wondered if Paddy had killed him, used Mark to hide this.'

Ellie shook her head.

'Unlikely,' she replied. 'Mark claimed his dad was on Paddy's take, but he was only blackmailed a few years later, when Monroe and I arrived at Vauxhall.'

'But he learnt the truth about his dad when he was freshly promoted to DC, and he was a DC here,' Delgado countered. 'Also, he's a lying piece of shit, so who knows what's true or not?'

She waved for a mug of tea from the counter.

'But the one thing that had come up was Andrew Slade's confession,' she continued. 'It was given to Mark Whitehouse. And half the time there's a large chunk of the interview where it wasn't recorded. You tell me what you think that means.'

Ellie nodded. She understood exactly what Delgado was suggesting.

The server from behind the counter walked over with a fresh mug of tea for Delgado, who sipped at it, grimacing before adding a couple of sweeteners. She stirred it and sat back, now staring at Ellie.

'I didn't tell you about Whitehouse because I didn't want it to trigger you,' she said. 'Let's be honest, I'd rather not deal with him, and I wasn't the one he managed to screw over.'

She looked around the diner as she took a sip.

'We used to come in here, you know,' she said. 'Now and then. Far enough from the unit to not feel like we're on duty still. Not too far that if something happened, we couldn't be called back. Want to know the weird thing? They had a staff changeover right after it all went down. First time I came back here, looking for something familiar, hiding out from the officers at Vauxhall all glaring at me, either blaming me for making them look bad or blaming me for making the *unit* look bad, depending on whether they believed you or not, I found there wasn't a single recognisable face here. Nobody who recognised me or could say hello, chat to.'

She sighed, cricking her neck as she did so.

'It's not the same anymore, Ellie. I'm considering handing it in, you know, maybe finding a country beat. I know they offered you one once.'

'You'd hate it,' Ellie replied. 'You're a city cop, just like me.'

She leaned forward, placing her elbows on the plastic table between them.

'You made mistakes and we've both dealt with that. The fact you've come back to start again says more about you than it does about the police. You need to stay at Vauxhall. Or if not Vauxhall, find somewhere else. You're a Detective Inspector now. Act like one.'

Delgado chuckled.

'What, you mean like you did?'

'Christ, no.' Ellie laughed for the first time. 'If anything, look at what I would do and do the complete opposite.'

There was a moment of silence as the two women stared at each other.

The server from behind the counter walked over with Ellie's ham sandwich. It didn't look like it had in the photo. It was limp and rather sad looking.

Ellie ate it.

'So, what haven't I been told then?' Delgado asked. 'I'm guessing you know something more.'

'There was a reparation fund,' Ellie explained. 'Five million held between the five areas of London. A kind of insurance policy to make sure that nobody goes out of line. Just so happens that the five people who control this owe me favours.'

Delgado leant back.

'Hey, if you want to ask a favour that gives you the money, I'm more than happy to take a percentage.'

'Not my thing,' Ellie chuckled through a mouthful of sandwich. 'But it is, however, Becky Slade's thing. I also know that Drew Slade is up for appeal. And there's a little part of me, a little spider sense, maybe my copper's intuition still hanging on by a thread, that says when a woman is looking to do everything she can, including burn someone else's favours to grab five million pounds the same time her dad goes for appeal, she's either looking to get an incredibly expensive solicitor—'

'Or she's looking to break him out,' Delgado finished the sentence. 'I see that.'

She pulled out her phone and started typing on it.

'I'll make sure I get placed on his detail,' she said. 'I'm pretty fluid at the moment, so I can bounce around from place to place. It's going to be at Southwark, I'm assuming, so they can't really stop me. If anybody tries to get Drew Slade out, at least I'll be feet on the ground.'

She looked back at Ellie.

'Although I'm guessing you'll be somewhere close by as well.'

'With luck, we won't reach that far,' Ellie replied. 'I think you were right when you told me to look into that murder. There's more there than was said. I think Mark Whitehouse will know more. I've applied to see him. But ...'

She trailed off and Delgado smiled.

'But you're not a copper,' she replied. 'It's a lot harder to get to see somebody when you don't have a magic warrant card, isn't it?'

'Oh, I still have a warrant card,' Ellie said. 'It's just it doesn't really work on internet portals.'

Delgado chuckled to herself.

'The great Ellie Reckless is asking me a favour,' she said. 'Maybe I should start my own collection.'

She sipped at her tea for a moment, contemplating the situation.

'He's at Wandsworth, but you already know that,' she

said. 'Make your way over there. By the time you arrive, you'll have the right paperwork. I'll make sure of it.'

She rose from the chair, sliding out of the plastic bench area as she did so.

'Keep me updated on this one,' she said. 'It might be personal to you, but it's definitely personal for me as well.'

Ellie nodded, still finishing her sandwich.

'Hey,' she said. 'I wasn't squeaky clean, you know. I was having an affair with an informant.'

'I'm aware.'

'I'm just pointing out that if you look at me, you, Alex Monroe when he was there and Mark Whitehouse, you're the only one of us who wasn't in any way dirty,' Ellie said, finishing up the sandwich and placing a ten-pound note on the table. 'I just wanted you to remember that before you went back.'

Delgado looked as if she was about to contest this or argue the point, but then stopped and tightly nodded before leaving.

Ellie sighed, clambering out of the plastic bench herself, dusting herself down and walking to the door.

As diners go, she preferred her own.

15

VISITING HOURS

Ellie parked her car and walked towards the imposing structure of HM Prison Wandsworth.

The grey facade loomed ahead as she approached the visitor's centre, where she joined a small line of people waiting to check in. The centre was a functional space, busy with activity, and she quickly found a locker to stow away her personal items, including her phone, which she knew from bitter experience was strictly prohibited inside, whether or not you were an ex-copper.

She presented her printed-out visiting order, fast-tracked and provided by Delgado, and her ID to the staff at the reception desk who checked her details against their system. After verifying her identity and purpose, she was handed a visitor's badge and directed towards the security screening area.

Ellie felt a knot of tension as she approached the metal detector, knowing the gravity of the meeting ahead. The last she'd heard, Whitehouse was trying for a plea deal against Paddy Simpson, and had been whisked away to a safe house, but now, months later, he was on remand, placed in a protective custody unit within the prison.

Looks like his plea deal information was as fake as he was.

Clearing security, she was escorted by a prison officer through a series of heavy, electronically controlled doors; the cold, institutional atmosphere of the prison was palpable as they walked down long corridors, the sound of their footsteps echoing off the concrete walls. She glanced at the barred windows and the occasional groups of inmates moving under watchful eyes, and was struck by how silent things were here; a stark reminder of where she was.

Finally, they reached the visits hall, a large room with several rows of tables and chairs, each sectioned off to allow monitored conversations.

Ellie scanned the room until her eyes settled on a familiar face. Mark Whitehouse was already seated, looking out of place in his prison-issued clothing. The officer escorting her indicated the table where she should sit, then stepped back to a discreet distance, keeping a watchful eye.

As Ellie sat down opposite Whitehouse, she took a deep breath. The man who had once been a colleague now sat across from her, his eyes haunted. Slim and tall, his hair was unkempt, his chin unshaven and stubbled. It was almost as if she'd woken him from sleeping.

She couldn't help it; just looking at the man made Ellie remember the last time they'd spoken. It'd been by phone, before she discovered he'd tried to kill Robert. He'd offered to help find out who did it, claiming the role of "loyal friend" until the bitter end.

But not anymore.

'I'm surprised to see you here,' Whitehouse spoke for the

first time, his voice hoarse and croaky. It felt as if speaking was something he had done little of in the last few months. Ellie realised that being in a secure room, he was pretty much in isolation, solitary even. Talking to people probably wasn't something he was used to at the moment.

'Yeah, well, I wasn't intending to turn up,' Ellie replied. 'Problem is, I need to ask you some questions.'

'I'm sorry,' Whitehouse frowned. 'Did I miss something? Are you police again?'

Ellie leant back, staring at the man in front of her. She remembered Mark Whitehouse well. But this man, this dishevelled, unshaven man in front of her, *wasn't* Mark Whitehouse. This was what was left after Paddy Simpson had chewed up and spat out anything good in the man.

As if realising he'd overstepped a line, Mark Whitehouse continued.

'How's Robert?' he asked, changing the subject.

Ellie went to snap at the jibe but then realised it probably wasn't. There was no way that Mark Whitehouse could have known that Becky Slade was now working with Robert Lewis. There was every chance this was a genuine contrition for what he had done.

'He no longer works with us,' she said. 'Went on sabbatical four months ago.'

'I'm sorry to hear that,' Whitehouse replied.

'You didn't exactly help there,' Ellie couldn't help herself. Her hands balled into fists under the table as she glared across at Whitehouse. 'You tried to kill him with an iron bar. You gave him injuries that he still hasn't recovered from.'

'I know,' Whitehouse replied, almost matter-of-factly. 'If you see him, apologise for me.'

'If I see him, I won't mention your name,' Ellie replied. 'In fact, if I see *anybody* who knows you, I won't mention your name. The only person who knows I'm here is Kate Delgado, and she told me to tell you to rot in hell, you traitorous shit.'

She allowed the sentence to fade off. The guard, standing a suitable distance away, was watching the other inmates and their visitors as they held their private moments.

'Kate wouldn't have said that,' Whitehouse replied.

'Maybe she did, maybe she didn't. You'll never know,' Ellie shrugged.

'So, what do I owe this visit to?' Whitehouse stretched out, hands and elbows now on the table, relaxed as he stared back at Ellie. 'I'm guessing you need something. Maybe I need something in return.'

'You don't even know what it is yet,' Ellie said.

'If it's brought you here, it's got to be important,' Whitehouse sighed and shrugged. 'Am I wrong?'

'Back when you started as a Detective Constable,' Ellie ignored the comment. 'Before we met, you told us you'd found out your dad had been working for the Simpsons.'

Whitehouse nodded.

'You also said that you'd found out about this when you became a Detective Constable, although it was years later when Paddy started calling on the debt.'

Again, Whitehouse nodded.

'How did you find out about your father?'

'I always knew something was wrong,' Whitehouse said. 'As it was, somebody told me.'

'Was it Cillian Slade? Or maybe Drew Slade?'

At the names, Whitehouse smiled.

'*There* we are,' he said now, back in control. 'That's why

you're here. Drew Slade's up for his appeal tomorrow, isn't he? What's it to do with you? Why do you care about a ten-year-old murder?'

He cocked his head to the side, watching Ellie carefully.

'You're on a case,' he said. 'Gaining a favour? No, you don't need favours anymore. This is something more than that, isn't it?'

'We're not doing *Silence of the Lambs*.' Ellie cut this down instantly. 'You can play detectives as much as you want, but I'm not giving you the satisfaction of working it out. Becky Slade's making a move on South London. And I think whatever she's doing is connected to Drew's appeal. Now I know you were the Detective Constable in charge of that case, and that you claim Drew confessed. But there are large periods of the recording that don't seem to have, well, *recorded*. And I'm curious whether Drew actually did it, or whether you'd been told to make sure he did.'

Mark Whitehouse shook his head.

'I'm a good cop, Ellie,' he said. 'Maybe not at the end, when everything I'd loved had been stripped from me, but when I was a Detective Constable, I wanted to be the best. I wanted to be the next Chief Superintendent. I wanted to be the guy who solved the crimes, no matter what it took.'

'So, what happened?'

Mark Whitehouse shrugged.

'London happened,' he said. 'It chewed me up and spat me out. And by the time you found me, there was nothing left.'

Ellie rubbed at her chin.

'What do you want?' she asked. The question was unexpected and seemed to throw Whitehouse for a moment.

'What do you mean?'

'I mean, Mark, that I still have a lot of favours owed to me,' Ellie said. 'If you want, I'll burn one for you. Is there something I can give you that would help you in here?'

She didn't want to say it, but she knew she had to.

'Or maybe help you with your case?'

Mark started to laugh now.

'Oh my God,' he said. 'This is important, isn't it? This is something you really need.'

He scratched at his own chin now, stroking the stubble as he considered the proposition.

'I'm in here for the long haul,' he said. 'I'm aware of that. What I did, I shouldn't be let out, at least until I've paid my dues. But there's a guy in here, another copper, did the wrong thing, found himself in prison. Even though he's looked after, being, you know, not a criminal class, he still gets beatings. You get him over to me to look after, I'll give you what you need.'

'And what is it you think I need?' Ellie asked.

'You want to know what happened that night,' Whitehouse replied. 'Not many people do. You see, I was the first on-site because I was, well ... on site when it happened, in the pub. Pure bloody chance. Hadn't meant to be. When I saw Cillian and Drew kick off, I knew it was nothing more than bluster; the son trying to prove to his dad that he was worthy. Problem is, the Slades were always pig-shit stupid.'

He looked away from Ellie as he spoke next, as if not wanting to catch her eye.

'You see, my dad, he was bought and paid for,' he said. 'Not by the Simpsons, but by South London. Sure, Paddy worked with him, and he looked the other way a few times, gave him the heads up when needed, but he also did the same for Cillian Slade, and a couple of other small-timers, even the bloody Turk when he was in town. In fact, he did this for anybody who wanted to give him money, drugs, favours, even a couple of prostitutes, at one point. I looked into it. I found out everything. My dad, he was an open-source corrupt copper. He wasn't exclusive to anyone. And Cillian, well, he wasn't as subtle about it as Paddy Simpson was.'

'Go on.'

'He found me in the pub, recognised me for who I was, said he knew my dad back in the day. Told me my dad was a "good friend to the Slades", and that he hoped I'd be as well. Of course, at this point, I was all piss and vinegar, and told him to sod off.'

His face darkened.

'Then he told me *unless* I helped him, he'd make damn sure I'd never get any further in the force. He'd tell the police everything about my dad. He'd make sure that there were enough loose threads to make them think that the apple never fell far from the tree. I'd never be looked at without suspicion again, all because I wouldn't do what he said.'

Whitehouse was glaring now as he stared at the floor, deep in his memory.

'When he started kicking off with Drew, I didn't get involved,' he said. 'And when he was killed, I saw it as a way out. Cillian held this over me? Well, hell, Cillian was dead now. Told the barman that I wasn't there, didn't need to scrub any CCTV because the bar didn't use it. Told the police as they arrived I'd been passing by, so was first on scene. It was close enough to my route home for me to get away with it.'

'Was it Drew?' Ellie asked. 'Who killed Cillian?'

Mark Whitehouse smiled as he folded his arms and faced Ellie.

'You get me my favour,' he said, 'and I'll tell you. Michael Swift is his name. You get him into my block and I can keep him safe.'

He looked over at the guard and waved.

'I'm done here,' he said. 'This is boring me.'

'Prison clothes look good on you,' Ellie said. 'I hope you're getting used to them. They look comfy.'

'I've got my own appeal coming,' he said. 'I've made my plea deals. When it finally gets around to trial, I'm sure I'll be sorted.'

'What happened to your promises of "willing to do the time for the crime" and all that?'

Whitehouse shrugged, his face set in a slight grimace.

'It's easy to say that before you spend time in prison,' he replied. 'Once here, you realise you'd rather be *anywhere*. So sure, my plea deal should help. Or maybe Paddy Simpson will have a nasty accident and I won't need to worry about it.'

The guard walked over now, motioning for Whitehouse to rise and follow him out the door. As Whitehouse complied, he said nothing more, turning away and walking off without a second word.

Ellie stared at his back as he walked off. This was a man who for years she'd believed had *her* back whenever they went into dangerous situations. And now, watching him, she realised just how little she knew.

But one thing was for sure. When Mark Whitehouse had been talking about his story, there was one person he hadn't mentioned.

Becky Slade.

Whether by accident or by design. The woman who'd been trying to stop her father from having the fight, who would have been there as it kicked off, had been strangely erased from the story.

Alone now, Ellie smiled to herself. *It was time to see if anybody else had been visiting Mark Whitehouse in the last, say, two months.*

She was pretty certain she'd find the surname Slade ... or worse.

16

OPENED VAULTS

'ROBERT LEWIS IS PLAYING A PRETTY DANGEROUS GAME,' CASEY said, as Ramsey entered the back office where he was currently working on his laptop, Tinker sitting beside him.

Ramsey frowned.

'I'm sorry, have I missed some get-together?' he asked. 'Why are you tutoring Tinker on how the internet works? There are certain areas that even she shouldn't be allowed to visit, you know.'

'Shut up and come and have a look at this,' Tinker replied, a smile on her face.

Wandering over, Ramsey stared at the calendar on the screen.

'It's a calendar,' he said. 'Why do I care about a calendar?'

'It's Robert Lewis's calendar,' Tinker said.

'I can see that,' Ramsey replied. 'His email's at the top. Gym. Dinner. Lunch with Peter. Sounds riveting.'

'Most of them are,' Casey said. 'All as riveting as this. But then, here and there, you get a couple of others.'

He scrolled backwards two weeks. And there, on a

Wednesday at 4 pm, a different coloured block was in the calendar.

'Check this out,' he continued. 'What's the name of the guy who runs that Vault place?'

Ramsey frowned. The "Vaults" were an underground secret – an off-the-books warehouse, once a more legitimate storage unit area, now used by those who wished to hide something from their rivals or police. Ramsey had once had a small locker there, but had stopped when he'd heard Nicky Simpson had booked out the whole third floor. They'd visited it a few times in previous cases.

'You mean Squeaky James?' he replied. 'He's the guy who mans the door, and signs up new accounts, if that's what you mean.'

'It's *William* James, right?' Casey pointed at the calendar. 'Here. Meeting a month back, William James, London Fields.'

'That's the Vaults, alright,' Ramsey sighed. 'I'll go see him right after this.'

'*We'll* go,' Tinker added. 'There's too much temptation there for you alone.'

'When you do, mention "Rosebud" to him,' Casey tapped on the "Notes" section of the event.

It was the only word showing.

'Bloody "Rosebud?" That man needs to get a life,' Ramsey muttered, as they both left the office.

THE VAULTS WEREN'T EXACTLY THE BUSIEST OF LOCATIONS, deliberately placed in a building near London Fields on the Blackstone Estate – an enormous, three-storey high, red-bricked building, maybe fifteen years old, with a large roller door to the side, large enough to drive a Luton van into, and a door to the right of it, surrounded by Screwfix stores, courier warehouses and what looked to be a pole dancing school. After all, if you were a criminal looking to hide your goods, the last thing you wanted was to turn up during rush hour; corridors of garage doors, each one locked and rising when opened, no questions asked to the contents inside.

But, as Ramsey and Tinker arrived, there seemed to be more interest than usual.

Two men were sitting in a car, watching them as they emerged from Tinker's Jeep. Ramsey had spied them first, deliberately keeping his attention away from the vehicle.

'Have you spied the ...'

'Yes,' Tinker interrupted. 'I've seen one of them in the south of London, so I know they're probably Becky Slade's people, checking to see who turns up here.'

An A4 sign on the other side of the wired glass door stated the location was "Open 24 Hours" but the door, as ever, was locked. There was a buzzer on the side, and Ramsey pressed it, aware the CCTV camera on the wall above them had rotated slightly and was now aimed at them.

'Yes?' The voice of Squeaky James spoke through the intercom. 'What do you want, Ramsey?'

'If I said "Rosebud" to you, would you think I was insane, or propositioning you?' Ramsey replied with a smile, and wasn't surprised to hear the buzzing of the door unlocking.

As they carried on into the vaults' main entrance, Ramsey heard a door slam and, glancing back, saw that the two men were now following them into the lobby; they'd used Ramsey and Tinker to bypass the security, and now Tinker was tensing beside him as they carried on through. There was a set of stairs to the side, and they made their way up into the bare white reception room. There was a small, no bigger than A2-sized window at the other end, a high table in front of it that looked through into another office, just as bare, the window likely bulletproof. Ramsey was aware one reason why this was done in such a way was if somebody tried to break into the vaults, whoever was guarding could shove a shotgun through the hole and start firing. Obviously, this had never happened; it was the threat of the action more than the action itself. But it made a chilling thought, especially as they found themselves now caught between the open slit and the two men behind them.

There was a rattling of keys and Squeaky opened the window, staring out at them.

'Ramsey Allen,' he laughed, 'about bloody time you turned up. Here to see your box?'

Ramsey went to reply in the negative to remind Squeaky, who had obviously forgotten, that he had stopped his membership in the vaults a while earlier, but a subtle nudge from Tinker paused him from replying. He altered his answer quickly.

'Just the two of us. They're not with me,' he pointed at the two men behind him.

Squeaky's eyes narrowed as he looked back at the newer arrivals.

'I've told you two to piss off,' he said. 'If you're not going to come in and look at a vault box, then you aren't allowed to keep coming in here.'

'We were told to keep an eye on whoever turns up,' one of the two men said.

'And what you're doing, mate, is giving yourself a little list of everybody who's got vault boxes here,' Squeaky replied. 'That ain't on, so you go and tell Slade that if she wants to play silly buggers any more, I'll close her vault and kick her crap out as well.'

The two men grumbled as Squeaky now closed the sliding door to the window and, after a couple of seconds, appeared at the doorway.

'Come on, Ramsey, I can take you to your box with your friend. These two will be pissing off.'

Ramsey followed Squeaky through the door, closing it behind him, and with Tinker beside him, they made their way down the metal staircase that led to the ground floor level.

Squeaky, once he was sure they were far enough away, turned back to look at them.

'I know you don't have a box any more,' he said. 'Which is a crying shame, in my opinion, and you really should consider returning with it. But I've got instructions.'

'What kind of instructions?'

'That if you, Miss Jones, or Ellie Reckless are to arrive at the vaults and say the word "Rosebud" to me, I'm to take you to Robert Lewis's vault.'

Ramsey glanced at Tinker.

'This is planned?' he said, before glancing back at Squeaky. 'We were actually given permission to look?'

'I was actively informed that if you turned up and said the word, I had to drag you here, no matter where you were going to look at first,' Squeaky said. 'You could have turned up to look at Danny Martin's box or someone else's, it didn't matter, I was still going to be dragging you here.'

He nodded back at the door.

'And it's something to do with those pricks and their boss,' he replied. 'Honestly, if it stops them hunting outside my bloody door, I am more than happy for whatever you need to do.'

Once they entered one of the smaller roller-shuttered rooms, Squeaky unlocking the padlock and placing it back on the catch once the door was opened, he stepped back.

'This is for you,' he said. 'I want no part of it. When you're done, lock up and leave through the back route. And don't be a stranger, Allen. There's not many of us around anymore.'

'I won't.' Ramsey shook William "Squeaky" James's hand as, walking away, the old man left the two members of Finders to stare into the tiny room that their long-lost member had seemingly left for them.

Robert had been busy, it seemed.

The walls were filled with pictures, photos taken from a distance, possibly through a long lens. Names were written on post-it notes and placed underneath them. There was string leading from one to another; photos of locations, often taken from what looked to be Google Street View, and receipts, or rather, photos of receipts, that had been printed out.

It was laid out in such a way that anybody who read it could see what was going on, which made Tinker wonder whether Robert had put this together on the off-chance that he wouldn't be around.

Ramsey was already examining the walls.

'What's this?' he asked, peering closer. 'Peterson Brothers. Aren't they—'

'Yeah,' Tinker finished the sentence. 'They're the people you go to when you want to get a vehicle that's, shall we say, untraceable? They specialise in industrial vehicles. Vans, lorries, that sort of thing. Fake cleaning companies and such like, armoured better than a tank.'

'Why would Becky be going to a car dealer like that?' Ramsey stroked at his moustache. 'Is she planning an armed robbery?'

He paused.

'Christ, she is planning an armed robbery, but it's not a bank we're going with. This is her father.'

Tinker nodded.

'If you wanted to stop a prison transport, you couldn't do it with a normal car, you'd need something a bit bigger. Peterson Brothers, well, they're probably the people to speak to about it.'

'Okay, so even if you had the vehicle, you'd still need to have some kind of armoury?'

'Here,' Tinker tapped at a receipt pinned to the wall.

'Griffin?' Ramsey shook his head. 'I don't know the name.'

'Griffin's from North London,' Tinker said. 'I know him because I know my guns.'

'Let me guess,' Ramsey pulled it off the wall, staring down at it. 'He's the person you go to when you want to buy off-the-books "shooters" and suchlike.'

'And the rest,' Tinker nodded. 'Assault rifles, grenade launchers, C4 explosives, the lot. So now you've got Becky Slade visiting a gunsmith, and a guy known for industrial off-the-books vehicles.'

Ramsey had moved over to the photos on the wall.

'There's Becky, meeting with Arun Nadal,' he said, tapping one of them. 'Arun's got a string attached, and it leads ...' he paused as he looked at it, 'straight to the Seven Sisters. But look, it threads off here and ends up on Johnny Lucas.'

'Well, we know he has a family connection,' Tinker replied. 'Maybe that's what this is about.'

There were papers strewn on a table to the side; the vault

Robert seemed to own didn't allow much space apart from this. It was just about large enough for the two of them to stand beside the table, staring at the wall.

But it was all that Robert Lewis had needed.

'He must have been coming in here pretending to be doing something else,' Tinker mused as she checked through the papers on the desk. 'Grabbing moments to come in here and add to this.'

She looked underneath the table and pulled out a small printer.

'Wi-Fi printer,' she said, looking at it and then back at the wall. 'He'd take photos on his camera or have photos sent to him from whoever took these shots, bring them here, print them out, stick them on the wall, then probably delete them off his phone immediately afterwards. There's an element of analogue to this that keeps him safe, but Christ, if he's caught before he gets here …'

She trailed off. She didn't need to continue.

Ramsey shook his head as Tinker now started looking back at the papers on the desk.

'There's the layout here of the route from Belmarsh to Southwark,' she said. 'This is definitely Drew Slade's prison transport. The van Peterson Brothers provided for them, it's an Iveco Daily panel van. Same make and model as UK prisons use.'

'And you know this how?' Ramsey raised an eyebrow quizzically.

'I have a friend who converts vans into campers,' Tinker replied, invoice in her hand. 'He's done a couple of these. But this? This isn't a bloody camper. Look. Here's a receipt for a spray booth. Looks like they've made sure the van is pretty much the same, with the checkers on the front and the orange line along the side. They're probably not expecting a close-up examination. A van the same colour and design would be enough.'

She pulled another sheet out from underneath and whistled.

'Christ,' she replied. 'They've got assault rifles, a rocket launcher, four pistols, a shit-tonne of ammunition. These guys aren't looking to get him out. They're looking to take him out.'

Ramsey looked back from the wall.

'Look,' he said softly, his face white. On the wall was a printout of a photo. It hadn't been taken of a live moment and sent to Robert, it was obviously a photograph of a photograph because the sharpie that had drawn an X through Drew Slade's head was part of the printout, rather than being drawn on top.

'That could be X marks the spot,' Tinker said, examining it. 'But it could also be X marks the target.'

She paused and found a handwritten note.

'Becky wants the money, but not for herself,' she read. 'Nadal has plans and Becky's part of them.'

She looked back at Ramsey.

'This isn't about Becky Slade. This is about Arun Nadal taking over London. If she's breaking Drew out, why the hell would Arun Nadal help bankroll his escape?'

Tinker shook her head.

'I don't think he is,' she said. 'I think Becky Slade's finally decided that bar the name, there's nothing that connects her father to her. And Griffin here? He works primarily with Arun Nadal in North London. Johnny Lucas told Ellie that Nadal was making a play for London, but he seemed to be a nobody who had big pockets, and Delgado mentioned him as a possible alliance for Becky.'

'Christ, we need to let Ellie know,' Ramsey frowned as he picked up another note. 'Who's William Peel? The name sounds familiar, but not in a "villians" kind of way?'

Tinker shrugged as Ramsey showed the Post-it note.

'He's circled the name like a dozen times,' he continued, now placing it to the side and flicking through the other papers. 'We should take these to the kid, see if he ...'

He stopped, pulling an invoice or, rather, a scan of an invoice, out from the pile.

'Now I remember the bastard,' he said. 'Ellie once told me that when she first met Robert, he was working for Bradwell Associates, and we know it seems Robert's returned there recently. This is an invoice for work – the hours claimed are by one of the partners, William Peel.'

'For the Slades?'

'No, it's not for Becky Slade, as we thought ... it's for a company called Pace Entertainment.'

Tinker whistled.

'Bradwell ... what do you bet he was Robert's old boss?' she asked. 'Back when he was there?'

'Maybe less of the "old", if Robert's returned there,' Ramsey replied. 'Either that, or Robert's being forced to work with him. It's definitely important enough for him to circle the name.'

He glanced at the papers on the table and wall.

'Now, of course, we have an additional problem,' he said. 'How the hell do we get all this to the office, without those two prats outside realising?'

17

SEVEN SISTERS

ELLIE HADN'T GONE STRAIGHT HOME AFTER WALTHAMSTOW. Instead, she'd driven in the car for a while, trying to work out what the next step would be. She hadn't meant to, but she found herself up in Tottenham, having effectively driven straight through London. Parking up, she stretched her back, getting out of the car and looking around.

This was *Seven Sisters* territory.

Janelle Delcourt held her own court above a block of shops; an international supermarket, a cab company and a Brazilian café stood shoulder to shoulder, facing the housing estate the other side of the road. A minute or two's walk south was Seven Sisters overground station. Above the shops were houses, and beside those was a Jehovah's Witnesses' church. The houses had been turned into effectively a manor house, hidden from the unsuspecting eyes of the people walking past. And so, steeling herself and making sure she had her old police issue extendable baton up her sleeve, she walked over to the Brazilian café, entering past the tables and chairs, moving through the mid-afternoon trade, walking up to the counter at the back.

There was a man standing guard.

Ellie understood that while the Sisters, the *matriarchs* had the power here, they still needed muscle to work for them. The men never gained too much of a level in the organisation, and Ellie was kind of okay with that, if she was being honest. There were enough criminal gangs being led by dickheaded men. It was nice to see one being led by a dickheaded *woman*, even if she was possibly not on the side of the angels in this one.

The man was young, barely twenty, a scrubbing of beard on his chin and a black baseball cap worn under a pale-grey hoodie, pulled up over his head. He grumbled to himself and narrowed his eyes as Ellie walked towards him, obviously immediately assuming that she was likely law enforcement.

'Mama Delcourt in?' Ellie asked.

'Depends who's asking,' the man replied.

'Tell her Ellie Reckless has come to parlay,' she said, using the word specifically. It was a term used when pirates would want to speak rather than fight, and she hoped that Mama Delcourt would take the hint and not come down with a dozen armed men.

'And should I give a shit about your name?' the man asked.

'Probably not,' Ellie smiled. The man was very much under her food-chain level. She rarely gained favours from these levels. 'Tell her it's in connection with Darnell Thompson and the reparation fund.'

The man sighed, pulled out a phone and dialled a number, putting it to his ear.

'It's me,' he said. 'Got a woman out here. Looks like a fed. Says she wants to speak to the mama.'

He paused, listening.

'No, I wasn't going to,' he replied. 'But she reckons she needs to – what was it again?'

'Parlay.'

'She wants to parlay, whatever the hell that means.'

The man listened for a bit longer.

'Yeah, I was thinking about that as well,' he smiled, looking back at Ellie. 'Shall I tell her to piss off, or shall I just give her a whack? Bitch looks like she could—'

'You didn't give my name,' Ellie said, interrupting him.

The man sighed.

'She said her name is Ellie something.'

'Ellie Reckless.'

'She said her name was Ellie Reckless—' The young man stopped now, as he listened to the now agitated voice speaking down the phone. Ellie couldn't hear the words, but she could hear that the voice had risen in both octave and pitch. After a moment, where he'd swallowed twice and turned off the phone, staring down at it like it was about to attack him, he slowly looked back up at Ellie.

'You can go in, Miss Reckless,' he said, suddenly incredibly subservient.

Ellie grinned. There was every chance that the person he had spoken to not only knew her name, but probably owed her.

Sometimes it was good to have that rep after all.

The man motioned for Ellie to follow him, and started up a set of stairs. At the top of the stairs, there was a thick, armoured door. The man rapped on it several times in a particular rhythm, and after a moment there was a click of a lock and the *shunk* of a bolt, and then what looked to be a fourteen-year-old boy opened the door, staring out balefully.

'Miss Reckless says she needs to speak to the Mama immediately,' the man said, suddenly sounding way more authoritative than he was a minute ago.

The boy nodded, probably already informed of this, and waved for Ellie to follow him; so follow him she did, walking into the main hallway.

The place was a labyrinth of narrow corridors and dim lighting, with walls covered in faded wallpaper and the air heavy with the scent of incense, and something else she couldn't quite place.

Eventually, she was led into a room that looked like a parlour. The wallpaper was expensive: gold patterns on a deep-red background. The carpet was burgundy; it was thick and obviously equally expensive. The lamps in the room were brass with misted-glass shades, but they were more of a brushed gold rather than a hard, shiny surface, making them warmer and more subtle. The furniture was antique mahogany or leather, and on the wall was an oil painting of Janelle and her son, Moses Delcourt, created a few years earlier when Moses was in his mid-teens – before he tried to take over the business – in an ornate golden frame.

'Can I get you anything?' the boy asked, motioning for Ellie to sit on a plush leather sofa.

'A water would be good,' Ellie replied.

The boy nodded and disappeared for a moment and after a few minutes, the door at the other end of the room opened, a woman led through by a younger teenage girl. Mama Delcourt had been blinded a couple of years earlier, when she'd been caught in a criminal conspiracy. She'd pulled the pin on a grenade rather than be taken, but it'd been a simunition "paint" grenade, and she'd been at point blank range. It had been during a time when her son had been looking to take over the family business, annoyed that only women had the vote, and over the next couple of years she'd slowly been regaining her sight, although the last Ellie had heard, it was still shapes and blurs. It hadn't stopped her from being a suitable leader, though, even if the clock was ticking and at some point, Ellie was aware, one of the younger women would make a pass at the role.

Ellie watched the younger woman, curious about her position here. Eventually, Mama Delcourt, sensing the quiet curiosity, or possibly because she could see better than she let on, patted the younger woman's hand.

'My niece Chantelle,' she said. 'This would have been Molly, my daughter, but well, sometimes the apple doesn't fall far from the tree, does it?'

Ellie nodded, then realised that Mama Delcourt probably couldn't see that, so she made an appreciative 'Mmm' noise.

'What do you want, Reckless?' Blunt and to the point, Mama Delcourt leaned forward. As she did so, the door opened and the young boy came back in, carrying two glasses of water. He placed them on the table between Ellie and Mama Delcourt, who smiled, waving at the closest glass.

'Only the best water here,' she said. 'Ellie, please, you've had a long couple of days, I hear. You must be thirsty.'

Ellie smiled, leaned forward, and took the glass in front of Mama Delcourt. It wasn't a power move, but she had heard how the Delcourts had used water and other drinks in the past to poison or at least incapacitate their enemies.

Even if she couldn't see what had happened, Mama Delcourt leant back as Chantelle whispered into her ear, probably telling her what Ellie had done, and Mama Delcourt chuckled.

'Don't trust me, eh?' she asked. 'Good instincts.'

'Feel free to drink the other one,' Ellie replied. 'I'm sure they're exactly the same.'

'I'm not thirsty,' Mama Delcourt simply replied.

Ellie decided she didn't want to risk either glass; there was every chance that Mama Delcourt might have known or even anticipated this, so she placed the water down before sipping from it. She could always grab something on the way home.

'You seem to know what's been going on for me,' she said as she straightened. 'Would that be because of Becky Slade?'

'I'm one of the Seven Sisters,' Mama Delcourt continued, shrugging. 'We hear everything north of the river and a lot of things that happen south.'

Ellie nodded at this.

'I'm also looking into Arun Nadal, heard he used to play with your son.'

At this, Mama Delcourt smiled.

'I wondered how long it'd take for someone to work out Nadal's link to the Sisters,' she smiled.

'There's a link?' Ellie raised an eyebrow.

'Oh, like the great Ellie Reckless doesn't know.'

The great Ellie Reckless doesn't know, Ellie thought to herself. *So what the hell are we talking about here?*

'Let's pretend I don't,' Ellie smiled. 'Humour me.'

Mama Delcourt frowned at this.

'You really don't know about Arun Nadal's father?'

Ellie sighed.

'Look, I could piss around for ages here trying to make

you think I did, but I don't have the time,' she said. 'Who is Arun Nadal's father?'

'Lad by the name of Mason Carter,' Mama Delcourt said. 'He died a while back, though.'

Ellie tried to think back; the name Carter was familiar.

'So, when I was on the beat, I heard a story,' she said. 'This was in Mile End, not Vauxhall.'

'Go on.'

'So, back then, there were stories of Anita Lucas. That she'd run off with a Russian, and that Jackie had killed him, forcing Anita to run to the Sisters, keeping the married name Taborska. That's all common knowledge and came out when we stopped her takeover, but there were other rumours.'

'Like what?'

'Like when she was in her twenties, she had a kid and gave it up for adoption. The talk was she'd been with the Turk, and he'd forced himself on her. She'd decided not to abort, and when the baby was born, she sent it off, so nobody would ever find it. Remember the stories about how Jackie went for the Turk, and they almost killed each other? The Twins and the Turk hated each other after that. No smoke without fire.'

It was a calculated guess, but it seemed to strike the mark.

'Was Mason Carter Anita Taborska's child?' Ellie asked.

Mama Delcourt nodded.

'We don't judge here.'

'And you knew that he was—'

'The result of a *rape?*' Delcourt's face darkened. 'Yes, we knew that as well, thank you for asking.'

Ellie nodded, and once more realising that Mama Delcourt probably couldn't see this, made another accepting sound.

'Hmm. Did you know the mother?'

'Sheera Nadal? We met a few times.'

Jesus. 'Did you also know at the time that his son was Arun Nadal?' Ellie asked next.

Mama Delcourt nodded.

'I knew Mason,' she said. 'We were around the same age, more or less. Sheera wasn't good for him. Flirted around with anyone. When he died in a drive-by shooting, I mourned. But then I moved on. So yes, I knew Nadal was Anita's – and the Turk, for that matter – he was their grandson, but we never funded him. I swear. So whatever war you have with him? It's not my problem. He's Anita's blood, not mine.'

She folded her arms.

'I'm guessing this isn't the only reason you came here,' Mama Delcourt continued. 'I don't owe you any favours, Reckless. So if you're here trying to gain some from me, or use some *against* me, you're sadly out of time, and I'm out of patience.'

'Becky Slade won't stop at South London,' Ellie quickly added. 'She wants to take over all of London. She's working with Nadal to do it. Whether she's working for him or he's working for her, we don't know yet. The one thing you've confirmed, however, is that they're related. Becky, we believe, is the illegitimate daughter of the Turk's son.'

There was definitely no surprise here at the revelation. Mama Delcourt had either known this already or had managed to rein in her emotions, playing the game a little more carefully.

'Go on,' she said.

'We know Arun Nadal is working in Shoreditch. We know he's moving into the North-East London area. We know he came from West London before that. And we *also* know he's being funded by somebody with deep pockets. Somebody with family connections, probably. The question is, of course, whether this is somebody connected to the empire that the Turk once ran, an empire I believed had been cut up into tiny little pieces and split between all of you, or whether it was somebody connected to the empire that his grandmother was trying to create. One that she almost got away with through your daughter.'

'Look as fun as this trip down memory lane is, we don't mention Anita's name here anymore,' Delcourt's eyes flashed. She might have been going blind, but the emotions still showed behind them. 'She's a cancer to everything we tried to do. She took my daughter and turned her into a weapon.'

'From what I can understand, it wasn't that difficult,' Ellie said, knowing that she was poking a bear. 'But let's put it this way. Anita Taborska isn't just connected to the Seven Sisters. The Russian that she married worked for the Turk, a man who probably owed her a lot after what had happened between them. She was also the older sister of the Lucas twins, which gives her East London. Now you knew about the Lucas's, and you knew about her son. So you must have realised there's every chance there are others playing here, using her as a pawn. And now with her gone, maybe they're using her grandson.'

'Why do you think she's gone?' Mama Delcourt asked. 'Because she's in prison? Don't make me laugh. She's still controlling things, still has people working for her. She also has her money. I could believe that she's controlling Arun Nadal quite easily from prison, but it could be others.'

'Like who?' Ellie asked. 'Please, if you have any information, I'd greatly appreciate it.'

Mama Delcourt considered this.

'He was in the Sisters, sure. His dad was, and he grew up in the world. He also spent time in West London, partly because of his ... well, let's just say his grandparent connections. Made a lot of his own connections there, too, and brought them across with him, when he teamed up with Moses. There's two or three people it could have been. But the question you've got to be asking yourself is, how many of them do you *want* to believe? I mean, it's easy for you to believe the ghost of the Turk could have risen and provided him with an inheritance that could build this empire. Or perhaps my rogue "Sister", the woman who tried to take my daughter from me, could have done this.'

Mama Delcourt took the water, sipping at it as she continued.

'What if it's more East-End related? He is, as you now know, the grandchild of Anita Taborska, a onetime Seven Sister, But that also makes him the great-nephew of her brothers, the Lucas Twins. And as you said, he's rising to prominence at the moment around the East of London.'

Ellie shook her head.

'Johnny Lucas has gone legit.'

'Because he's a Member of Parliament? Don't make me laugh,' Mama Delcourt chuckled to herself. 'I've known Johnny Lucas since he was a shifty little teenager, with a better-looking and slightly older brother. Don't for one second think that I believe *anything* he says about his reasons for joining Parliament. And while he's doing that, he'll need someone to keep his interests okay. And it won't be any of those meatheads in his gym. It'll be somebody he can trust.'

She smiled a thin, narrow, vicious grin.

'It'll be family,' she replied. 'Now you said there was something else you wanted to talk about?'

'We think Becky's going for London.'

'You said already,' Mama Delcourt shook her head. 'Even with Johnny behind her, she can't do it. She doesn't have the capital for what would be needed.'

'She would if she took the reparation fund,' Ellie argued.

At the name, Mama Delcourt paused. It was as if she was suddenly playing a game of statues.

'What do you know about the fund?' Her voice was low now.

'I know there's five names, and one of them works for you,' Ellie said. 'I also know that all five of them owe me favours – and Becky Slade is going to a lot of effort to gain those favours from me. Which to me says she wants your money. All five million.'

Ellie leant forward, lowering her voice to match Mama Delcourt's.

'So, tell me, how far could you go in taking over London if you had five million and the mentorship of people in both the North, East and Centre of London?'

There was a long, quiet, almost-awkward moment of silence, then Ellie shook her head, almost as if she was disappointed.

'You've got a Scottish bare-knuckle boxer with a chip on her shoulder who might end up with five million pounds, who comes from a legacy older than anybody else,' she continued. 'But you don't seem worried. What do you know?'

Mama Delcourt said nothing, and Ellie considered what she'd been told.

'You think Nadal and Slade won't work together?'

Again, nothing, but this time there was the slightest of knowing smiles.

'Arun Nadal will never work with the Slades.'

At this cryptic comment, Ellie leant closer.

'Mason Carter's drive-by shooting,' she continued. 'You said you mourned. Did you look into the attack?'

'Oh, we know who did it,' Delcourt replied. 'It was never proven though, but people talk.'

Her eyes narrowed.

'It was Drew Slade,' she said. 'He'd butted heads with Mason, and took offence. Cillian was furious, sent Drew away for a while. But like all rotten apples, he came back.'

Ellie nodded at this.

'So, Arun's father was killed by Becky's,' she said. 'Although that latter part's debatable. But you didn't say Arun Nadal wouldn't work with Becky, you said "Arun Nadal will never work with the Slades" which is different, if Becky isn't actually a Slade ...'

She trailed off as a horrifying thought came to mind.

'How many of the Seven Sisters exist right now?' Ellie asked.

'What do you mean? There's always been Seven Sisters.'

'I get that,' Ellie replied. 'You need seven so that there's never a tie in a vote. But with Anita gone, did you already cast a replacement?'

'It's something we're looking into.'

Ellie smiled.

'Jesus.' She shook her head. 'Please don't tell me you're actively considering inviting Becky Slade to become the seventh Sister.'

Mama Delcourt said nothing, and Ellie shook her head, rising from the sofa.

'I think we're done here,' she said. She turned and walked towards the door, but before she reached it, Mama Delcourt's clipped voice broke through the room.

'I can tell you what the deal is,' she said, carefully.

'And why would you do that?' Ellie asked.

Mama Delcourt paused, looked towards Chantelle, and motioned for her to leave the room. The younger girl did so, and it was only after the door closed that Mama Delcourt turned to face Ellie.

'It's true there's talk of getting Becky Slade to join the Sisters,' she said. 'We know she's likely to win whatever happens in London. We know she has money behind her. It makes sense.'

She sighed audibly.

'But we already have candidates for the current seventh Sister vacancy,' she added. 'Unfortunately for me, if the Sisters do vote to bring Becky in as well, it looks like it will be me that loses the role, and I'm not particularly happy about that.'

Ellie grinned.

'Well then, Mama Delcourt,' she said as she watched the gangland leader from the door. 'Looks like you might end up owing me a favour after all.'

ELLIE HAD PLANNED TO RETURN TO SOUTH LONDON AFTER this; for a start, she wanted to check in on Millie to make sure she was okay, having been left with Nicky Simpson's assistant. But after one phone call, where all she could hear were baby noises in the background and someone off speaker playing with Millie, she knew she didn't need to worry. Millie was having the time of her life, and the voice off-camera sounded remarkably like Nicky Simpson himself.

She'd considered returning to the boxing club, maybe

seeing if Johnny was around, but paused as she reached her car, texting what she'd learnt so far to Casey, in case it helped anything he was currently looking into.

A man was standing next to her car.

'Ellie Reckless?' he asked as Ellie eyed him up and down. He wasn't more than mid-twenties, in a black jumper, joggers and white sneakers. His "bling" was understated, nowhere near the level of most men his age. He was stylish and dangerous.

Ellie ignored him, walking to her driver's door. The man went to pause her, but stopped as she turned to face him.

'You're not with the Sisters and I can't see you working for the Slades, so you're with Nadal, yes?' she asked.

Surprised, the man nodded.

'I'm guessing you've been sent to pick me up, and take me to Shoreditch to meet with him?'

Again, now off balance, the man nodded. Bar the question about her name, he hadn't spoken.

'Good,' Ellie smiled as she opened the door to her car. 'Off you trot, I'll follow.'

'I was supposed to bring you personally,' the man replied uncertainly, looking around.

'And you will,' Ellie climbed into the car. 'But there's no way I'm leaving my car here, so chop-chop, we've got a wannabe gangland leader to see.'

18

MICHAEL BAY'S KEYRING

Casey was still working through the calendar files at Nicky Simpson's health club by the time Ramsey and Tinker had returned with a shoebox filled with papers. Ramsey had followed Squeaky's advice and exited out of the back door, and luckily for him, the goons who had been told to watch the front door hadn't considered that such a thing would happen. Tinker, meanwhile, had walked out the front, grabbed her Jeep, and driven around the back, picking Ramsey up and carrying on south. As she'd driven, Ramsey had texted with the information he'd found, so by the time they slammed the box full of documents onto the boardroom table, Casey had been pretty much brought up to speed.

'I've been looking into Arun Nadal,' Casey said, once they'd settled. 'There was a meeting in Robert's diary a month back: Nadal and Becky. Robert wasn't in the meeting, so was probably told to stay outside. I started digging, and I think I fell down a rabbit hole.'

He swapped desktops on the screen, swiping to the right, and a new Discord forum window opened up.

'So, Nadal's only twenty-four, right?' Casey explained. 'Turned up about two years ago, apparently from nowhere. Seemed to come up in West London, but the Tsangs never utilised him.'

'Maybe he knew Jeffrey, the one that died in Tsang City?' Tinker suggested. 'That was West London.'

'Maybe, but the thing here is he's come from nowhere, then he started hanging around with Moses Delcourt, who was apparently Mama Delcourt's son—'

'He went for the throne and failed a couple of years ago,' Tinker commented.

'Which matches the time here, and someone must have funded him after that,' Casey replied. 'I checked into him. Has money in Shoreditch properties, but has a rep for dark stuff. Expanded into drugs, illegal immigrants and female trafficking, for a start.'

He pulled up some threads, and Ramsey could see Casey had been digging deep into this.

'He's the son of Mason Carter,' he explained. 'Mason was a nobody, nothing more than fodder.'

'Fodder for who?'

'Mama Delcourt,' Casey looked back at Tinker and Ramsey, smiling. 'Seems Mason was a foundling, had been brought into the family as a teenager on a personal request from ...'

He opened another browser and a new face turned up – one of an elderly, stick thin woman who bore an uncanny resemblance to Johnny Lucas.

'Anita Taborska, one of the Seven Sisters, and onetime sister of Johnny and Jackie Lucas,' he said triumphantly. 'Mason Carter turned up around sixteen years later, in ninety-six, and Anita made sure he was looked after. There was talk he might have been her secret son, from a forced attack from the Turk.'

'You got that from these channels?' Tinker was impressed.

'No, Ellie was told by Mama Delcourt, and then texted me,' Casey grinned. 'She didn't text it to you? She must love me more. Anyway, a few years later Carter had a child with Sheera Nadal, but then died in a shoot-out a year on from that.'

'Christ,' Ramsey stared wide-eyed at the other two. 'Arun Nadal is Anita and the Turk's grandson? No wonder he's being bankrolled. He has claims on Central London, North London and East London. I wonder if Johnny knows this?'

Tinker shrugged, unable to think of anything else to say for the moment.

Suddenly, Ramsey Allen felt sick.

'Oh hell,' he muttered. 'I just remembered what Arthur Davenport told me and Ellie.'

'What?'

Ramsey thought back to the moment.

'He said Drew's wife Charity, apparently there's talk she cuckolded Drew with the Turk's son, Baris, and Becky was the result.'

He shook his head.

'That'd make Arun Nadal and Becky Slade bloody *cousins*,' he muttered. 'No wonder they're working together. But who's in charge?'

He looked around suddenly, as if remembering something.

'Have you seen Davey at all?'

'She's off-grid,' Casey said, still scrolling through the calendar. 'She's burning some favours for Ellie, making sure that our family are safe.'

'And how would you know that?' Tinker frowned. 'Or are your computer skills now to the point where you can actually hack into people's heads?'

Casey looked up and smiled.

'My mum called me,' he replied. 'She said two men from Milton Keynes had turned up, saying they'd been informed by a friend of a friend of a friend that they needed to look after her for the next day, keeping it quiet, like. Suffice to say, she's pretty pissed off.'

'No, I get that,' Tinker said.

She was about to continue, but Casey held up his hand.

'Don't get me wrong. She's pissed off, but she likes the fact she's being looked after,' he said. 'She's worried about me, but I think she's also kind of given up on me.'

He paused as he reached a month and a half earlier on the calendar.

'Something else?' Ramsey asked.

'Familiar names,' Casey said. 'Nothing major, but he's marking down meetings here with a property services company named Baillies. He's also visiting Pace Entertainment ... I've seen these names before.'

'One of them was on an invoice we found,' Ramsey said as he started rummaging in the shoe box. 'William Peel and Bradwell Associates are working for Pace.'

'Are they connected to Becky somehow?' Tinker asked. 'They have to be, right?'

'You know, I actually don't know,' Casey was frowning, shaking his head now. 'But Ellie did say she thought Becky Slade had to be backed by someone, and I know somebody who might be able to confirm this.'

'Please, God, no,' Ramsey muttered. 'Anyone but him.'

'Yeah, I've heard of those names,' Nicky Simpson said, sitting back on his chair, the desk between him and the others. 'I never used them, just like I never used Peterson or Griffin, but they worked a lot with North London.'

'Anyone in particular?'

Simpson nodded.

'Let me guess. Arun Nadal?'

Simpson nodded again.

'You've heard of him, then? He's turned up quite recently, bankrolled by somebody. No idea who. Definitely not one of the normal players. But the one thing I can tell you is that he's been trying to make a run on London for as long as, well, I've known him.'

'Have you met the man?' Ramsey glanced at Tinker as he spoke, a slight shake of his head to remind her to keep quiet on the revelations they had on Nadal, until it was confirmed as gospel. Simpson didn't notice as he continued.

'A few times. He's insane. Spends a lot of time around Shoreditch. Acts like he's a businessman, an entrepreneur, but really everybody knows who he really is.'

He frowned.

'But Pace, Baillies ... these are all companies that are owned by him,' he said. 'They're shell companies, but I can pretty much guarantee if you look into them, you'll find his name attached.'

'So why is Robert Lewis sticking them in his calendar?' Casey asked.

'I think the question's more why is Robert Lewis going to these places in the first place?' Simpson replied. 'I'm guessing he's going there because Becky's going there, and if Becky's going there, then maybe she has an alliance with Nadal, using them for off-the-books meet-ups.'

'And it looks like Bradwell Associates are working for Nadal, if the invoice we have from William Peel is correct, and if Robert's back with them, and he's with Becky, they have to be together,' Tinker mused.

Simpson pursed his lips at the thought.

'Problem is, Nadal doesn't play well with others,' he said. 'He's got his own problems here and there, but he's got sway, big-time sway. He's been known to bring in major league hitmen when needed, and with a click of his fingers, he can bring in muscle that even I couldn't really consider at my strongest.'

He smiled.

'Hypothetically, of course. You know that I've never really been a criminal.'

Ramsey shook his head. Now wasn't the time for fake humility.

'There's one of three options, then,' he said. 'The first is that Becky's working with Nadal. The second is that Nadal is working for Becky—'

'And the third is that Becky's working for Nadal,' Tinker finished. 'What if that's what's going on here? What if this isn't some woman trying to gain back her family's land? What if she's being aimed at us by Nadal?'

'Why?' Ramsey asked.

'We're a day before her father is put on appeal,' Tinker said. 'We're seeing arms and vehicles being planned. She's trying to take favours off Ellie that would gain her money.'

'What if Nadal is doing all of this as a Michael Bay?' Casey asked.

'A Michael Bay?' Simpson shook his head. 'I don't know the term.'

'It's not a term,' Casey said. 'It's the director. You know the guy who does the Transformers movies? There's a known comment about his style of films, which is he doesn't really need to worry that much about the plot. He just likes to jangle a shiny ring of keys. And the noise and the glinting of the shiny keys will keep your attention away from the fact that there's not much going on.'

'Don't look behind the curtain,' Ramsey said. 'Wizard of Oz.'

'Similar, sure,' Casey replied, irritated that Ramsey was trying to take away from his analogy. 'But Michael Bay does great movies. They're action-packed. They're wonderful. But whenever there's any kind of plot hole, he distracts you, makes you look elsewhere. Maybe all of this happening with Becky right now is just Arun Nadal jangling his keys.'

Ramsey looked back at Simpson.

'You claim you're still in with all the gangster types,' he said. 'Is there anything that we need to know about what's going on in North London right now?'

'Not that I can think of,' Simpson shrugged. 'Although no one's really heard from the Seven Sisters in quite a while. Mama Delcourt has gone strangely silent ever since, well, her daughter tried to take over London.'

Tinker nodded.

'Yeah, we remember that one, thank you. I also remember you didn't seem to do much to stop it.'

'Wasn't really my place to do something,' Simpson argued.

'We should look into that,' Tinker decided, patting Casey on the shoulder. 'Do your computer stuff. See if you can find out if Nadal is aiming everybody at Becky while he does something else.'

'But all he's doing is aiming Ellie at this,' Casey frowned. 'He's not aiming the police or anyone else.'

'Maybe he's expecting Ellie to tell the police.'

'No,' Simpson shook his head. 'Becky Slade turned up and told Ellie she was making a play for London. The first thing Ellie did was pull in me, Kenny Tsang, and Mama Lumetta. All of us are now watching South London to see what Becky's going to do next, when maybe we should be looking at North London. She could be purely trying to get Ellie to take her eye off the ball. Or maybe it's not as complicated as we think and she is just working with Nadal on something.'

He shrugged.

'Personally, not my monkey, not my circus anymore. I've got a health club to run. Sorry I can't help you anymore, guys, but enjoy the ride.'

He paused, holding up a finger as he looked back at his computer.

'I'm not a bloody dog,' Tinker growled, unaware of the irony.

'Sorry, it's just that there was something,' Simpson said, scrolling through a list of emails. 'Ellie asked me to check in with my sources about Lavie, the nephew that got beaten.'

Triumphantly finding the correct email chain, he looked back up with a beaming smile.

'I was told Lavie worked for a guy named Mickey—'

'We know,' Casey muttered. 'And I'm checking into it, asking around on the forums.'

'Gangsters use forums now, do they?'

'There's a few encrypted sites, usually Telegram channels

or other such places where people talk about where to find drugs. We know Lavie dealt them. It wasn't hard to work up the chain,' Casey smiled. 'I am a genius, after all.'

'And did you find Mickey?' Simpson raised an eyebrow.

'Well, no.'

'Of course not. You see, Lavie Kaya worked for Mickey, but Mickey is actually called Vito,' Simpson explained. 'Vito Lombardi, who's a middling-level gangster working for Angelo Turner, known as "Cash" Turner.'

He read the email again.

'Cash is part of the crew run by Megan Harris,' he said, looking back at Tinker. 'And Megan is a lieutenant who now works for Becky Slade.'

'Wait,' Tinker frowned, shaking her head. 'That can't be right. You're telling me that Becky Slade actually owned the gang that ran Lavie Kaya?'

'Looks that way,' Simpson nodded. 'Although whether or not this was a recent movement of resources, we don't know.'

He trailed off as there was a movement at the door, and the receptionist from the health club downstairs appeared, looking around in confusion.

'Is one of you here called Alan?' she asked.

'Alan?' Ramsey frowned. 'Do you mean Allen with two-Ls and an E?'

'I don't know.' The girl shrugged. 'I've got a woman downstairs named Sandra, asking to speak to Mister Alan.'

'That'll be me then,' Ramsey sighed, but then paused halfway out of his chair. 'Sandra?'

He looked back at Tinker.

'The server at Caesars?'

'Maybe she's got information on what happened,' Tinker said, frowning.

'Maybe Becky's been back,' Casey added.

'Well, you're a little ray of joy, aren't you?' Ramsey muttered. 'Still, I'd better check.'

He looked back at the receptionist, who still stood there, looking confused.

'Did she say where to meet?'

'Oh, she's in the health club café downstairs,' the receptionist replied, already leaving. 'Not impressed with the place, if you ask me.'

'That's Sandra, all right,' Ramsey said as he followed.

19

NEW TENANTS

Sandra, the server from Caesar's Diner, was indeed sitting in the café at the base of the building; a small area to the side of the health club where people could sit and drink macrobiotic smoothies and the occasional barista-made coffee. She was sipping at a paper cup, grimacing as she did so, as Ramsey sat down with her.

'They claim this is tea,' she muttered. 'Isn't any kind of bloody tea I know.'

Ramsey smiled as he sat opposite her.

'I must admit I'm a bit surprised to see you here,' he said, frowning as he did so. 'Please tell me you're not missing me and the others already.'

'Christ no,' Sandra shook her head. 'It's been quite quiet without you guys there, although Ali's a bit annoyed that his takings are down. It's amazing how many breakfasts you guys would put away. He told me he'd kicked you out, and the suits at your swanky offices said you'd decamped...'

She looked around, sniffing, and Ramsey wondered if she

was jealous, that there was a belief somewhere deep inside, that they were *cheating on her diner*.

'...here,' she finished.

'So, what do I owe this visit?' Ramsey asked.

Sandra looked uncomfortable, and Ramsey knew she didn't want to be there.

'Look,' she said, 'I wanted to come along because you guys have always been good to us, yeah? I mean, I don't like the dog being in, and half the time you guys are pains in the arses, but you're good clients, you're regular, and regulars deserve to know the truth.'

Ramsey leant closer.

'What exactly is the truth?' he asked.

Sandra shifted in her seat, trying to take another sip of the tea before grimacing and just pushing it away.

'How much do you know about Caesar's Diner?' she asked.

'Well, I've gone through your menu five or six times, I'd say that's pretty good.'

'You know I mean the history of the diner.'

Ramsey shook his head.

'Not much,' he said. 'I mean, I know it's attached to the building where *Finders* is based. I know the building itself was built around 2015, so you've been there maybe eight years, maybe less. I know I've been eating there three, maybe four years now.'

He shrugged.

'What else is there to know?'

'Do you know how we got the lease?'

Ramsey frowned.

'Are you saying you're more than just a server, Sandra?' he asked. 'Are you secretly the owner and I've been taking the piss out of you all this time without realising how powerful and rich you are?'

For the first time, Sandra actually smiled.

'I'm a partner, but I don't own it,' she said. 'It's shared between me and Ali.'

She leant back, staring at Ramsey for a long, quiet moment, almost as if she was deciding whether or not she should give away this secret. Eventually, she sighed, clicked her tongue against the top of her mouth twice, and then nodded to herself.

'Robert Lewis,' she said.

'What about him?'

'Before he worked for Finders, he was a solicitor at Bradwell Associates,' Sandra said. 'He was still going through his secondments when I first met him, so this is a good ten years ago. He'd do six months in criminal, six months in property, that kind of thing, some kind of rotation with the company he worked for. Anyway, he was working on the criminal defence side when we first met him, through a case that we were connected to.'

'What do you mean, a case you were connected to?' Ramsey frowned now. 'What aren't you telling me?'

'Look,' Sandra held her hands up in a surrendering gesture, 'I'm doing my best here, you've got to bear with me, yeah? But Ali used to own a pub, right? And I worked behind the bar, that's how we got to know each other back in the day. Things happened in the pub, it closed down, we moved on. Bradwell Associates had been involved, and when we started looking for new opportunities, we spoke to Robert, who had, at this point, moved into property law. Ali wanted to change the work he did; he was sick of working in pubs, he wanted something different. He had always wanted to work in food.'

A smile crossed her face.

'In fact, he used to own a Turkish restaurant years ago with his cousin – well, he worked *for* his cousin in one, back in the day, in London. That's how he moved into becoming a landlord, managing pubs and all that.'

She shook her head.

'Sorry I'm rambling, I apologise. This is difficult.'

'Okay,' Ramsey replied. 'Take your time.'

'Look, it was Robert who suggested the diner, and he found the location for us. This is 2014, 2015. The building was being built, they were looking for tenants for the ground floor, and a diner was a nice choice for the optics. It needed to be more than a truck stop, though; it had to be a posh retro kind of style, which was fine because we'd always wanted to do some kind of fifties diner. That's how Caesar's was created,' Sandra explained. 'Robert would come and eat there when he was in the area, and then a few years later he found himself chatting to a partner at Finders over a cheese toastie one lunchtime. They offered him a job, and he took it on shortly after he'd closed the Ellie Reckless case.'

Ramsey nodded, understanding now. Robert Lewis had created the diner that they all ate in, and in doing so, had actually provided himself an opportunity to move to the company they now all worked for.

'There's more to this, though,' he said. 'You're not just here to talk to me about the diner.'

He frowned, thinking back to what she'd said.

'Holy hell! The pub you worked for,' he asked. 'Was it the Lord Palmerston in Deptford?'

At this, Sandra looked to the floor, unable to catch his eye.

'Oh my god,' Ramsey was stunned. 'Are you telling me

you and Ali ran the Lord Palmerston the night Cillian Slade was murdered?'

Again, Sandra stared at the ground.

'Look,' she said, 'we didn't know anything was going on. Ali's cousin needed someone to manage the place, you know? At the time, Ali was younger, eager to prove himself. And here was an opportunity.'

She shrugged.

'I was already working behind the bar when Ali came in. It's how we met. I got used as the expert, in a way. I could tell him what was going on and he'd carry on doing it. We were there for a good few years. Then Ali's cousin died.'

Ramsey narrowed his eyes.

'Ali's Turkish, right?'

A nod from Sandra.

'His cousin wasn't "the Turk", was it?'

Sandra looked away.

'Are you telling me that the Turk, the guy who owned most of London in the eighties and early nineties, was *Ali's bloody cousin*?'

Sandra shook her head.

'Incredibly distant,' she replied. 'But you know families. Everyone's a bloody cousin in a group like that. And it wasn't relevant to this, apart from the fact that Ali found himself landlord of a pub that had its fair share of fights over the years, but ended with a brutal murder outside. We got out as quick as possible; didn't want to be involved. Then the pub got closed down, and we moved on. Ali had been left some money, and he used that to create Caesar's Diner.'

She leant closer now, almost as if not wanting people to listen to this.

'Problem here, though, is Becky Slade,' she said. 'You see,

the message that you were told by Ali, that she'd wanted Ellie involved in this wasn't completely true. When she found Lavie, it was deliberate. She wanted Ellie, she wanted her favours, but there was a second message given to Ali, and to me, to keep his mouth shut, no matter what happened.'

'No, that was to Ellie,' Ramsey frowned. 'She said, "tell Ellie to keep quiet about the past, before she ended it permanently".'

'*Ali* and *Ellie* sound the same to a terrified kid having the shit kicked out of him,' Sandra replied. 'I only realised last night this was a message to us. "Tell Ali to keep quiet about the past, before she ended it permanently."'

Ramsey understood. 'This is about Drew, isn't it? The night of Cillian's murder?'

Sandra shrugged as she rose from the chair.

'Look, all I know is a decade ago, we sidestepped some serious shit, and now it's haunting Ali,' she muttered. 'If you and Ellie can fix this, I'll allow the bloody dog in.'

'The dog's already allowed in, Sandra.'

'Fine, then. I'll pretend I like the fact the bloody dog's in.'

Ramsey grinned.

'Can't say fairer than that,' he said. 'One last thing. You mentioned that you first met Robert Lewis during all the fallout of the pub, working on the criminal defence side when you met him through a case you were connected to. This was Cillian's murder?'

Sandra nodded, as if realising she'd missed something.

'Sorry, yes,' she said. 'We were interviewed as witnesses, but nobody ever claimed we were part of it, mainly as a detective was drinking in the bar when it happened.'

'Handy, that.'

'You don't know the half of it. But we still had to give

written evidence for both prosecution and defence,' Sandra replied. 'Robert was the associate that took our statement. His company was the one defending Drew Slade; Bradwell Associates, and his boss, a guy named Peel was the guy who collated everything.'

Ramsey leant back, watching Sandra here.

'William Peel?'

'No idea. Why?'

'We believe Becky Slade is the daughter of Baris, the Turk's son,' he replied. 'Which makes her family, not only to Ali, but to a wannabe gangster named Arun Nadal. You recognise those names?'

Sandra shook her head as Ramsey continued to observe her, waiting for something to happen. He didn't know what it was yet, but his gut was screaming *this wasn't right*. Ali hadn't sent Ellie on this mission for just ...

There.

'He knew,' Ramsey whispered as he realised. 'Didn't he? When he confronted Ellie, really plied the guilt on her ... he *bloody knew* the message had been for him.'

Sandra said nothing, simply staring down at the table.

'When Becky found Lavie, she asked if he knew Ellie,' Ramsey continued. 'It wasn't Ellie though, was it? It was if he knew *Ali*. And Ali knew if he threw Ellie at this, it'd get sorted.'

Ramsey rubbed his chin as he considered the words he'd been hearing.

'So, how did you find him?' he asked, eventually.

Sandra looked up, her face an expression of innocence and confusion.

'Cut the shit, Sandra,' Ramsey snapped, glancing around to make sure he wasn't being watched. He needn't have worried; the surrounding people were so intent on checking their Instagrams and TikTok feeds they weren't paying attention to the two old people sitting near them. 'Ali told Ellie that Becky Slade seemed to go for Lavie directly, knew his name. The meeting wasn't accidental in any way whatsoever. We thought that meant she'd gone to find him knowing he would get to Ali, which would eventually get through to our Ellie, but it wasn't.'

He shifted, and Sandra flinched slightly at the movement. Ramsey frowned as he continued.

'Becky Slade went to Lavie already knowing about Caesars and your clientele,' he shook his head. 'None of us would have said anything to her, and that includes Robert, who currently seems to be involved with Becky Slade.'

He held up a hand to stop Sandra's inevitable question.

'Long story, just know for a fact that from what we can work out, I don't think he would have dobbed you in, which means to me and my old man analogue brain that somehow Ali slipped. What did he do?'

Sandra leant back, uncomfortable at the direction the conversation was now going. Ramsey knew this was because she was very much aware that he was correct.

'Look,' she said, 'six months back, when all that stuff was going on with Nicky Simpson, yeah? He had a photo taken in the diner with two teenage girls, fans of his. At the time, he'd faked his death, it hit the internet, people went a bit wild. We had people contacting us; they'd worked out it was in Caesars, and well, one thing led to another.'

She shrugged, now resigned that this was the conversation they were having.

'It was no secret that Nicky Simpson had eaten in the café, and to be honest, there was a small sales bump from people turning up to visit. You know, like that diner that was in *Sherlock*, the BBC TV show, yeah? That place has made thousands because it was the place next door to 221B Baker Street. Ali thought he could gain a bit of money from it. The problem was, once the story came out that Ellie Reckless had helped Nicky Simpson—'

'It wasn't hard to work out that Ellie Reckless worked for Finders, and Finders was in the same building as Caesar's Diner, so therefore Ellie Reckless and the diner must have been connected,' Ramsey finished the statement.

'And then the people from South London started to visit,' Sandra sighed.

'Ali said nothing about this when he spoke to Ellie earlier on,' Ramsey replied.

'That's because he didn't want Ellie to know,' Sandra shook her head. 'He's not a bad man, Ramsey. But he's got a past, you know? Anyone checking through the details would have known this, and as we already know, Becky Slade was waiting for Simpson to slip so she could make her move.'

Ramsey nodded, he understood.

'How well did Ali know the Turk?' he asked.

'They were distant cousins—'

'I didn't ask what their familial relationship was,' Ramsey interrupted. 'I asked how well he *knew* him.'

At the question, Sandra paused, shaking her head as she frowned.

'He worked for one of his businesses, he saw him at events.'

'Did he know the son, Baris?'

Sandra said nothing, just nodded.

'In passing.'

'Did he ever realise that Becky Slade could be Baris's illegitimate daughter?'

'Not that I know of.'

Ramsey went to move, possibly to rise from the chair he was sitting on, but as he did so, Sandra grabbed his hand.

'He tried to break away from the life,' she said. 'When Ellie started bringing in those ... those *people*, I could see it affected him, but he knew she was a good one. He knew she'd always make sure that the downtrodden was looked after. People like us.'

Ramsey stared hard at Sandra.

'Before you go anywhere,' he said, 'I want you to do me a favour.'

He pulled out his phone and opened up a voice recorder app.

'I want you to tell me everything you remember about that night ten years ago –and I don't want the police report. I want the *real thing*, Sandra.'

He waved to the Health Club cafe's counter.

'Can I get one of those sick green smoothie things?' he asked. 'Put it on your boss's tab. And make it to go.'

20

YOUNG PRINCE

It was mid-afternoon now, coming up to what was known as drive-time – happy hour in most places – as the black-clad, sullen messenger brought Ellie into the *Shoreditch Light Bar*, a onetime power station-turned-bar and restaurant. It had been revitalised over the last few years, merging its historical roots with a far more East-London, contemporary touch. The interior was built almost as a tribute to the power station's past, with the original mechanical pulley system, exposed steelwork, and glazed-brick adding to its "rustic yet modern charm", according to the sign on the glass door.

Another sign showed the levels of the bar itself. There was the "Engine Hall" on the main ground floor, where the space was open and lively; above, the "Copper Bar" looked to offer a more intimate setting, built as a space where cocktails and memories of early millennium East London parties mingled; while the top floor apparently housed the "Timber Loft", a more secluded area with skylights that bathed the space in natural light.

But the bar didn't seem that happy as Ellie entered. In

fact, if she was being honest, it looked like somebody had had a funeral.

There was a man standing near the stairs who was checking his phone, and he looked innocuous to most, but Ellie watched as someone walked towards the stairs. A glare and a slight shake of the head were all it took to send the patron somewhere else.

The messenger led Ellie across the bar and walked directly up to the man, waiting for him to acknowledge them both. As he did a swift once over, his eyes scanning upwards and downwards, Ellie smiled.

'I've seen you before, haven't I?' she asked.

The man, who up to this point had been expecting some kind of argument, frowned.

'Dunno,' he replied. 'I don't know who you are.'

'Yeah, I'm sure I've seen you before,' Ellie continued. 'Or maybe it's somebody you know, or used to work for. Somebody connected to you. I'm sure we've crossed paths.'

'And your name is ...'

'Ellie Reckless.'

Ellie took her time saying the name, slowing it down, emphasising every syllable. She might not actually know this man in front of her, but she was pretty confident that the name would be known. Especially as, after all, she lived in the manor.

She had expected the guard to perhaps raise his eyebrows, or nod, maybe even speak into his phone. What she didn't expect was him to back against the wall, as if facing the most terrifying opponent he'd ever faced.

'I ain't got no problem with you,' he blurted, looking around. 'I didn't do it, and you can't prove it.'

'Oh, this is an interesting turn of events,' Ellie smiled, stepping closer. 'What didn't you do?'

'Look, you don't know my name and let's keep it that way, yeah?' the man said, pointing up the steps. 'You wanna see the boss up there? I ain't involved.'

Ellie paused.

'I know where I've seen you,' she said. 'You hung around with Matteo Lumetta, didn't you? When he tried to take over the family business?'

The man paled.

'Look,' he said, 'it was a paid gig. Please don't do anything.'

Ellie grinned widely.

'Do a lot of the Lumettas now work for Nadal?'

'Some do.'

Ellie nodded slowly. It made sense. Once Matteo Lumetta had failed in his attempt to take over and had been arrested, many of the lower-level goons would have found themselves without employment. Henchmen always needed a supervillain, after all.

'Listen,' Ellie said, leaning in close,

'I don't know your name. And you're quite happy for that to be the case. But here's the thing, if I find that you double-cross me or screw me over, I will find out your name. And if I've got anything that's owed to me that relates to you, I will be using it.'

She paused, looking up the stairs.

'Who's he meeting with?'

The messenger glared at Ellie, and she felt a little sorry for him, as he'd probably realised by now he wasn't the one in control as he thought he'd be.

'Everybody.' Ignoring the obvious gaze from the messenger, the guard shrugged. 'One by one, every half hour, someone comes in to bow and scrape before him.'

Ellie didn't mean to ask, but it seemed like a prime moment.

'Who's bankrolling him?'

'Nobody,' the messenger now replied, butting in. 'He's his own man. And he's waiting for you.'

Realising something more was going on here, the guard shook his head.

'I ain't saying anything,' he replied. 'And I think you know why.'

Ellie did. And in a way, it confirmed her suspicions. Arun Nadal had somebody bankrolling him, who was even scarier than he was. And from the guard's point of view, currently, by the fact he was backing off and allowing Ellie to walk up the stairs, to him, Arun Nadal wasn't as scary as Ellie Reckless. Which, by sheer mathematics, meant whoever he feared was probably a lot scarier than Ellie could ever want to be.

Arun Nadal was holding court on the top floor, in the Copper Bar, at a simple wooden table to the far end. On one side were two chairs, the other side a bench, cushioned and leaning against the balcony. Resting casually on it, his arms stretched out on the balcony itself, was Arun Nadal. He was young, a faded and trendy haircut above a white hoody, gold chain glinting on top. He had stubble, but no beard, although the slightest hint of a goatee was appearing. The man in front of him was young; Ellie didn't recognise him, but when he looked over to see who had entered the meeting space, his eyes widened.

Once more, it was good to be recognised.

Ellie went to walk forward, but then Nathan's voice, that

onetime comment about being mugged once more echoed through her mind, about how the underworld feared her.

She shook it from her head. For every young man with a scared expression when they heard her name, there was a Becky Slade.

He'd now seen Ellie approach, and after speaking quickly to the man in front of him, he waved him off, motioning Ellie towards the now empty seat in front of him. Ellie quickly scanned the area as she walked into it, regretting that she hadn't brought Tinker to Mama Delcourt's with her.

Nadal had two men, one on either side of the bench. But the fact he was stretched out, with his arms out to the sides, meant that his jacket had opened, and she could see there was no weapon.

Of course not. Nadal wouldn't need one. The men he had on either side of him and the man downstairs would have been his weapons.

Ellie sat.

'Mister Nadal,' she said.

'Miss Reckless,' Nadal replied calmly, and the cards were on the table. They each knew each other's name. 'I didn't know if you'd come.'

'I'm a walk-in,' Ellie shrugged, holding her hands up in a "what could I do" kind of way. 'A friend of yours said I should have a chat with you.'

'My "friend" must hate you,' Nadal replied, flashing his gaze quickly over to the messenger, now hiding at the bar. 'Not many people want to talk to me.'

'I dunno,' Ellie smiled, waving her hand around. 'Pretty place like this?'

'It's nowhere near as good as a fifties diner, I suppose,' Nadal smiled back. 'Or some kind of posh health spa.'

Ellie kept her face emotionless, but inside was noting the fact that Arun Nadal knew where she was currently working.

Of course he did. If he was working with Becky Slade, he'd know everything.

'I'm missing a trick,' she continued, keeping her face emotionless. 'I should be investing in bars.'

'Oh, I don't have any money in this place, that's all PR bollocks,' Nadal gave a self-deprecating shrug; it didn't suit him. 'But I do spend a lot in here. Are you about to burn a favour? Am I about to get a phone call from someone asking me to do something terrible, because they owe you and I owe them?'

'Would you like that to be the case?' Ellie asked.

Nadal shrugged.

'It is what it is,' he replied. And his demeanour, the calmness of his speaking, was grating on Ellie. There was something *off* here.

She leant back.

'Let's cut the shit,' she said. 'If you're going to play silly buggers, I'm just going to get up and walk out.'

Ellie half rose from the chair, but Nadal raised a hand.

'It's pretty ballsy of you,' he said, 'agreeing to come to me, instead of scrabbling around looking into her, still.'

By "her", Ellie knew he meant Becky Slade.

'Last time I met with "her", she punched me in the face and shouted down at me in a boxing ring,' Ellie shrugged. 'I decided I didn't really want to do that in the immediate future. But don't worry ...'

She leant closer now, placing her elbows on the table.

'We will be meeting again,' she finished. 'We will have that deciding match.'

'From what I heard, you'd need two matches,' Nadal

replied. 'You'd need to obviously beat her to bring yourself up to even-stevens and then, well, beat her *again* to prove you're the better woman.'

'So I'll beat her twice,' Ellie replied calmly. 'I'm going to get quite a few opportunities, I feel, in the near future.'

She'd expected Nadal to make some kind of witty line but instead he just started laughing, a bellowing laugh of genuine amusement.

'Oh, I picked the wrong horse,' he said. 'I should have teamed with you, shouldn't I?'

'Is that a confirmation that you're currently working with Becky Slade?'

'What do you think?'

Ellie straightened. The cards were well and truly on the table now, and she couldn't back out if she wanted to. She considered the question, running her tongue along her teeth as she worked out how to tactfully reply, while at the same time showing that she wasn't unaware.

'I think you're bankrolling her,' she said. 'I think you're *using* Becky. And whatever she wants to do as a distraction is to take away from whatever you're trying to do up here.'

Arun said nothing, nodding for Ellie to continue.

'I know her father killed yours, and no, I don't mean Baris, I mean the guy she shares the surname with, Drew. So I think there's animosity there that you're either using to your advantage, or you're the one being played.'

'You think that, do you?'

'Well, you see, I don't know if you're actually the person I should be talking to,' Ellie continued. 'I've got a proper feeling there's a hand behind the throne here. Somebody who bankrolled you, started you on your path, maybe still tells you what to do from the shadows.'

She could see that the two men on either side of Nadal were listening, so she raised her voice a little as she asked the question she wanted to know.

'So tell me, Nadal, are you the organ grinder or the monkey?'

'I ain't no one's monkey,' Nadal snarled, his voice ice-cold, emotionless, almost angry at the concept.

'And yet you came out of nowhere,' Ellie replied. 'Moses Delcourt's little buddy. I speak to a few of Moses' old crew here and there, and you know what? Not one of them's done even remotely as well as you have.'

'That Moses' people lack ambition is neither surprising nor unexpected,' Nadal replied. 'I always knew I was the intelligent one in that crew. I even told Moses to back down, said it wouldn't work. When Anita—'

'You mean "when my grandmother", right? I mean, you're basically a gangster nepo-baby.'

Arun ignored the interruption.

'When she came over to me asking if I'd help with placing Molly on the throne – and yes, I know you were involved in that as well – I said no. It was nothing but a land grab, after all. Nothing but money. She was a distraction.'

'Is that where you got the idea from?' Ellie asked.

Arun Nadal chuckled to himself.

'What do you want, Reckless?' he asked. 'Do you want me to let Becky go? If I side with you instead of her, you need to offer me some sweeties. Because I can tell you now, I'm getting all the sweeties in the world from her. She wants to take over South London, and give me five million reasons to play with her. And the best bit? I don't even have to lift a finger. Sure, I'll provide her with some muscle, but it's all on her.'

'And her father,' Ellie added. 'You've got to remember Drew.'

'Andrew bloody Slade is a nobody,' Nadal replied. 'He couldn't see the bigger picture. Went up against his father and failed.'

'And got arrested for it,' Ellie shook her head. 'But never charged for killing *your* father, I saw.'

'My father died when I was a tot,' Nadal snapped back. 'I barely remember him, so that doesn't alter my opinions, sorry to piss on your chips there. But he was careless. Arrested by a detective constable, too. Not just any detective constable, though, was it?'

Nadal waved at the barman for another drink, shaking his empty tumbler, the ice rattling inside it.

'It was your ex-partner, wasn't it? Is that why you're here and involved? Trying to clean up that? Does he owe you a favour now for sorting that?'

He shook his head.

'You know they paid him to free Drew, don't you?'

'What do you mean?'

'I mean that back then, when Becky got hold of your partner, or whatever he is to you now, she threatened him with everything she had to make him walk away, to say someone else did it. But you know what happened? Someone else paid *more* for his talents. Probably Paddy Simpson. And they pressured him to make sure that Drew got taken for it. Whether it was the police, whether it was somebody else, who knows? One thing I can tell you, though ...'

Nadal smiled now, a wide, beaming grin, like the cat who had caught the canary.

'Becky Slade has no problems with her dad going to prison. So if you think that ten years on, Becky Slade's going to risk anything to get her dad *out* of prison, then you don't know the woman. I don't know what she's doing on a day-to-day basis, but I do know one thing. She's got her eyes on a far bigger prize than saving her dad.'

'Let me guess. Would the term "reparation fund" come into it? The five million reasons you mentioned?'

Nadal checked his watch.

'This has been a fun conversation,' he said. 'I've always wondered what you'd be like to talk to. But you currently have no idea what you're playing. This is a chess game; I've brought my pieces to the table, and you've just brought some Monopoly figures. That idiot in the top hat and the little doggie.'

He made the motions on the table of moving a piece as he spoke.

'You can learn a lot with Monopoly,' Ellie said calmly, standing up slowly, making sure that Nadal's men didn't think she was making some kind of sudden move. 'I appreciate the advice, and I agree; it was nice talking to you. And if it's okay with you, I'll leave you alone now.'

Nadal nodded his head.

'If you ever need anything, Ellie Reckless, if you ever have any favours that you want to burn to give yourself some kind of advantage, you can always come and have a chat with me. I understand you've got a fair amount of favours in your pocket. Someone like you could be a real pain in my side. I'd rather not have that.'

'I wouldn't worry,' Ellie said as she turned and started back towards the stairs and the downstairs bar. 'If anyone's going to have a problem with me, it'll most likely be the guy who funds you. Not *you*, Arun.'

And, as Arun Nadal chuckled, Ellie headed out of the bar,

her mind awhirl. If Becky wasn't trying to save her father, then what was she doing? What was Arun's part in this? And why did Ellie Reckless feel that he'd been absolutely correct when he said that she was bringing *Monopoly* pieces to a *chess game?*

All she hoped was that Ramsey, Casey, and Tinker were doing better.

21

NEXT STEPS

By the time Ellie returned to the makeshift Finders offices at Simpson's Health Club, she found pretty much total chaos.

Casey was shouting at Ramsey while waving his tablet at some kind of forum on the screen, and Ramsey was shouting back, something about how "analogue was better than digital any day of the week". Tinker, meanwhile, was sitting in a chair, watching this with amusement and bemoaning the fact that she hadn't been allowed to punch anyone, while Millie was running around the boardroom barking excitedly, in the way Spaniels do, convinced this was all some kind of magical game arranged purely for her.

Eventually, as Ellie arrived, they paused.

'What did you get?' Tinker asked. 'From Whitehouse?'

'Oh, I've had a far more interesting day than just Whitehouse,' Ellie said. 'In the space of, what, three hours, I've seen Mark Whitehouse, Mama Delcourt and Arun Nadal.'

'You've seen Nadal?' Tinker's eyes narrowed. 'Your choice or his?'

'It was more a case of him thinking he was in control and then realising he really wasn't,' Ellie smiled. 'What do we have?'

'An entire box full of printouts and receipts,' Ramsey replied, waving a couple of them in an almost menacing fashion. 'Although your wunderkind child seems to think that online forums are much better than paper proof.'

'Paper proof's fine,' Casey said. 'It's just I'm finding the same things out on my tablet here, while you're rummaging through all that.'

He shook his head sadly.

'You know the criminal thing here is the fact that these are all scans from Robert's phone,' he continued. 'He's literally taken digital photos and turned them into paper, the complete opposite of what you're supposed to do.'

'I don't think he wanted to get caught,' Ellie replied, checking through the documents. 'So, tell me about this solicitor.'

'Well, it looks like Robert's returned to his old company,' Tinker said. 'A company that, from what we can work out, has worked with a variety of South London wrong 'uns. When Drew Slade was in court for the murder of his father, they defended him.'

'Not very well, it seems,' Ramsey muttered, looking up from the papers. 'Although from the looks of things, the deck was pretty much stacked against them.'

'How so?'

'I managed to get a copy of the court transcript,' Casey said, waving the tablet. 'You know, from these forums that I'm being told are completely pointless.'

'I thought transcripts were supposed to be locked?'

'They are,' Casey smiled. 'Anyway, from what I can work

out, Drew Slade was claiming he was "not guilty", said that he never made a full confession, that Detective Constable Whitehouse was lying—'

'Which we know he does as easy as breathing,' Tinker interjected.

'And then the following day completely changed his plea to "guilty", claimed it was self-defence and went down, seemingly willingly. Whether this means he was told to do it, or he was trying to be a good father ...'

'Why a good father?'

'Because it looks like it was Becky that shot Granddad in the face,' Tinker said. 'A lot of word on the street says so, anyway.'

'But Drew would have known Becky wasn't his by then,' Ellie frowned. 'So she didn't care about him, but he'd sacrifice himself for her?'

'Chump,' Casey muttered from the tablet as he scrolled through files on the screen.

Ignoring this, Ellie started going through the papers.

'So, what do we have then?' she asked.

'William Peel worked for my grandfather,' a voice spoke from the door, and Ellie jumped as she spun to see Nicky Simpson standing there like some kind of apparition.

'You really need to announce your presence,' she said irritably.

Simpson smiled.

'Your dog's fine, by the way,' he said, crouching and stroking the now calming Millie. 'I've been keeping her company.'

'And feeding her E-numbers or amphetamines, from the looks of things,' Ramsey muttered irritably, moving through the papers. 'Why didn't he put these in any kind of order?'

'He did, there was string connecting them all on the wall, remember?' Tinker replied from the chair. 'You tore them all down.'

'If I recall, we were trying to get out quickly, and with a minimum of fuss,' Ramsey muttered, pretty much to himself as Simpson walked into the boardroom, made a theatrical wink and pointed at the stand-up of himself, then sat down at the head of the table with the arrogance of a man who knew he could do whatever he wanted in his own building.

'Did you take a photo of the wall before you did that?' Casey asked, not noticing as he stared at his screen.

'Of course I bloody did,' Ramsey snapped, slamming his phone onto the desk. 'It's on there.'

'It won't jump into my computer by magic, old man,' Casey grinned. 'Email me it. Or airdrop... actually, I'll do it myself.'

Ramsey muttered obscenities to himself as he looked over at the now arrived Simpson.

'William Peel was used by my grandfather a few times,' Simpson said, 'but he was also used by the Slades, and by some others.'

He frowned.

'I even think Johnny Lucas might have used him at some point, but I might be wrong there.'

Ellie watched him carefully. Simpson never made throwaway comments like that. He was deliberately leading her in a direction, but she didn't know why.

'Why would Robert circle the name?' she asked. 'We'd know he was working for Peel if he returned, so why is he so important right now?'

'Oh, because the guy was as corrupt as anything,' Simpson replied calmly. 'He was open source for whoever wanted him. He had no qualms. He had no conscience. And he was also the lead solicitor on the Drew Slade case, so it makes sense he's probably the guy who's leading the appeal.'

Ellie nodded.

'So, we're being aimed at the guy who's trying to sort that out,' she said. 'Am I still feeling that we're being led by the nose?'

'Have you worked out who's funding Arun Nadal yet?' Simpson asked, and Ellie spun to face him.

'You know, it'd be a lot easier if you just bloody told us what you knew,' she growled. 'It's obvious that you've got clues.'

'I just think that this entire problem has been about family,' Simpson replied, shrugging. 'And, as somebody who has no ownership interest because my family's not involved, I think you need to be looking at the others.'

Ellie looked back at the papers, flicking through them, but her eyes weren't focused, her mind a thousand miles away.

'What happened after the Turk went?' she asked.

'What do you mean?'

'The Turk was killed, possibly by Jackie Lucas. Definitely in a drive-by shooting,' she said. 'Baris was his son, but I've not heard anything about him recently.'

'Armed robbery. Vicious thing. Went down for twenty-seven years,' Simpson replied calmly.

Casey looked up from his laptop at this.

'He's done sixteen of them. He'll probably be out in a year with good behaviour.'

'That's convenient,' Tinker said.

'Baris was arrested and imprisoned. The Turk was killed. His lieutenants fell apart,' Simpson replied. 'The Tsangs took over chunks of Central London because they pretty much controlled Chinatown. The Lumettas took a chunk for themselves, too. Realistically, everybody was having a free-for-all. There was nobody as important as the Turk, shall we say, to come in and unify anything. God knows, people tried.'

Ellie stared back at the sheets of paper, trying to make sense of them. *What was Robert trying to say here?*

'Okay,' she stated, bringing herself back to the present. 'We know Drew is up for an appeal tomorrow, we know William Peel is likely to be there beside him, but we also know Robert, who's been beside Becky, has passed us Peel's name to look into this.'

'We also know Arun Nadal is making a play for the middle of London, and Becky's probably promised him the reparation fund,' Ramsey continued. 'Although why he hasn't gone for it himself ...'

'That's it,' Ellie looked up at the comment. 'Why *hasn't* he? And why drag Robert around all these places, allowing him to take sneaky photos, knowing he'll betray you at the first opportunity?'

'Because she wants this to be betrayed,' Casey suggested. 'Perhaps she never meant to divert the transport? She just wanted us all there when it happens?'

Ellie was pacing now.

'If you really want to walk, you could start with walking your Cocker Spaniel,' Simpson muttered. 'As for the notes, I could speak to Peterson and Griffin; we've worked together in—'

Tinker had risen from her chair, walked up to Nicky Simpson, and then, before he could finish, she punched him hard in the face, sending him sprawling to the ground.

'What the hell?' Wiping the blood from his lip, Simpson

started, but Tinker hadn't finished, crouching down, placing a knee on his chest, and glaring at him.

'You bloody knew,' she said. 'You knew what was happening. You told us you'd never used Griffin and Peterson, yet here you are, offering your help. In fact, you've offered your help every step of the way, haven't you? The location, the phones, the Wi-Fi connection ... always appearing while we're discussing the case, and Becky Slade always being one step ahead ... are you informing on us?'

Simpson struggled to sit up, pushing Tinker off.

'Of course I bloody am,' he hissed. 'I have a reputation to uphold. And Slade is hurting people I care about in South London. So, I've been making new alliances.'

'With Becky?' Ellie asked, before shaking her head. 'No. You genuinely hated her when I saw the two of you together. You're allying with Arun, aren't you?'

Tinker stood up now, staring at Simpson as he stayed sprawled on the floor.

'Arun isn't just controlling Slade, he's setting her up, isn't he?' she said eventually. 'He knows Robert will get us to look into the court appeal, so he aims her at it too, giving her a reason to focus there. Not to save dad, but to *kill* him – hoping we'll be there with the police. Meanwhile, he goes and grabs the five million reparation fund Becky thinks she's gaining.'

'A hypothesis, nothing more,' Simpson muttered.

'If you want to take her on, you've got two things you can do,' Tinker said quietly to Ellie. 'We stop her doing whatever it is she intends to do tomorrow, whatever it is, in connection with her father, and we stop Arun gaining the money.'

'Or you do it first,' Simpson said, holding his hands up to stop Tinker from kicking off again. 'I'm serious. When we first sat down, all of us – Mama Lumetta, me, Kenny, you – we said that with her, you couldn't just have her arrested, you had to make a statement.'

Casey nodded.

'He's right, boss,' he added. 'You can't kill her – I mean, please don't kill her – but you can pull her teeth out. De-fang the snake.'

Simpson shrugged.

'It's been done before,' he said. 'You know how it is; remove the leader, cut off the head, whatever you want to call it. You need to break Becky down into her most base components, and leave her exposed, raw, bleeding.'

'No offence, Nicky, but I don't think you really saw what happened in that fight,' Ellie replied. 'She kicked the living crap out of me.'

'True,' Simpson smiled. 'I'm aware of that, but she didn't fight fair. You came for a sparring session, she came for a *murder*, so this time you don't play fair.'

He walked over to her now, staring deep into her eyes. It wasn't a romantic moment, however, it was a sizing up.

'If you had the right situation, could you beat her?'

Ellie thought for a moment and then shook her head.

'I genuinely don't know,' she said.

'What if you had help?' Ramsey asked.

'What do you mean?' Ellie frowned.

'Exactly what I said,' Ramsey smiled. 'You find a way to fight her in public, in front of everybody, but you stack the odds in your favour. There's nothing Becky could do. You'd make her look foolish. And, in the meantime, we'd make sure Delgado had everything she needed to nail Becky Slade to the wall.'

Ellie considered this.

'It'll take a lot to get done,' she said. 'And we're talking a short amount of time if we want to do it before ten o'clock tomorrow morning.'

'I was thinking more in a couple of hours,' Ramsey grinned. 'And I know just the place.'

He made a mock, sad expression.

'Of course, you might have to burn a couple of favours to get it all perfect,' he finished.

'Now that is something I know I can do,' Ellie smiled. 'What else do you need?'

'I'll need Davey back, I have a plan for her.'

Ellie nodded.

'Done. Casey, get hold of Davey. Tell her to come out of the cold, we have a new job for her. Ramsey, do whatever it is you need to do, to get this going—but keep me in the loop.'

'And me?' Simpson asked, and Ellie wasn't sure, but sensed he was actually unhappy he wasn't involved. She glanced back at Ramsey.

'This is your play,' she said with a smile.

'I need you to make a last-minute booking,' Ramsey said to Simpson. 'If it's already taken, I need you to do whatever you need to, just to make sure we get it.'

'And what about me?' Tinker asked, a suspicious expression now on her face.

'Book out a studio in the gym downstairs,' Ramsey smiled darkly. 'You have an hour to teach young Elisa how to fight dirtier than she ever has before, before she goes and visits an old friend again.'

Casey fist-pumped into the sky.

'Hell yeah,' he laughed. 'We've got a *Rocky* montage.'

22

CAR SHARE

JOHNNY LUCAS ENJOYED BEING AN MP, BUT THERE WERE certain moments of glad-handing where he could have happily passed them on to someone else. Even when he was running East-End ganglands, he wasn't spending so much time in the public eye.

He called this the "kissing babies" part of his job – showing the people of Bethnal Green and Bow that he was there for them, while arranging clandestine meetings with various business owners who wanted to add infrastructure to the town. He had entered politics with the best intentions, finding himself with a clean slate by effectively throwing all his criminal activities onto his brother, now believed publicly to have been Anita Taborska, after the events of a year earlier. He used this opportunity to move into politics, never shying away from his history. In fact, in a way, he leaned into it, showing that, as a former criminal, he was more in touch with the people of London than the millionaires and investment bankers that ran against him.

Tonight was no different – an early evening get-together

with tiny vol-au-vents and canapes, cheap wine, and beer if you weren't happy with that. If you didn't drink, like Johnny now didn't, you could have apple juice or the exciting water – not even sparkling mineral water, just plain tap water.

But he was fine with that. His days of partying were long gone.

As he waved farewell to the constituents and walked outside Bethnal Green Library, a two-storey red-brick building in a late Victorian, classical style with columns either side of the door, he saw his car, a black SUV, waiting for him at the end of the courtyard, with Peter, his erstwhile companion and current driver, waiting in the front seat.

Peter looked off; Johnny couldn't explain it, almost like he'd had bad news.

He gave one more wave to the crowd following him out, walked over to the SUV and climbed in the back, and immediately realised why Peter had such a dour expression.

'Evening, MP,' Ellie Reckless said, sitting on the other side of the back seat.

Johnny groaned.

'I have surgery hours, you know,' he said. 'You could make an appointment, like all of my other constituents.'

'Is that what you thought when you broke into my apartment?'

'That was more of an extreme situation,' Johnny glanced back at Peter. 'You did this?'

Peter shook his head.

'I owed her a debt,' he replied. 'She called it in.'

Johnny Lucas looked back at Ellie with sudden respect.

'You burned a debt just to see me?' he smiled. 'I'm honoured.'

'I wouldn't be,' Ellie replied. 'I'm about to burn another one.'

She moved closer to Peter.

'You might not want to be here for this conversation,' she said. 'It involves things you might not know about.'

'That's fine by me,' Peter replied. 'I'll just pop into the Library and use their toilet.'

As Peter climbed out of the car, the press no longer paying attention to the vehicle, Johnny looked back at Ellie, folding his arms and pursing his lips.

'So, what's this about?' he asked.

Ellie shifted in the seat, obviously uncomfortable to be there.

'You remember you owe me a favour too, right?' she said.

'I thought I'd paid that back.'

'You did. And then you said that I could have another one because I gave you loads of gold,' Ellie smiled.

Johnny winced, remembering.

'What can I do for you, then?' he said.

'You know how the debts work?' she asked.

Johnny nodded.

'I give you whatever you require, at a time or place of your choosing, as long as it's within my remit,' he said. 'So, I ask again, Ellie, what is it you want?'

'I need to ask you two questions, and then ask you to do something,' Ellie replied. Her tone was cautious, careful. 'But I want you to know that I take no pleasure in this.'

At the words, Johnny frowned.

'That doesn't sound ominous at all,' he mocked.

'Regardless of what I ask you, and therefore what you're forced to answer truthfully, I want you to know that I still respect you a lot, and I hope, after all this is done, that I'm still allowed to visit your boxing club.'

Johnny was really not enjoying this conversation now.

'Should I be getting a solicitor?' he asked. 'I have Fabian Kleid on speed dial.'

'I have two questions and a favour, that's it,' Ellie shook her head. 'Are you happy to do this?'

'Sure,' Johnny laughed. 'You never had to burn a favour to ask me questions. I've always been open for you.'

'I need you to be honest this time,' Ellie replied. 'And that means I need to *force* you to answer the questions. You might not want to reply to some of the things I'm asking. By making you pay back the favour, I'm guaranteeing the answer I need, as the first part of the favour owed is that you answer them honestly, simply. No Member of Parliament double-talk. Simple yes and no answers. I don't have the time for anything else and this has taken way too long already.'

She leant back in the chair, rubbing her eyes.

'I've already spent the day talking to criminals and gangsters and it hasn't even finished yet,' she sighed. 'Are you ready to pay back your debt?'

'Just bloody get on with it,' Johnny snapped. 'It's been a long day for me as well, you know.'

'Okay, question one,' Ellie nodded. 'How long have you known Arun Nadal was your sister's grandson?'

Ellie wasn't sure, but she thought Johnny was prepared for the question, because he didn't flinch the moment she asked.

'I found out a long time ago about Mason Carter,' he admitted. 'I mean, we all knew the Turk had raped her, we all knew that Mason came out of that. Jackie had kicked off a massive war because of it, and then Anita walked off from the family, and married one of the Turk's lieutenants, like nothing had happened, again causing more problems.'

He shrugged.

'We paid little attention to Mason. He was a nephew, sure, but Anita had made it pretty damn clear she didn't want anything to do with us. And then he died. End of.'

'And Arun?'

'It was a few years back, maybe five, six years ago. He was eighteen, and we heard the Seven Sisters had started grooming him a little. He had no dad, as Mason died in a drive-by, and his mum was in a dangerous place. She turned up in the boxing club one day and asked us to keep an eye on him while she got clean – poor cow never did. We used our contacts to get him some experience, working with Jeffrey Tsang, who at the time was pretty much a kid himself. He got to know a few of the Tsangs and the West London crowd, and we left it alone. By this point, we were having our own problems.'

Ellie nodded. She knew he meant his double personality had arrived in force at that point, and she hadn't missed the fact Johnny had continually stated "we" when talking about the decisions.

Johnny clicked his teeth for a moment.

'We'd heard rumours,' he continued, 'that he was back with the Seven Sisters. I know when Moses Delcourt made his attempt, Arun was around, but ...'

He trailed off.

'So yeah, I've known. Next question.'

Ellie let the moment sink in and then spoke quietly.

'And when did you start *funding* Arun Nadal's criminal empire?' she asked.

Johnny went to reply, a smile breaking out on his lips, and

Ellie knew immediately he was going to fob this question off and make a joke, holding her hand up to head it off.

'Remember, you're paying a favour,' she said. 'This debt isn't over if you lie to me.'

Johnny paused, and the smile dropped.

'Who told you?' he asked.

Ellie kept quiet.

And Johnny, not really expecting an answer, continued.

'It was when Moses made his ill-advised attempt against Janelle,' he said. 'I realised at that point I needed somebody in the Sisters, somebody who could give me information. But with Moses gone, his crew were pretty much dumped out. Anita was already starting to make her play, grooming Molly, you know, the obvious heir being female. Arun was lost, turned up one day, just like his mum did, asking what to do. I said I'd help him out, started funding him a bit here and there, making sure he was working in the right direction. And then Anita made the play and destroyed London, as it was. By the end, Benny was dead. Kenny was injured. The Sisters were broken, with Molly in prison – well, wherever you send teenage kids who want to kill the world. Anita was removed and ...'

He sighed.

'Well, you know how it was, you were there. I realised I had an opportunity to go legit. But the problem was if I did that, I had no eyes on the ground. There was nobody in East London who would be scared enough to keep away if they knew I wasn't watching.'

'And so you made Arun Nadal the new you.'

'I gave him the money to become so, yes,' Johnny nodded quietly. 'I never made him my heir apparent, but I don't have kids and he *is* family. I always felt that perhaps I could retire from this life and he could just carry it on, follow on the family tradition. But, if I'm being honest, he's been a bit of a letdown. He's too modern, too brutal for what I wanted. More Jackie than Johnny, if you get what I mean.'

'And yet you still allow him to do what he needs to do.'

Johnny nodded, laughing.

'I'm Doctor Frankenstein here,' he replied. 'And he's my monster. I created him to replace me, but I've created something that's way worse. You see, for as much as he's my DNA, he's also Anita's and the Turk's. I should never have tried to do it.'

'Do you still fund him? Do you still *use* him?'

'I think we're getting past more than two questions now,' Johnny replied. 'But I'll answer that because it is connected. Yeah, he's still funded by me. If he didn't have that behind him, the chances are he'd lose his men. A lot of them are previous Moses Delcourt family, some of them are ex-Paddy Simpson's, and a couple are even Mama Lumetta's boys, from when Matteo was trying to take over.'

He chuckled.

'In a way, Ellie, his army was built because you kept taking down his rivals. You're as much to blame for his rise as I am.'

He paused, frowning.

'How did you know?' he now asked.

'You told me back in my apartment,' Ellie replied. 'Remember? *"If I did have to pass the baton, I'd rather it was to family, no matter how distant."* I thought you were giving me a back-handed compliment, but it was actually Nadal you spoke about.'

There was a long, silent moment in the SUV now.

'How did you keep away from this?' Ellie eventually

asked. 'I mean, you're a Member of Parliament. The cameramen outside the library, outside this car show that you're constantly being watched.'

Johnny nodded.

'I used a solicitor,' he replied. 'Someone who used to work south of the river. A man by the name of William Peel, at Bradwell Associates.'

Ellie raised an eyebrow.

'We're hearing a lot about Robert's old boss right now,' she said.

'Yeah, I heard Robert was under him. When William was a partner, Robert was a junior associate. He primarily based himself in South London, and I thought by using somebody from an unfamiliar area –well, I couldn't use Fabian, my usual go-to solicitor for this – people wouldn't notice. But moving my off-books legal affairs down to Nicky Simpson's stomping ground, well, that was a different matter. I could quietly hide the background. I hadn't really considered how much it would link to you guys.'

'Did you know that Nadal would end up working with Becky Slade?'

'I hadn't even considered Becky Slade,' Johnny admitted. 'I wasn't lying when I saw you in your apartment. The Slades are scum. We had enough fights with Drew as it was. It's one reason why I'd aimed Arun up to North-East London rather than back down south. The fact he's trying to take over surprises me.'

'You don't think he is?'

'No,' Johnny replied. 'And I also know that you've been to visit him, because I had a call while I was in the middle of a speech. The voicemail left said you'd been seen at the Light Bar in Shoreditch. Did you get what you wanted?'

Ellie shook her head.

'Between us? No,' she replied. 'You see, I thought this was originally just Becky wanting to take over London. She wanted my name so she could take my favours and create an empire. Now I believe she wants the five million.'

'The reparation fund.'

'She's knows all five of your signatories owe me. Then I find Arun Nadal's there in the middle. I find she's breaking Drew out of prison, possibly during his appeal.'

'Appeal?'

'Yeah, because every case Mark Whitehouse was involved in is now being retried and examined,' Ellie explained. 'Then the next thing I know, maybe she *doesn't* want to bring him out. Maybe she wants to *kill him* because she's not actually his daughter and she's related to Arun Nadal.'

Johnny shook his head.

'It doesn't count. Once a Slade, always a Slade.'

'What's Nadal's plan?' Ellie asked. 'And I know I've asked the questions and you don't have to tell me, but I can't see him spending time with Becky and enjoying it. He seems more like the Nicky Simpson style of gangster. Swish, relaxed. He even talked to me about playing chess while I was playing Monopoly with him.'

'You don't think that's apt?' Johnny asked.

Ellie's face darkened.

'If he thinks I'm playing Monopoly, then what the hell does he think Becky's playing? Guess Who? Connect Four? Top Trumps? There's no way they're working on the same level, which means he's controlling her, because having met him, I can't believe Becky Slade's controlling Arun Nadal in any way. And if you're funding him, then you know exactly what his game plan is.'

At this statement, Johnny now grinned.

'So you've had your questions answered,' he said. 'What's the request you ask of me? What do you want me to do?'

Ellie considered this for a moment, checked her phone to see if any new messages had arrived, placed it quietly back into her pocket, turned to fully face the MP for Bethnal Green and Bow, Jonathan Lucas ...

And told him *exactly* what she expected him to do.

23

DEALS WITH DEVILS

Joanne Davey had spent the day burning favours, and it was something she felt she could definitely get behind as a full-time job. It was one thing walking into rooms filled with criminals, but there was a certain buzz from waving a piece of paper in the air saying, "I have a favour requested by Ellie Reckless", and watching the men in the room shit themselves, wondering which of them was going to have to do it.

She'd managed quickly to find the people needed to protect the targets that Becky Slade had created. Davey had also double-checked her list, making sure she had missed no one, and now had every single loved one under guard with a list of numbers that, the moment she called, would lead to very scary, incredibly armed people who would immediately whisk them away to somewhere quiet and unknown.

Ellie had sent a message half an hour earlier explaining Ramsey's plan. She'd also given a small list of people from whom she needed to gain new, *incredibly specific* favours; again, off books and making sure Becky Slade learned nothing about this. Luckily, these had been nobody that

Davey had already spoken to, the favours were still in play, and knowing this, Davey had confirmed to Ellie the second part of the plan was completely doable.

She'd smiled as she did so; Ramsey was a thief, Casey was a hacker, Tinker was muscle, but Davey was forensics. Davey could sort a crime scene out, but at the same time, Davey knew chemicals and certain substances that could make someone's day go really well or really *bad*.

And finally, she was about to be allowed to do her job.

She'd been given *another* job, however, to go alongside this; an invitation to all and everyone of note, to a very important event. She had worked out the maths and knew this would burn another six or seven favours to make sure this happened, but every single player in London, every main name, every made man or woman who had a say in what was going on would be available if required.

She looked at the location she currently stood outside, a posh-looking bar in Shoreditch. She paused at the door, took a deep breath, and then walked through it, heading towards the top floor, apparently known as the Copper Bar.

A man stood in front of her, blocking her way.

'Ellie Reckless sent me,' she said. 'Do you want to do a long conversation and banter back and forth, or shall I just walk past you and carry on?'

The man, on hearing the name, just stepped aside, waving her on, and Davey gave him a smile, walking up to the top floor and finding Arun Nadal still in his cushioned bench office.

'I don't know you,' he said simply, almost dismissively, as he examined her.

'Good,' Davey replied, sitting down in front of him. 'I'm fine with this staying that way. I'll have a Magners with ice. If they don't do that, find me some kind of sweet cider, maybe some kind of fruit-based one would be nice.'

'And why am I buying you a drink?'

'Because I'm going to have a long conversation with you,' Davey smiled. 'And I'm going to get parched; also, I don't really want to drink any more water. I've been drinking quite a lot and there's only so many toilet breaks a woman can take without feeling like she's got some kind of medical problem.'

Arun Nadal didn't smile at this. In fact, if anything, he looked pretty irritated that this woman was sitting in front of him.

'You're from Reckless,' he said, a statement of fact rather than a question.

'I am,' Davey nodded, reaching into her pocket slowly so that nobody reached for weapons and pulled out the paper that Ellie had written for her. She showed it to Arun, who took it from her, read it, nodded, and then proceeded to tear it into small pieces.

'I don't owe Ellie Reckless any favours,' he said, as he tossed the shreds onto the table. 'Why should I care that this paper gives you the right to ask favours on her behalf?'

'I was showing it to you as a courtesy,' Davey smiled. 'But the message wasn't for you. You see, I know at least three of the people on this floor alone owe favours to Ellie. Some of the men downstairs do as well. We know who funds you. We know who's controlling you – he owes a favour too, although that might have been called in this evening – and we know pretty much what we need to do to destroy you if we so wanted.'

Arun started to laugh at this.

'You are ballsy,' he said. 'I mean, I thought Ellie was pretty ballsy, but you ... you're just ...'

He shook his head.

'Does she surround herself with people like you?' he said. 'Because honestly? You're a gang that I'd want on my side.'

'And we can be,' Davey replied. 'If the night goes our way. Me? I left the police after I kind of helped a group of serial killers get murdered. I pissed off the Colombian Embassy to the point I'm banned from the country, and most recently tasered someone in the face, which didn't go down well. Sure, we have experts in a variety of different things. Myself? I trained in forensics under Doctor Rosanna Marcos, a woman who taught me very, very carefully how to make sure a body is never found, how to kill someone without it being realised as murder, and how to do a tonne of other things.'

She chuckled.

'She dated a Tsang, you know,' she said. 'And they're terrified of her. So what do you think that makes me?'

Arun held a hand up.

'You don't need to pitch any more,' he said. 'You're scary. Woo. What do you need from me? What is this favour that I'm going to be asked for?'

'For you, it's a request. Nothing more,' Davey replied, leaning closer. 'You see, you don't owe a favour. Your people do, and we could use them to make your life hard, but we want to give a show of faith.'

She pulled another piece of paper out of her pocket and placed it on the table.

'Be there in two hours. Bring whoever you want. It's not a trap. But I think you'll be very interested in what happens.'

'And why would that be?' Arun asked.

'Let's just say debts are being paid and family is being revealed.' Davey rose, shaking her head. 'I am disappointed, though, I thought you'd at least have given me a drink.'

Then, before Arun Nadal could say anything, Joanne Davey walked out of the bar and carried on with her mission.

She had three more people to speak to, and a fight to fix before the hour was over.

After two meetings in as many days with Ellie Reckless, the last thing Kate Delgado expected was another meeting with someone from Finders, so she was quite surprised to find Ramsey Allen and his teenage sidekick waiting for her in reception as she finished her shift.

'Shouldn't you be a hundred feet away from the building or something?' she asked Ramsey as they exited the Vauxhall Crime Unit together. 'You know, so when the lightning strikes you for being anywhere near a police station, we don't all get caught in the blast range?'

'You're funny,' Ramsey said with a deadpan expression. 'Hilarious, isn't she?'

He said this to the boy, Casey, who nodded with the look of someone brought here against his will. Delgado understood that.

Ramsey placed a hand on her side as he led her to the right of the building, as if making sure they weren't being watched.

'Don't go home,' he said. 'I know your shift is over, as the desk sergeant said so as we arrived, but you really don't want to do that.'

'Oh, and what do I want to do? Delgado raised an eyebrow. 'And honestly, Allen, what happened to you? You went from master thief to messenger boy?'

Ramsey smiled.

'We need you to go to an address,' he said, pulling what looked to be a black leather wallet from his inside jacket pocket. 'It's on a Post-it note, in here. Bring a few officers.'

'And a camera,' Casey added. 'Believe me, you're gonna want to snap a few photos of this.'

As Delgado took the wallet, Ramsey and Casey now walking away, she opened it up to find it was a police warrant card.

Her police warrant card.

And, as Ramsey had said, in it was a Post-it note with a single address of a pub down the road.

'Hey!' she shouted after Ramsey, checking her pocket, realising he'd picked it while moving her to the side. 'Impressive.'

Ramsey turned back to her with a smile.

'Not just the messenger boy,' he said, and the two of them turned the corner out of Delgado's sight.

She looked back down at the paper, noting once more the address and suggested time.

With her jaw set, she turned and entered the building once more, as it looked like DI Kate Delgado would be working some overtime now.

IT WAS GETTING LATE IN THE EVENING WHEN ELLIE ENTERED the Shackleton pub for the second time that day. This time, however, there wasn't a fancy book launch happening, and the locals seemed less likely to care about such stories and launches. There were no vol-au-vents or canapes being passed around, and the waiting staff had long gone.

William Peel was an elderly man. His hair was short,

almost shaved, the top of his head pretty much bald. It was a gunmetal grey and matched the horn-rimmed glasses he wore. He was slim, actually quite muscled for his age and, unlike most of the lawyers Ellie met over the years, he wore a pair of chinos, a blue shirt, and a navy-blue blazer, no tie, his collar loose.

'I understand you wanted to speak to me?' he asked, leaning back onto the chair as he sipped at his drink, what looked to be some kind of whisky and tonic mix on the rocks.

Ellie nodded, taking a seat opposite.

'I understand your company defended Drew Slade ten years ago,' she said.

William nodded.

'We've defended many people,' he replied. 'Some were innocent, some were guilty. We don't differentiate. If somebody claims to be innocent, we give them every opportunity to prove it.'

He smiled.

'You're the one Robert defended against murder, aren't you?'

Ellie smiled in return, giving a slight nod.

'Guilty as charged,' she said.

'Well, there you go then,' William replied. 'You're a case in point.'

He took another sip of the drink.

'You know he left us shortly after that,' William scratched at his chin. 'I always wondered if it was you that convinced him.'

'Don't look at me,' Ellie held her hands up, a defensive gesture, warding away the comment. 'From what I can work out, he was already moving out of the industry.'

'Fair point,' William nodded. 'So, what do you want to know about Drew?'

'He's up for appeal,' Ellie said, settling in her chair. 'I wondered if you were defending him.'

'He's gone elsewhere this time,' William shook his head. 'And, to be honest, if we were asked, we probably would have said no. As I said, we give everybody a chance to prove they're innocent. Drew Slade was not innocent.'

He checked his phone. Ellie couldn't work out if he was looking at the time or waiting for a message.

She knew, however, that a message would arrive soon for him. And she *really* wanted to be here when it happened.

'You know why the appeal's happened, don't you?' he asked, looking back up. 'It's your friend, Whitehouse. Since they proved he was corrupt, every case he's been involved in has been examined. Andrew Slade is claiming he was screwed over by Whitehouse, that it was self-defence; that Whitehouse promised he would get him off and then screwed him over based on orders from a rival crime family.'

'Let me guess,' Ellie replied. 'The Simpsons?'

William didn't reply, a slight nod his only answer.

'It doesn't matter,' he replied. 'There's enough information out there to head it off before it even happens.'

He watched Ellie carefully.

'But this isn't about the appeal, is it?' he said. 'I've worked with many people, Miss Reckless, over the years, and I've learned I can read people well. What's happening with Robert?'

'Why do you ask that?' Ellie asked.

'Because he turned up on my doorstep two months ago and started working for me, pretty much immediately.' William folded his arms now, his body language showing that this was no longer a comfortable conversation. This was turning into an interrogation.

Fine, Ellie thought. *Two can play at that game.*

'You want the truth?' Ellie replied. 'Robert Lewis works for Becky Slade now. But then you already knew that, didn't you?'

'How would I know this? I don't work with the Slades.'

'Yes, but you work with Pace Entertainment, owned by Arun Nadal, and I'm sure he's mentioned it in passing, or perhaps when – maybe through him – you sent Robert on secondment with Becky,' Ellie continued. 'Or maybe Johnny Lucas told you about it when *he* contacted you last.'

William considered the statement, nodded to himself, then took another mouthful of his drink.

'Robert always went for the winning teams,' he said, ignoring the accusations. 'Although I heard the accident didn't help him.'

'Accident?' Ellie snapped. She was sick of dancing around. 'Mark Whitehouse beat him half to death with an iron bar. That was no accident.'

'I was being polite,' William replied; his eyes were narrow and cold. 'I could have just said he was never the same after working for you put him in such a hazardous position that he almost died. Would you have preferred that?'

Ouch. Ellie knew she deserved it, but she hadn't expected it to really hurt.

'Look,' she said, 'Becky Slade's not a good person. I think we can both agree on that. The Slades, as a family, aren't exactly angels. I'm trying to find a way to stop her.'

She looked around the bar. There were a couple of familiar faces, and Ellie wondered whether they were truly alone.

'You don't represent Drew Slade anymore, do you?'

'I've already told you that,' William shrugged.

'Yeah, but you haven't said the real reason why,' Ellie replied. 'You're not representing Drew because you represent his daughter, don't you? Through her association with Arun Nadal?'

She recognised one man by the bar. He was definitely the kind of person who would drink in a pub like this, and the last she'd heard, he'd been working for the Simpsons.

Easy to swap across.

She almost laughed as she looked back at William.

'Call her out,' she said. 'I'm guessing she's watching somewhere. Get your boss to speak to me because I'm sick of dealing with the monkey.'

William didn't seem surprised by the statement, didn't seem insulted, even. He simply glanced at the bar and held his hand up, waving.

The man at the bar, the one Ellie had recognised, tapped something on his phone, obviously sending a message, and a minute later the doors to the bar opened and Becky Slade walked in.

Three steps behind her was Robert Lewis.

'Oh, look,' William said. 'There's Robert, and there you were worrying if he was okay.'

24

WEIGHING IN

ELLIE STOOD, FACING BECKY ACROSS THE BAR, REALISING, AS SHE did so, that there were at least three other men in the pub who were watching her conversation with more interest than she'd expected.

As Ellie stared at the newcomers, William Peel leant back, wearing the expression of a cat that not only got the cream but had managed an entire cake as well.

'You see, Miss Reckless, you were right. Robert never worked for Becky Slade. He worked for me, and I work for Arun Nadal, and Robert's owed me, ever since the days he was a trainee solicitor ... you could even say, ever since he helped put Becky's father away in prison.'

Ellie snapped her head back to William at this.

'What do you mean helped put him in prison?' she said. 'Your job was to keep him *out* of prison.'

'Was it?' William asked. 'Maybe Robert might have thought that, but we always knew where we wanted Drew to be, and it certainly wasn't in a position of power.'

He looked back at Becky.

'I believe you wanted to speak to this lady,' he said.

Becky continued towards Ellie, and Ellie couldn't help but notice that the way she walked, with her hands by her side, was exactly the same as the way she'd paced around the boxing ring when she'd faced Ellie earlier that week.

'I know what's going on now,' Ellie said casually. 'Took me a while, but I got there in the end.'

Becky paused at this and, although she wanted nothing more than to attack, there was a curiosity in her eyes, a question of whether Ellie Reckless had actually worked out what was happening.

'Please,' she said. 'Enlighten us.'

'I know who your real father is,' Ellie said. 'And I know who Arun Nadal's grandfather was. Second cousins, isn't it? That must be fun at Christmas.'

Becky shrugged.

'You're fishing,' she said. 'So Drew wasn't my father. So what?'

'So, you're not a Slade,' Ellie said, raising her voice a little to make sure that everybody around overheard. 'There you are, stating your position, but actually you're just cosplaying a gangster.'

She looked down at William.

'Does *she* know that you've been working for Johnny Lucas too?' she asked. 'Funding Nadal's rise to power?'

She noticed a flash of surprise on Becky Slade's face at that.

Got you, you bitch, she thought to herself. Becky had thought she was in control here. Ellie wasn't going to give her that joy.

Then, as if on cue, William Peel's phone buzzed as a text message came through. He pulled on a pair of reading glasses and peered down at the details as, ignoring him, Becky Slade focused on Ellie as she continued.

'The problem you've got, Becky, is you thought you had everything you needed, but there's a massive list of things you forgot,' she explained. 'You've aligned with a man who's using you as a distraction, keeping everyone watching you while he takes over North London. He's throwing you to the wolves, because at the end of the day, family is everything, and you ain't family to him.'

Becky's eyes narrowed.

'I don't have family,' she said. 'My real father's in prison. My grandfather, he's dead, killed in a drive-by shooting. Drew, he's nothing to me. Cillian, well, he was a racist old man who needed to be put down.'

'Then why use the Slade name?' Ellie asked, holding her hands out. 'Honestly, there's no reason you couldn't turn around and state that as the granddaughter of the Turk, you're claiming what was his.'

'I don't want Central London,' Becky replied. 'I want *South* London. It was Slade territory, and thanks to both Slades and Simpsons, the Turk's name causes anger and distrust rather than loyalty. I grew up wanting it, watching Paddy Simpson piss it away, and then Max Simpson destroy it. Don't even get me started about little Nicky.'

Ellie decided not to reply to this and just waited to see how far Becky would go in her ranting.

'So, go on then, Ellie,' Becky said. 'Tell me what I'm going to do. You seem to know about my history and my alliances, but you haven't yet said what Becky Slade is going to do this week.'

She narrowed her eyes, smiling darkly, no hint of humour to it.

'Or is this the point where you smile enigmatically and inform me that "ah, the time's not right to be told" and all that bollocks, meaning I have to wait, wondering whether the great Ellie Reckless really knows what's happening, as you desperately try to find a way out of this? You see, not only do I know I've beaten you physically, I've beaten you mentally as well. I'm playing chess, and you're—'

'Let me guess,' Ellie interrupted. 'I'm playing Monopoly with the little top-hat man and the dog? Yeah, I've heard that one from Nadal already. If you're going to give me some kind of great soliloquy, at least think of an original one for yourself.'

Ellie turned slowly around in a circle, taking in the whole of the bar, including William Peel, who had placed the phone down now and looked as if he was about to be violently sick, most likely realising that everything Ellie had done since entering the bar had not only been planned, but pretty much an orchestrated setup.

'But no, I'm not going to keep it to myself. I'm going to tell you exactly what you're going to do. Tomorrow, your stepfather, fake father, whatever you want to call him, appears in Inner London Crown Court in Southwark, appealing a sentence because of problems with the detective who arrested him, claiming a mistrial,' she started. 'I know that, bankrolled by Arun Nadal, you've gathered yourself a nice collection of weaponry and an armoured van, painted to look just like the one transporting Drew. I'm guessing you've got yourself a nice team, and tomorrow morning you'll be intercepting it.'

'You think I'm going to break my father out of prison?'

'No,' Ellie shook her head. 'I think you're going to *execute* him. You see, I know Drew killed Arun's real father, Mason

Carter, and if Arun Nadal is giving you backing, he's going to have his own requests you need to take on. And I think part of it was to remove Drew Slade. But you don't really care much about that, do you?'

'And why would that be?'

'Because even back in 2014, you didn't care about your family. It was you who killed Cillian, wasn't it? Drew was correct when he said he'd been set up. But, he hadn't been set up by the police, he'd been set up by his own daughter. Tell me, did you know he wasn't your father at that point?'

Becky Slade was no longer smiling.

'I learned a couple of years earlier,' she said. 'I never understood why Cillian hated me. He'd loved me so much when I was a kid. And then, when I turned thirteen years old, he berated me, hit me, belittled me. I didn't understand why. As I became a teenager, I realised the truth. I didn't look like my family. Sure, I had my mother's looks, but I had this olive complexion. Perhaps it was genetics. But Cillian, ever the racist, would throw jibes in. One day around then, my mum came to me, broken and battered and sick of the life she'd been leading, told me everything, explained who my father was, explained why my grandfather was so cruel to me, why my father – the man I believed to be my father, that is – had disowned me. Then she climbed into a car, drove to Bluebell Hill in Kent, parked up overlooking the fields, and blew her head off with a sawn-off shotgun.'

She paused, reliving the moment, her face blank before continuing.

'I never understood why Cillian hated me, but yeah, I killed him when I had the chance. I wasn't going to let the same thing happen to me as happened to Mum. But I also knew if I did it cleverly, waited till the right moment, I could kill two birds with one stone as everyone wanted Drew to fall. So, I shot him with his own gun, begged Dad to clean things up and then blackmailed your buddy Whitehouse to get the confession. And he was more than happy to throw a Slade under the bus.'

Ellie nodded. 'So, now you're going to kill Drew tomorrow morning?'

Becky shrugged.

'I thought you were clever,' she sighed. 'That you knew all that was happening? You've not even got past the prologue.'

'Oh, I know that's not all,' Ellie said. 'I know you want the five signatories, that you want the reparation money. But I've got something bad to tell you. It's gone.'

Becky's eyes narrowed and her lips thinned as she glared back at Ellie, shaking her head.

'No, no, no,' she said. 'No, that's not how it works.'

'Yeah, it is,' Ellie smiled. 'You see, before I came here, I burned five debts. Can you guess what they were?'

You could have cut the atmosphere in the bar with a knife, as Becky Slade's eyes gave a glare that, if it could have been weaponised, would have destroyed anyone crazy enough to cross her. However, as a gaze couldn't become such a thing, Ellie simply smiled back sweetly in response, waiting for the next move.

'What did you *do?*'

The voice was emotionless, cold, and slow as Becky Slade moved closer, her fists gripping and ungripping uncontrollably and most likely unconsciously.

Ellie, drawing the moment out, shrugged.

'The money's gone,' she said. 'It's been removed and passed back to the relevant parties, that being Mama

Delcourt, Johnny Lucas, Nicky Simpson, Kenny Tsang, and Mama Lumetta.'

Ellie paused, frowning.

'The Turk didn't put any money in, did he, on account of being dead for many years at that point? So, I don't think there's anything in the pot for you ... or your cousin.'

At this, she gave an even wider smile.

'Although the last I heard, Arun was on good terms with his Uncle Johnny, so maybe he *will* make some money out of this. You, however, not so much. Your father will get his day in court, and more importantly, you'll be outed as the person who *actually* killed Cillian Slade. We have statements from witnesses.'

'There were no witnesses,' Becky started, but then paused, smiling.

'Oh, well played,' she said. 'You got the Diner guy and his bitch to speak. Nobody's going to believe them.'

'True,' Ellie shrugged. 'But I'll also have your father's word, and I'll also have the word of the police officer who arrested him, who was told by you – as you just told this room of witnesses, including a solicitor there – to make sure Drew suffered.'

Becky snarled, almost knocking aside the member of bar staff, a red-haired woman who walked up beside her, a pint of cider and black in her hand.

Realising what it was and grabbing it, she downed the first half-pint of it.

'Okay, so there's a court case,' she said. 'William Peel there's *my* lawyer. I'll get him to go down and pressurise the judge, make sure it doesn't go through.'

'I'm sorry,' William looked up at Becky, with a face that resembled a dog eating a wasp, 'but I need to recuse myself;

not only from that case, but also from working on your behalf. I'm paid by Mister Nadal, not you.'

'You're *leaving* me?' Becky was incredulous.

'Yeah, he just got a message from the person who actually pays his bills, telling him to quit you,' Ellie smiled. 'Guess why that happened? Go on. I'll give you three guesses.'

Becky didn't need to. She knew Ellie had burnt a favour to have this happen. And, watching her work it out, Ellie had a slight flash of triumph pass through her.

Johnny Lucas had come through with the last part of his debt.

'But don't worry, *Bradwell Associates,* not Peel have recently returned to service as the solicitors for Drew Slade,' Ellie smiled again. 'Happened oh, about half an hour ago. And thanks to you, the man standing beside you currently works for Bradwell Associates.'

Becky slowly turned to face Robert, who looked at her, gave a slight smile, and shrugged.

'She's got a point,' he said. 'When you put me on your books, you did it through Bradwell Associates, claiming my old connections so it didn't lead back to you. And, well, if William Peel is recusing himself, and Bradwell are taking Drew back on, then *I'll* have to be the one that stands in court tomorrow, telling them everything I know, won't I?'

Becky opened and shut her mouth a couple of times, and Ellie knew this was the moment where things could go badly quickly.

'That's not all,' she said quickly, pulling the attention back to her now. 'The whole point of this for you was to gain a seat at the table, so that Arun would share the money that you'd made him. The five signatories, all giving the millions across. But as I said, that's gone, so you've lost that as well.'

Ellie shook her head.

'Looks like you've lost.'

Becky, forcing her face to stay emotionless, reached into her inside pocket, likely for a weapon, but then paused as the doors to the bar opened, and Kate Delgado walked in, two officers behind her.

'DI Delgado, Vauxhall nick,' Kate said loudly as she stared at the group, waving her warrant card around. 'We had an anonymous call that something illegal was happening here.'

Becky pulled her hand away from her pocket, looking back at Ellie, who grinned.

'Sorry, DI Delgado, you must be mistaken,' Becky said. 'There's just a meeting of old friends here.'

At this, Robert stepped across the divide, now standing beside Ellie as he looked back at Becky Slade.

'I'd like to say I quit, but let's be honest, you never hired me,' he said calmly. 'So, how about I say that you're no longer a client of mine and I suggest you find new legal representation?'

He glanced at Delgado before continuing.

'Probably as soon as you can,' he finished.

'You think you've won,' Becky's voice was terrifyingly cold. 'See if Drew gets off. I doubt it. See if you can prove anything on me.'

She turned to face Robert.

'You think the police are going to stand here and help you? Every person you love is dead right now.'

She looked back at Delgado.

'Hypothetically, of course, officer.'

'Hypothetically, they're not,' Ellie grinned. 'You thought you had everything sorted, that you were one step ahead of me. The problem is, and this is something I said to your cousin, you keep throwing around Monopoly as if it's a dumb game, but you're missing the bigger picture. In Monopoly, you learn negotiation: trading properties, making deals, and manipulating situations. Just like in the London underworld, it's about who you know and how well you can play the game.'

Becky went to reply, but Ellie held a finger up to stop her, now in control as she continued.

'In Monopoly, strategic planning is key. You think several moves ahead, anticipating actions and adapting strategies. In the criminal world, it's the difference between a lucrative heist and a stint in the nick. Decisions have consequences, and understanding the risks is vital. One wrong move, and it could all come crashing down. The game teaches adaptability; being quick on your feet when circumstances change. Patience and persistence are crucial. Those who stay calm under pressure and keep pushing forward are the ones who survive. And the social dynamics? Building alliances, navigating conflicts ... these skills are indispensable in our world.'

Ellie looked around the room.

'So, you see, Monopoly isn't just a game, where a little metal doggie barks around a board. It's a microcosm of the real world. It teaches you how to think, adapt, and survive. Underestimate it, and you're only playing yourself.'

'I'm gonna kill everybody you ever loved,' Becky replied as a matter of fact rather than a comment.

'Doubtful,' Ellie shrugged. 'You see, while you've been pissing around concentrating on me, I've had one of my team —Joanne Davey, remember her? No? Looks like Robert didn't tell you everything, doesn't it? Anyway, I've had her run around, burning favours on my behalf, and those favours have removed every single person from your grip.'

She looked around the room and saw that the more she spoke, the more the men and women who had been standing around Becky Slade were questioning their loyalties.

'You see, this is the problem you've got,' Ellie smiled. 'You thought you could blackmail me by threatening my friends. Well, that's off the table. You thought you could take a man I care for, who I would do anything for, and hold him over me. Well, as you can see, that hasn't benefitted you either. And then you have Arun Nadal, who you thought you could control but who's actually been controlling you, and I'm sorry to say has been doing it with far better skill than you seem to have.'

She shook her head.

'I mean, let's be honest, you were kind of caught between a rock and a hard place, weren't you? I'm guessing he wanted you to kill your, well, whatever he is – onetime father, stepfather – to show your loyalty to the family, but also, he allowed you to create mistakes.'

Becky shook her head.

'You don't know what you're talking about,' she snapped.

Ellie leant closer, her voice dropping as she continued.

'You've been set up from the start. Arun Nadal told you he was going to take the money that you were providing him, and share it with you. To gain this percentage though, you'd have to kill Drew Slade before he provided proof in his appeal that you killed your grandfather ... because he *is* the one that has the proof, isn't he? He's the one who could have you put away for the murder. Especially if some new forensics and a favour or two, recently offered to us from some police friends can connect you to the gun, and the murder itself...'

Ellie could see the muscle around Becky looking

nervously at each other at this comment. Some of them were older than Becky, and Ellie wondered whether they had been around since the days of Cillian ... and had long memories.

'Face it,' she continued. 'You're screwed either way. Once Arun realises you can't kill your father, you're done. Even if you do, it sounds like you've been screwed over to where everybody knows you're planning to do it, and the police will be waiting. You'll never be able to take any form of ownership of South London. At best, you'd gain a couple of million, the most expensive hit-woman in history, and you'll spend the rest of your life looking over your shoulder.'

She clicked her fingers as if remembering something.

'Ah, snap,' she said. 'You can't do that cause the money's gone.'

The room was deathly silent. Ellie allowed the moment to draw out.

'It looks to me like this makes us even,' she finished. 'You might have beaten me in the ring, but I seem to have beaten you quite badly here. So, how about we fight a deciding bout? We both know there's a boxing ring upstairs, and I can think of nothing I'd like more than to smash your teeth in. Becky Slade versus Ellie Reckless. Right here, right now.'

25

FIGHT NIGHT

BECKY AGREED WITHOUT EVEN CONSIDERING IT. DOWNING THE second half of her pint, she slammed it on the table, wiping the back of her hand against her mouth as she already started to pull off her jacket.

'You want a fight?' she said. 'Let's do it right here.'

'Upstairs,' Ellie shook her head. 'We do it there, in the ring where Henry Cooper once trained to fight Muhammad Ali.'

Becky's eyes narrowed.

'I'll beat you here, I'll beat you there,' she said. 'But this time, when I'm finished with you, you'll be sucking your food through a straw.'

Ellie said nothing, turning and walking to the back of the pub, the others following her. She started up the stairs, and it was only when they reached the top that she knew Becky would have realised something different to a simple fight was happening.

The upstairs room of the ex-pub was not empty.

The ring, cleaned and ready to go, had a man wearing the

shirt of a boxing referee on inside it. As Becky saw him and looked around the pub, she recognised more than a couple of familiar faces.

Arun Nadal was there.

Mama Lumetta and Kenny Tsang were standing in a corner.

Janelle "Mama" Delcourt sat at a table near them, her niece beside her.

Even Johnny Lucas, freed from Parliament for the night, was to the side, almost skulking in a nook beside the bar. In fact, as Becky looked around, she saw pretty much every major player in London was standing there.

All of them had entered through a back entrance while Becky had hidden downstairs, waiting for her grand entrance.

'What the hell is this?' she said, spinning around to stare back at Ellie.

'This is an intervention,' Ellie replied, climbing into the ring and already pulling off her jacket. 'You see, I could have you stopped right now. I could have you arrested and you could be charged for what you did to Cillian Slade all those years ago, and I'm sure that we've got enough to show the terrible things you've been doing recently. You'd do some time, but that's not enough. There needs to be a lesson given on what happens to people who piss on my chips, and stomp them into my turf.'

'*Your* turf.' Becky chuckled as she suddenly saw Nicky Simpson and the other members of Finders walking into the room at the back. 'If anybody, it's *his* turf, and he gave it up willingly.'

'I don't know what you're talking about,' Simpson shrugged. 'But I can tell you now you're going to have your arse kicked. And then the nice DI over there is going to dump you in a nice dark cell.'

'Technically we should be doing that now,' Delgado replied, the slightest hint of a smile on her lips as she looked at her officers. 'But I can't turn down the opportunity of seeing Ellie Reckless repeatedly punched, first.'

Becky turned back to face Ellie.

'Fine,' she said. 'I'm going to take you apart piece by piece. I'm going to break you into little bloody gibbets, leave you on the floor. They're gonna need to comb through the pieces just to gain your identity. And then I'm going to carry on doing everything I was going to do, but without you being a pain in my arse.'

She glared at Delgado.

'And my solicitor will have me out of custody before you even get me to the cell.'

Delgado simply shrugged, in an "of course you will" kind of way as she settled back to watch.

'Funnily enough,' Ellie smiled, allowing Leroy, who was now standing in her corner, to wrap her wrists, 'I was pretty much going to do the same to you, but without all the hyperboles. I was just going to beat the living shit out of you and leave you here for the police.'

She looked up, straight into Becky Slade's eyes.

'You attacked my family,' she said. 'You went for my friends. You're lucky I don't burn *more* favours, and have a lot worse done to you. But this, as you've said before, is personal, and I will always pay my own debts.'

By now, Becky had wrapped her wrists and smacked her fists together, cricking her head left and right to knock out any knots in her neck. She was wearing a tank top and jeans, trainers on her feet, and with her stocky frame, she looked dangerous. Ellie, meanwhile, was wearing a pair of simple trousers, a blouse, and two rather oversized boxing gloves.

'I'm going to split you apart, bitch,' Becky said, as she had someone help her gloves onto her hands.

'Ready for the deciding bout?' Ellie replied, moving into the middle. 'But know this, when I beat the living shit out of you and leave you on the floor beaten and broken, every single gangland leader who has a say in London is going to see. Do you think you can climb back up after that? Christ, you'd better *hope* you're arrested, because everything you've gained will be taken in a second.'

Ellie smiled a very dark, evil smile.

'And anything that hasn't been taken, I'll burn every remaining debt I have to make sure it is.'

Becky went to reply but didn't have time to. Before she could even put in a mouth guard, Ellie had moved in, swinging hard, catching her off guard. Becky held her hands up, shaking away.

'I'm not ready,' she grumbled. 'You're not playing fair.'

'I'm sorry, did you just say something to me about playing fair?' Ellie said, walking back to the corner and allowing Leroy to put her own mouth guard in. 'You've got some nerve.'

Becky had placed her mouth guard in now, but was shaking her head, wiping at her forehead, which was breaking out in slices of sweat, as she stared at Ellie.

'No, no,' she said. 'This isn't right.'

She said nothing more because Ellie had already moved in, slamming two vicious jabs into her face. Becky stumbled to a knee, and the crowd straightened, like an audience seeing blood in the water.

Becky was slower now, her breath laboured. Ellie walked

over and pulled her up, and then started once more, hammering punches left and right, pushing Becky back as she tried desperately to defend herself.

Ellie circled Becky, her eyes locked on her opponent's sluggish movements. Becky threw a jab, but it was slow, almost lazy. Ellie ducked, the punch whistling past her ear. She countered with a sharp right hook, connecting solidly with Becky's jaw. Becky stumbled, her legs wobbling, but she managed to stay on her feet.

The small, specifically invited audience roared, sensing the shift in momentum.

Ellie pressed forward, landing a series of quick jabs. Becky's arms struggled to rise as she tried to defend herself, her movements becoming more erratic with each passing second. Another punch slipped through her guard, crashing into her cheek. With no headguards on, there was nothing to soften the blow; blood sprayed from her mouth, and she blinked, dazed, swinging wildly, a desperate attempt to regain control, but Ellie easily dodged.

Ellie could see the confusion in Becky's eyes, the frustration at how badly this was going for her. She stepped in, delivering a brutal uppercut that snapped Becky's head back.

Becky staggered, her vision blurring. She tried to raise her hands, but her arms wouldn't respond.

Ellie seized the opportunity, pounding Becky with relentless blows. Each punch landed with a sickening thud, driving Becky further back into the ropes. The referee watched closer, ready to step in, and Becky's knees buckled as she fell to the mat, gasping for breath. She tried to rise, but her body betrayed her, collapsing again under its own weight.

Ellie watched as the referee moved in to start the count,

but she stepped forward, an arm out to stop him, shaking her head.

'Not yet,' she said, her voice firm. 'A statement needs to be made here.'

The referee hesitated, looked at the audience watching and yelling to let her continue so, realising the amount of high-level gangsters he'd be pissing off if he *didn't* do what they asked, he simply nodded, stepping back.

Becky, on her knees, reached out desperately, grabbing Ellie's legs. She clung on, trying to pull herself up, trying to stop the barrage of punches. Ellie gritted her teeth, shaking Becky off with a swift knee to the ribs. Becky groaned, her grip weakening, but she rose just enough to wrap her arms around Ellie's waist, holding on for dear life. Ellie's fists pounded down, trying to break Becky's hold, but Becky's determination to stay upright was the only thing keeping her from collapsing completely, holding on tightly as she fell back, stumbling until the two of them were in a corner, falling against the ropes.

It was here, close and unhindered, that Ellie now whispered into Becky's ear.

'You think you covered all this? You think you saw everything?' she hissed. 'You didn't see the woman who gave you your drink tonight, did you? That's the thing about a forensics officer. They know lots of nasty little chemicals and ingredients that can be put into something, say, like a cider and black.'

Becky's eyes widened like saucers as Ellie retreated across the ring and looked to the side, where now standing at the back, still wearing the white shirt of a server, was Joanne Davey, grinning.

'You tricked me!' Becky snarled, looking back at the crowd. 'She poisoned me!'

'We saw nobody poisoning you,' Robert shouted out. 'And if you're that worried, I'm sure we can have somebody do a blood test once you've finished this match. If you *have* been poisoned, I'm pretty much sure that it'll show.'

'Stop looking for excuses!' Ramsey shouted out. 'You're simply not good enough!'

'I wouldn't be *too* sure about finding anything in a blood test,' Ellie whispered again into Becky's ear. 'Davey's *very* good at hiding things.'

Becky, now realising she was rapidly fading, glanced back at Ellie.

'You couldn't beat me in a fair fight,' she hissed.

Ellie replied by swinging hard, catching Becky under the jaw, sending her to her knees, her hand out, holding her up from collapsing completely to the floor.

'I never said I was going to,' she replied. 'When we first met, I wasn't prepared for what this was while you were. This time I'm simply returning the favour. And now it's time for you to go bye-byes.'

She hammered down with another punch. Becky's hand, the one holding her up, failed, and she slumped to the ground.

'Stay down, bitch,' Ellie said, mimicking the words spoken to her in a different boxing ring. Becky tried to clamber back up, but this time Ellie crouched down, and in the same way that Becky had earlier, punched her hard in the face.

'I said stay down,' she replied.

Two more punches rained down. In the process, Ellie

noticed that Becky's nose had been split open, blood pouring down the sides of her face as she lay on her back, her eyes glazed; although, whether that was from the fight, or whatever drugs Davey had spiked into her drink, Ellie couldn't be sure.

As Becky stared up at the ceiling, Ellie walked over to the corner of the ring and, with a little trouble thanks to the boxing gloves, picked up a vicious looking Maglite torch that had been placed there. Half a metre in length, it was a heavy metal club, and she slapped it into her hand, walking back to Becky.

'Recognise this?' she asked, holding it out over the prone woman. 'It's the same type of torch you used on Lavie Kaya to get my attention, remember? The one you said you broke his forearm with, your little personal touch, while you threatened Ali and Sandra as well?'

She stood over Becky now as the woman beneath weakly waved her gloves to ward Ellie away.

'I wanted you to understand that I'm as serious as a heart attack,' Ellie said, mirroring Becky's own words. 'Now stay still, or this is going to hurt a lot more.'

Viciously and with significant force, she swung the torch down, the metal light connecting—

—With the canvas floor no more than an inch from Becky's head with a hefty *thunk*.

There was a moment of stunned silence in the room, only broken by the slightest of whimpers, a breath from Becky herself as she saw the torch embedded into the canvas beside her.

'That was for Lavie Kaya, you bitch,' Ellie hissed. 'And the next time I see you in *my* manor, I won't pull the blow.'

This done, and Becky now lying prone on the floor, Ellie

stood up, catching her breath and looking around at the audience.

'This woman claimed she was going to take over,' she said. 'This woman who lies at my feet.'

She turned to face Arun Nadal.

'You'll stop what you're doing,' she said. 'Your funding has been paused until you can prove you're a grown-up.'

Arun went to snap a reply back, but noticed Johnny Lucas shake his head. Ellie saw this too and smiled; this had also been part of her debt – to stop funding momentarily for Nadal, and change Peel's loyalties. She'd known the latter was done, but she'd worried Johnny would baulk at the first part.

Ellie looked back at the audience.

'It's my fault that London's like this,' she said. 'We took down bad people and we let worse in the door. There's nobody to police you.'

She looked back at Delgado.

'No offence.'

Delgado shrugged, looking back at her officers.

'I think we need to leave now,' she said, 'before we hear anything incriminating.'

Delgado looked back at Becky, now still unconscious on the ring canvas.

'Pick up that piece of crap and bring it with us as well,' she said. 'When she wakes up, she's got a lot of questions to answer.'

Ellie waited as the two officers took Becky's prone form and removed her, then once again turned to the crowd.

'The reparation fund of five million was held aside to stop you fighting against each other,' she said. 'But now half of you have retired, and the land is still falling apart. The new gangs have nothing that'll stop them in the same way that the old gangs did. So we've been having conversations.'

She looked around the room.

'Mutually armed destruction is a plan,' she said. 'But, when you retire, it doesn't really work. So, the money's been returned to the groups who placed it there in the first place. People who have retired or moved on now have a small windfall. But some of that money, and I'm not saying who from or why, has been kept. That will fund a new deterrent.'

Boxing gloves still on, she placed her hands on her hips as she turned slowly around in the ring, spitting out the mouth guard as she did so.

'That deterrent is *me*,' she said. 'I've burnt a lot of favours in the last couple of days. But I still have a lot to go, and the big ones are still in my pocket. It's been suggested to me that if I wanted to, I could be the next Becky Slade. That I could make a play for one of the London Boroughs. But I don't want it. This might sound surprising to all of you here, but I don't want to be one of you. I don't want to be a gangland leader.'

She smiled.

'But that doesn't mean I don't want the power,' she continued. 'It doesn't mean I won't tell you when you're out of line. So that's how we're going to move on. It'll take time to get it working, and it'll be a tough journey. But me and my team ...'

She glanced back down at Tinker, Ramsey, Casey, Joanna Davey, and now Robert Lewis standing beside them.

'We'll sort your various problems out like we always have. And we'll still operate with favours. Gaining them and burning them. But we will not have this city that we love so much destroyed by gangland warfare. And if you think that we're not strong enough to stop you from whatever you want to do ...'

She waved a hand around the ring, an inviting gesture.

'Then get in here right now, and I'll prove it to you.'

There was a long, quiet moment, then, slowly, a low murmuring from the audience; acceptance as to what was happening.

Ellie hadn't expected a rapturous round of applause. It wasn't a speech worthy of *Independence Day* or other such films. But she felt like a Rubicon had been crossed. She was no longer the cop for criminals. Now she was something *bigger*. And, with luck, she'd be something a lot more useful.

Clambering out of the ring, she allowed Leroy to help pull off her gloves. Grabbing her jacket, she walked over to her team.

'Let's get out of here,' she said. 'We've got work to do.'

26

CRUSHING DREAMS

Mark Whitehouse sat once more in the visitor meeting room of Wandsworth, this time alone as the doors opened and his visitor entered.

He'd been told it was Ellie Reckless, and he shuffled eagerly in his seat, expecting her to be subservient to him, explaining what would happen with Michael Swift's transfer. After all, he'd said he wouldn't answer any questions until Swift turned up.

Instead, it was a man with dirty-blond hair and a white scar in the parting. A man that Mark Whitehouse recognised instantly.

Robert Lewis walked over to the table where Whitehouse was and sat down, placing his hands on top of the table. He said nothing for a moment, simply staring at Mark, and then nodded to himself.

'I didn't know what I'd say to you when I saw you,' he said. 'I thought I might be angry, might decide to hurt you. I had visions of being dragged off by guards as I tried to strangle you with my tie.'

He sat back in the chair, checking his watch.

'I haven't got long,' he said. 'I've got to be in court in an hour and a half. Drew Slade's appeal.'

He smiled.

'I'll see you there, won't I?'

Mark Whitehouse frowned at the casual nature of this conversation.

'I was told Ellie was coming.'

'Yeah, that's not happening,' Robert shook his head sadly. 'You see, you said you'd give her the answer she needed if she brought in Michael Swift for your protection, right? Poor man was being victimised, and you were going to look after him. Copper saving coppers.'

He shook his head.

'Problem is, I know you'd been asked by Arun Nadal to terrify him into *keeping quiet about certain events* he was privy to, a way for you to gain Nadal's protection in here because, actually, it's the other way around, isn't it? You're the one being victimised, held in solitary effectively for your own safety.'

Robert sighed, shaking his head.

'Must really suck, being stuck here all alone, unable to do anything about it.'

He moved closer.

'Just so you know, the problem Ellie had – the problem I had as well? Well, that problem's gone. Which means that we don't need you to answer questions anymore. And that means we don't need to move anyone.'

He stood up now. Mark Whitehouse still hadn't spoken.

'Interestingly, Michael Swift was *very* helpful when we asked why Nadal would want him dead. It seems you have a lot more to be answering for, especially as, if you hadn't demanded it, we wouldn't have known to look. I'm afraid that also there won't be a plea deal for you, Mister Whitehouse. You're no longer of importance.'

'Now wait here—' Whitehouse spluttered, but Robert Lewis wasn't listening anymore, as he turned and walked out of the room, leaving Mark Whitehouse alone with his thoughts.

LIAM KENNEDY HAD HEARD NOTHING FOR THE LAST TWENTY-four hours, but a job was a job, and he'd been paid handsomely to do it. He sat in the driver's seat of a white panel van, an Iveco Daily panel van, at the corner of Bermondsey Street and Long Lane, dressed in the dark blue-grey clothing of a prison guard. In the back, hidden from view, were five men, vicious-looking, masked, and armed with a variety of dangerous weaponry. He'd been hired by Becky Slade to do one thing: stop an armoured prison van from attending Inner London Crown Court, pull the prisoner out, pass a very personal message, and shoot him in the head. It was a risky move, but Becky Slade had promised enough money for this so that Liam, if needed, could disappear for years in Spain or some other non-extradition country.

They'd made sure the usual route up the A2 was blocked, a lorry on fire, and that left the backup route up the A2206, and then a right to cut across to the A2198, straight up Bermondsey Street and past the waiting Liam.

He checked his watch. Five minutes to go.

He glanced across at the man sitting beside him, Nash Hopkins, a certified psychopath. He'd used him several times in the past, allowing Nash's berserker rage to instil fear, shock and awe into the victim's minds; he found it always made them more pliable, susceptible to suggestion. Today's suggestion was to get the prison guards to allow Drew Slade to be dragged outside and shot, something that he felt Nash would be uniquely qualified to help with.

Four minutes.

He stretched, preparing himself for the oncoming event, but then paused as a woman walked up to the door beside him and tapped on the window.

He rolled it down, glaring at her.

'We're on official business, love,' he said. 'Move along.'

'Oh, I know what kind of business you're on,' Ellie Reckless smiled. 'But I'm just here to tell you Becky Slade isn't running things anymore, so you don't really need to do what you're going to do here. I mean, even if you did, she won't be paying you, so you're shit out of luck, really.'

'What do you mean Becky Slade's gone?' Liam frowned.

'Oh, didn't you hear? She got arrested last night,' Ellie shrugged. 'About five minutes after I beat the living shit out of her in the middle of a boxing ring.'

She held her hand up and gave a little wave.

'I'm Ellie Reckless,' she said pleasantly. 'And I'm here to tell you that you're on my turf, and I'd appreciate it if you'd just drive this van back to Peterson and Son's and tell them you'd like a refund.'

She went to leave and then paused.

'Oh, and you can keep the money they gave you for it all,' she said. 'Class it as a kind of kill fee for the project, although I'm aware that I'm probably using the wrong terms. I'm still new to this.'

With a tap on her forehead with her hand in a slight salute, she turned and walked off. Liam couldn't help but notice that she was currently walking a Cocker Spaniel, pulling on the lead in front of her. To anyone watching, it was simply a dog walker having a chat with someone in a van.

He looked back at Nash.

'Do me a favour,' he said. 'Phone our source. That was Ellie Reckless, and if you've not heard that name before, then you're an idiot.'

Nash shook his head.

'We should go,' he said. 'I've got a bad feeling now.'

Liam considered this, but then looked towards the end of the road, where, turning into their street, they could now see an identically designed van. He gripped the steering wheel tightly.

'Screw it,' he said. 'We got paid for this, we ought to do it.'

He turned on the engine, preparing to pull out in front of the van as it got closer. At the required moment, he placed his foot on the accelerator, moving out into the street—

Only to stop as the surrounding doors opened up and armed SCO-19 officers came bursting out, weapons aimed directly at the van.

'Put the guns down, get out of the van!' they shouted. 'Drop your weapons, get on the floor!'

Liam turned, confused, to Nash, expecting him to go out in a blaze of glory. His first instinct was to grab Nash, to stop him from leaping out with a weapon in hand. He'd heard rumours of how mental this guy was, and the last thing he wanted to do was kick off a gunfight where he could be taken out.

But he was surprised to find Nash calmly sitting back, placing his weapons down and holding his hands in the air.

There was something about his demeanour that grated.

'You told them,' he said.

Nash shook his head.

'No, but I knew this was happening,' he replied.

'You set us up,' Liam hissed.

'Sorry, bud,' Nash simply shrugged apologetically. 'I'm afraid I owed a favour to Ellie Reckless.'

Liam slumped against the driver's seat as armed police opened the back door and brought out the five confused mercenaries, all dropping their guns.

Another woman walked over and rapped on the door. It wasn't Ellie Reckless and her dog again this time, but the woman held the same energy and held up her warrant card.

'DI Kate Delgado,' she said. 'Vauxhall police. I'm afraid you won't be removing Drew Slade from his court date.'

She nodded at the van, now blocked by his own.

'In fact, he's not even in that vehicle. If you'd made it in there, you would have found some more SCO-19s with their guns aimed directly at you.'

Liam wanted to scream. He should have listened to Ellie Reckless.

Delgado motioned for him to leave the van.

'Don't worry,' she said. 'It could have been worse. She could have demanded a *favour* from you.'

Liam sighed heavily and stepped out of the van, hands raised.

'Fair point,' he replied.

ELLIE HADN'T EXPECTED TO SEE JOHNNY LUCAS FOR A WHILE after what had happened. She knew that she had effectively outed him as Arun Nadal's secret employer, and that was something that would probably bite him on the arse down the line. She knew also that he would be angry.

As it was, he was waiting for her when she arrived at the boxing gym the following day for her regular sparring session. Leroy was nowhere to be seen but, as Ellie strapped her gloves on, Johnny pulled off his jacket, now in his shirt and trousers, clambering in to face her, placing the pads on his hands.

'I'll be with you today,' he said.

Ellie raised an eyebrow.

'Are we okay?'

Johnny shrugged.

'Why wouldn't we be?' he asked.

Ellie nodded, accepting the conversation as done, and started to work through a few of her movements.

'I thought I'd give you some heads up,' Johnny continued. 'There's an election coming, probably at the end of this year, maybe next year. I've decided not to run.'

Ellie stopped.

'You'll no longer be the MP for Bethnal Green and Bow?'

Johnny shook his head.

'When I realised I had a clean slate, after all the dodgy shit I'd done had been passed on to somebody else, I thought I could make a difference,' he replied. 'Take my notoriety and help the people of Bethnal Green and Bow, but you get nothing done in Parliament. Trust me, I've done my best for the last year or two, but a lot of the time you're just smashing your head against the wall while other people get rich from their plans. And then you made my mind up.'

Ellie felt a shiver slide down her spine at the comment.

'Look,' she said, 'I didn't mean to out you.'

'Oh God, no, I don't mean that at all,' Johnny said. 'I had no fear of that. Everybody in that room knew who the hell I was. What I mean is, standing in that boxing ring, you showed true leadership. With what you've done, taking on the role of effective arbitrator, you've changed London more than I did officially. I realise that if I want to make London a better place, I have to return to what I'm best at.'

He smiled.

'You know, running a boxing gym.'

'Yes, of course,' Ellie laughed. 'Well, as much as it pains me to say it, I think you'll do a better job. But what does that mean about your grandnephew?'

'You're wondering if he's going to want recompense for what you did?' Johnny shrugged. 'I warned him off you, said you're more useful when you're on his side. But he's a young man, passionate. He might try to score some points against you.'

He held up the pads once more, motioning for Ellie to start again.

'But you're ready for it, Reckless,' he said, as she started striking at the pads in order. 'You'll find a way to fix that problem, in the same way you fix all the others.'

Ellie started the drills once more, as Johnny Lucas barked out numbers. There was a moment of unease that had gone through her when Johnny had mentioned how he was going to quit Westminster. But there was also a feeling of relief. Things were returning to the natural order. Johnny Lucas would be running East London.

Whether or not he had Arun Nadal with him was a different matter.

'With luck,' she said eventually after finishing a routine, 'I won't have to see that much of Nadal, anyway.'

At this, Johnny laughed.

'Oh, I think you might be seeing more of Nadal than you thought,' he said. 'He's quite the entrepreneur, you know.'

EPILOGUE

THE FIRST THING ELLIE WANTED TO DO, ONCE EVERYTHING WAS sorted, was see Ali at Caesar's Diner. But when she arrived, she found the doors closed and a sign on the front.

Opening soon, new management.

Ellie stared at the door. She had guessed that there would be problems with Ali and Sandra returning to their life, especially after having to give a statement about Becky but, for some reason, she had expected the world to stay the same. Caesar's Diner would still be there, her meetings would still be taken.

This was a shock.

Tinker shook her head sadly.

'Please,' she said, looking back at Ellie. 'Let me be the one to tell Ramsey?'

Ellie didn't reply; this was the first actual proof nothing was ever going to be the same again.

She was about to speak when there was a movement in

the background, behind the door, and a figure walked out, making their way to the entrance where the two women stood, unlocking it and opening it for Ellie and Tinker to enter.

'Alright, guys,' Nicky Simpson said.

Ellie frowned.

'You're the new management?'

'More of a franchisee,' Simpson explained, making a small, mock theatrical bow as he did so. 'When I heard that Ali and Sandra wanted to disappear, I thought, "Why shouldn't I take this place? Real estate's good. It's north of the Thames, which means I'm not anywhere near my usual stomping ground." Made sense to me.'

He looked around the diner.

'There's a couple of locations nearby where I could create another health club. This would be a fun distraction.'

'Ramsey won't like it,' Ellie shook her head.

'Why would that be?'

'Well, you'll change the menu, make it full of healthy, macrobiotic shit.'

Simpson laughed.

'Not at all,' he replied. 'I intend to keep the menu exactly as it is. I even have some enhancements of my own; unhealthy ones I think he'll enjoy.'

Ellie looked around the diner.

'Are you going to allow dogs?' she asked.

'Of course,' Simpson nodded. 'Everything the old diner had, this will have as well.'

'So, they're really gone?' Tinker asked. 'No chance to say farewell?'

'I'm sure they'll pop in from time to time,' Simpson

replied. 'But yeah, as of right now, Ali and Sandra feel it's best if they stayed away. I do have a message for you, though.'

He turned to Ellie, lowering his voice.

'He says sorry.'

'Does he now?' Ellie couldn't help it; her face betrayed the irritation at the comment. She had hoped that Ali would have at least turned up himself to apologise in person for what he had done.

'He knows he pissed you off, he knows he used you,' Simpson continued. 'But he was in a tight spot.'

'This is more of his apology, or are you just deciding this?' Ellie snarled.

Nicky Simpson simply smiled back.

'I know what I would have done in his position and you would have done the same, so don't give me that shit,' he replied. 'Ali was in a place where he was screwed. She'd come for him and he needed her removed. He couldn't go to the police; he was a cousin of the Turk, he was effectively being blackmailed for his criminal past ... and, let's face it, you're Ellie Reckless, the cop for criminals. I'm sure you'll see him again, but right now ...'

He waved around the diner.

'... Welcome to my empire.'

He checked his watch.

'I'm afraid I have to kick you out,' he said. 'I have a meeting with my business partner.'

Before they could leave, however, he paused Tinker, lightly touching her arm.

'You still owe me a date,' he said.

'You still gonna wear a dress?' Tinker asked, a vicious looking smile on her lips.

'Of course,' Simpson looked hurt she would expect anything else. 'I'm a man of my word.'

'I'll believe that when I see it,' Tinker chuckled.

Ellie waved for Tinker to follow her out, shaking her head as she did so. Emerging outside Caesar's Diner, they started towards the Finder's offices.

At least with Becky gone, they could return to their old life there.

'Are you actually going to go through with that?' she asked, and was surprised to see Tinker redden slightly.

'I made a bet, so I kind of have to,' she replied, but Ellie was sure there was a glint in her eye. Excitement, perhaps?

Better her than me.

Ellie didn't know why she did but, as they were walking away, she turned to look back at the diner and had to admit she wasn't that surprised to see Arun Nadal and two of his goons entering in their place.

It seemed Nicky Simpson's business partner was a little more East London than Nicky was.

Entering through the lobby, Ellie was surprised to see a custodian changing the letters on the board, removing "Finders" from one of the three floors that it rented from. Surprisingly, it was on the floor where Ellie and the others had their offices.

'Are they closed?' she asked, tapping at the now blank line.

'Depends who you are,' the man replied. 'I've just been told to change the sign so ...'

He trailed off, showing the elevators to the side.

With a frown Ellie, Tinker following and Millie at her feet, took the elevator up to the floor and the glass-walled Finders' offices. It was true they hadn't been there for a couple of weeks, having moved to a more South London venue before taking a well-earned break for a few days, but she hadn't expected Finders to change the locks while they were away.

As it was, the office seemed the same. Sara, the receptionist, sat there, nodding as Ellie and Tinker walked past and, as they reached their offices, Ellie saw a welcome sight; Robert Lewis sitting at his own desk, working through his papers.

Tinker, seeing this as well, took Millie's lead from Ellie's hand.

'Go speak to him,' she said.

Ellie nodded, tapping lightly on the door, before she entered the room.

'Are we being evicted?' she asked as a way of introduction, followed by, 'Glad you're back. You look good in that chair.'

Robert looked up and smiled. For the first time in many months, possibly since before the Zoey Park case even, he seemed at peace.

'Finders have rented this floor out to another company,' he said. 'Everything's being changed as we speak.'

'When do we need to move out by?' Ellie asked, annoyed that such a decision had been made without her consent, but aware that, to be honest, all she really was, was an employee.

'We're not leaving,' Robert smiled. 'You see, while you've been cleaning up the fallout from Becky Slade for the last few days, I've been dealing with the other problem.'

'Problem?'

'Your speech about how we're now the arbitrators of the underworld,' Robert shrugged. 'Not to mention the seven-figure war cabinet we were given by Mama Lumetta. Oh, and obviously, the little amounts by Simpson, Kenny Tsang, Mama Delcourt – who, by the way, says that she owes you a favour if you ever want it – and Johnny Lucas.'

He leant back in the chair.

'It's a good amount of working capital for what we intend to do here, but we can't do it under the Finders' name. As much as they would want us to work with them – and we are still consulting for them on a case-by-case basis, hence why we can stay in these offices at a reduced rental rate – we are now ...'

He trailed off, picking up a piece of paper and passing it to Ellie.

Ellie read the sheet, her eyebrows rising.

'Reckless and Company,' she said. 'This is your work?'

'Mine and Casey's,' Robert replied. 'Ramsey helped.'

He smiled.

'It makes sense, Ellie, and it's a logical step. You worked for Finders while you were looking to clear your name, and you've done that. But you were always destined for bigger things. This way, you get to do them. You can consult for Finders whenever they need us to solve a case. And you can ... indulge ... your more criminal activities.'

Ellie stared back down at the piece of paper.

'Right then,' she said. 'I'm guessing Sara's part of this. She's been seconded to us?'

Robert nodded.

'On a plus note, it means you don't have to use the diner downstairs for your meetings anymore. Especially with the new owners.'

Ellie chuckled. *Of course, Robert Lewis would know about it.*

'And what about you and Bradwell Associates?' she asked. 'Do you have to give some kind of notice period?'

'No,' Robert laughed. 'In fact, I think we might use them as well as time goes on. I have a feeling having a solicitor at our call that isn't me is probably an excellent thing, and even though you effectively blackmailed William to step away, you made quite an impression on him.'

There was a moment of silence in the room, as if neither of them quite knew how to progress the situation. Eventually, it was Robert who spoke first.

'I've missed you,' he said.

'I've missed you too,' Ellie smiled back. 'Later, once we get through all this, can we have a chat?'

'About?'

Ellie walked over to the desk, leaning over it so she was only a foot or so from his face.

'Us,' she said simply.

Robert's face broke into a smile.

'I'd like that,' he said. 'I'd like that a lot. But maybe not with an audience?'

He nodded to the boardroom, rising from his chair. Ellie looked into the room and saw that Casey, Ramsey, and Davey were already waiting. Tinker, having settled Millie down and provided her with some food and water, entered and sat beside them.

Ellie, with Robert following her, walked into the boardroom.

'Right,' she said, sitting at the head of the table. 'I believe the first meeting of Reckless and Company is in session.'

There was a small round of applause from the others, and Ellie smiled.

'So,' she said, 'who's been naughty recently … and what do we need to do about it?'

Ellie Reckless and her team
will return in their next thriller

TAKE
—THE—
KING

Coming Early 2025

ACKNOWLEDGEMENTS

When you write a series of books, you find that there are a ton of people out there who help you, sometimes without even realising, and so I wanted to say thanks.

There are people I need to thank, and they know who they are, including my brother Chris Lee, who I truly believe could make a fortune as a post-retirement copy editor, if not a solid writing career of his own, Jacqueline Beard MBE, who has copyedited all my books since the very beginning, and editor Sian Phillips, all of whom have made my books way better than they have every right to be.

Also, I couldn't have done this without my growing army of ARC and beta readers, who not only show me where I falter, but also raise awareness of me in the social media world, ensuring that other people learn of my books.

But mainly, I tip my hat and thank you. *The reader.* Who once took a chance on an unknown author in a pile of Kindle books, thought you'd give them a go, and who has carried on this far with them, as well as the spin off books I now release.

I write these books for you. And with luck, I'll keep on writing them for a very long time.

Jack Gatland / Tony Lee,
  London, July, 2024

ABOUT THE AUTHOR

Jack Gatland is the pen name of *#1 New York Times Bestselling Author* Tony Lee, who has been writing in all media for thirty-five years, including comics, graphic novels, middle grade books, audio drama, TV and film for *DC Comics, Marvel, BBC, ITV, Random House, Penguin USA, Hachette* and a ton of other publishers and broadcasters.

These have included licenses such as ***Doctor Who, Spider Man, X-Men, Star Trek, Battlestar Galactica, MacGyver,*** BBC's ***Doctors, Wallace and Gromit*** and ***Shrek***, as well as work created with musicians such as ***Ozzy Osbourne, Joe Satriani, Beartooth, Megadeth, Iron Maiden*** and ***Bruce Dickinson.***

As Tony, he's toured the world talking to reluctant readers with his 'Change The Channel' school tours, and lectures on screenwriting and comic scripting for *Raindance* in London.

As Jack, he's written several book series now - a police procedural featuring *DI Declan Walsh and the officers of the Temple Inn Crime Unit*, a spinoff featuring "cop for criminals" *Ellie Reckless and her team,* and a second espionage spinoff series featuring burnt MI5 agent *Tom Marlowe*, an action adventure series featuring conman-turned-treasure hunter *Damian Lucas*, and a standalone novel set in a New York boardroom.

An introvert West Londoner by heart, he lives with his wife Tracy and dog Fosco, just outside London.

Feel free to follow Jack on all his social media by clicking on the links below. Over time these can be places where we can engage, discuss Declan, Ellie, Tom and others, and put the world to rights.

www.jackgatland.com
www.hoodemanmedia.com

Visit my Reader's Group Page
(Mainly for fans to discuss my books):
https://www.facebook.com/groups/jackgatland

Subscribe to my Readers List:
https://bit.ly/jackgatlandVIP

www.facebook.com/jackgatlandbooks
www.twitter.com/jackgatlandbook
ww.instagram.com/jackgatland

Want more books by Jack Gatland?

Turn the page…

LETTER FROM THE DEAD

"BY THE TIME YOU READ THIS, I WILL BE DEAD..."

A TWENTY YEAR OLD MURDER...
A PRIME MINISTER LEADERSHIP BATTLE...
A PARANOID, HOMELESS EX-MINISTER...
AN EVANGELICAL PREACHER WITH A SECRET...

DI DECLAN WALSH HAS HAD BETTER FIRST DAYS...

AVAILABLE ON AMAZON / KINDLEUNLIMITED

THEY TRIED TO KILL HIM...
NOW HE'S OUT FOR **REVENGE**.

NEW YORK TIMES #1 BESTSELLER **TONY LEE** WRITING AS

JACK GATLAND

THE MURDER OF AN **MI5 AGENT**...
A BURNED SPY **ON THE RUN** FROM HIS OWN PEOPLE...
AN ENEMY OUT TO **STOP HIM** AT ANY COST...
AND A **PRESIDENT** ABOUT TO BE **ASSASSINATED**...

SLEEPING SOLDIERS

A **TOM MARLOWE** THRILLER

BOOK 1 IN A NEW SERIES OF THRILLERS IN THE STYLE OF
JASON BOURNE, JOHN MILTON OR **BURN NOTICE**, AND
SPINNING OUT OF THE **DECLAN WALSH** SERIES OF BOOKS

AVAILABLE ON AMAZON / KINDLE UNLIMITED

"★★★★★ AN EXCELLENT 'INDIANA JONES' STYLE FAST PACED CHARGE AROUND ENGLAND THAT WAS RIVETING AND CAPTIVATING."

"★★★★★ AN ACTION-PACKED YARN... I REALLY ENJOYED THIS AND LOOK FORWARD TO THE NEXT BOOK IN THE SERIES."

JACK GATLAND
THE LIONHEART CURSE

HUNT THE GREATEST TREASURES
PAY THE GREATEST PRICE

BOOK 1 IN A NEW SERIES OF ADVENTURES
IN THE STYLE OF 'THE DA VINCI CODE'
FROM THE CREATOR OF DECLAN WALSH

AVAILABLE ON AMAZON / KINDLEUNLIMITED

EIGHT PEOPLE. EIGHT SECRETS.
ONE SNIPER.

THE BOARD ROOM

HOW FAR WOULD YOU GO TO GAIN JUSTICE?

NEW YORK TIMES #1 BESTSELLER TONY LEE WRITING AS
JACK GATLAND

A NEW STANDALONE THRILLER WITH A TWIST - FROM THE CREATOR OF THE BESTSELLING 'DI DECLAN WALSH' SERIES

AVAILABLE ON AMAZON / KINDLE UNLIMITED